Ariella

and

The Curse of Dawnhaven

Owen Crane

This book was written for Beth, Joe and Isaac.

My love, my inspiration and my world.

Your greatest adventures are ahead of you.

"Fairy tales do not tell children that dragons exist. Children already know that dragons exist. Fairy tales tell children that dragons can be killed."

G.K. Chesterton

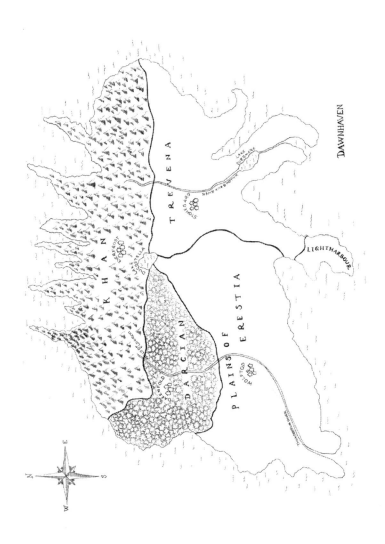

1

The Announcement

The roar of the crowd behind the curtain filled Ariella's ears, making her head swim with the fears she'd been nursing for the past week. She may not have been able to see their faces, but the vibrations she could feel through the floorboards confirmed that the whole of Lightharbour was gathered on the other side of the plush hanging fabric. Nerves had already got the better of her in the morning, and she'd been sick twice, narrowly avoiding detection from her mother.

This is it Ari, no going back now. In a few moments, the whole city will know.

She tried to appear calm but her stomach was churning and her palms were clammy with sweat. Her mother was standing next to her, a picture of serenity waiting patiently to be welcomed onto the stage.

"Are you all right dear?"

Ariella smiled weakly.

"Do you think you'll recognise any of them? They'll be the same age as you," her mother smiled. "Fifteen seems much too young to begin the Journey to become a Guardian. They must be so nervous, waiting out there for the announcement."

You think they're nervous? You have no idea.

The crowd beyond the curtain was momentarily silenced by the blast of a dozen trumpets sounding out across the city square, announcing the royal entrance.

Ariella's mother turned and smiled. "It's time," she whispered as she took her hand and the curtain in front of them parted.

I think I'm going to be sick.

Beyond the curtain, Ariella could see the mass of people cheering as her mother led her onto the stage. She tried to smile and wave, but she was starting to feel dizzy.

Thankfully her mother was fully absorbed in the moment and did not notice her daughter's distress. She led Ariella to the two grand chairs that had been placed on the stage for them. The crowd continued to cheer until the trumpets let out a long blast. From the far side of the stage stepped a tall, handsome man with a broad smile. His skin was dark, a stunning contrast to his bright silk clothes. He walked with natural confidence, approaching Ariella and her mother and bowing low.

"Your Majesty," he began. "May I begin the Announcement?"

Her mother paused for a moment then smiled, "You may, Hakeem." Hakeem bowed again and flashed a glance at Ariella.

What was that? Does he know? How could he know? The test is secret, no one knows. Is there anything that goes on in this city that Hakeem doesn't know about?

Hakeem walked to the front of the stage, the crowd silent as if they were collectively holding their breath. He paused, allowing the tension to build. After what seemed like hours to Ariella, Hakeem reached inside his jacket and, with a flourish, withdrew a thin scroll bound with green silk. He took his time untying the silk and unrolling the scroll. The crowd seemed to lean in, waiting.

Hakeem's voice rang out clear and strong across the city square. "By decree of the Guardians of Dawnhaven and the royal household of Lightharbour I hereby make this announcement: the ten who have been chosen to begin the Journey are…"

Ariella's heart began to race. She sat on her hands so nobody would notice them shaking. Hakeem slowly read out the names, and one by one, the crowd roared their approval as those chosen made their way to the stage.

Seven names were called, then eight, then nine. Ariella held her breath, trying to concentrate on what Hakeem was saying, desperately hoping she could keep it together.

"The final person to be announced is…Ariella Lightharbour."

Silence fell over the crowd. Ariella felt her mother stiffen as she turned slowly to face her. Hakeem was looking at her, his expression impassive.

Ariella rose to her feet and walked to stand with the other nine. Still, no one spoke, nothing breaking the silence. Then, painfully slowly, the crowd broke into applause. It rippled through the square building to a crescendo, shouts of approval finally filling Ariella's ears. She smiled weakly and managed a hesitant wave before casting a glance over her shoulder towards her mother. Her face was like marble, unreadable except for her eyes. Her eyes were burning with anger.

2

Gargoyles in the Library

The Lightharbour palace library was the envy of the world. For centuries it had drawn scholars, philosophers, dreamers, treasure hunters and prophets. They came for the riches contained in the thousands of bound volumes and rolled scrolls.

Hung on the walls were the first maps of Dawnhaven, drawn before the Breaking, before the five kingdoms were formed. Recorded here were the great scientific discoveries, their tomes neatly filed. Experiments with flight, fire and steel. Every venture and misadventure logged for all time. Given an equal place were the myths and legends of Dawnhaven: tales of Darcian, firstborn of the unicorns, mighty and majestic; songs of Kalasa, the mighty mountain chieftain who first tamed the gryphons of Khan.

The library was a place of wonder and beauty for Ariella. She had spent countless hours there while growing up in the palace. It was her escape, a chamber of peace and solitude, but most of all, a place of dreams. Somewhere she could live out the adventures she heard in the stories told by the sailors of Lightharbour. She unleashed her imagination in the library, as she read the ancient sagas. In her mind, she soared on the winds with the grace of the eagles. She had dreamt about diving from the falls of Elderod and charging down the rapids of the Thunderrun river. She imagined scaling the vast ranges of the snow capped Khan mountains and fighting off vicious Ghost Raiders as they sought to plunder the coasts of Dawnhaven. In the library, Ariella made her own choices, walked the path of her choosing. In the library, she was free.

It was in the library that she now waited. She was trying to be calm, behaving as if she was not nervous, trying to act as fearless as the palace guards. She was failing. She took a book down from the shelf. A random choice. She was not even conscious where she was standing in the library.

She took the book to a nearby table and let the pages fall open. The chapter title stood out in bold print: 'The Effects of Dragon Fire on Stone Walls'. Ariella smiled to herself as she spoke aloud. "It's a pity the dragons died out. I'd much rather be facing a dragon today."

"So would we!"

Ariella jumped as the bookshelf next to her slid silently to the side. Behind it was a sloping passageway and the grinning faces of her younger brothers, Osias and Calixto. She glared at the twins. "Mother is going to lose it with you two if she finds you skulking down the passageways again."

"I think our wonderful mother has other people in her sights today," laughed Calixto.

"You're hilarious." Ariella was not in the mood for her brother's particular brand of humour.

"It'll be okay, Ari," Osias chipped in. "I'm pretty sure that she's not going to lock you in the dungeon. Although I could've sworn, I heard someone calling for the jailor."

She threw the book she was reading across the room towards her brothers, but the bookcase was already sliding back into place. The hefty tome thudded to the floor with a dull echo. The laughter from her brothers grew fainter as they withdrew down the hidden passage.

The Palace of Lightharbour was riddled with these passages. Ariella had heard many tales of what the passages were built and used for. The popular stories were of escape tunnels if the palace was besieged. Some of the sailors would sing songs of midnight rendezvous, unrequited love, tragedy and torment, all made possible by the tunnels.

Some of the darker tales were of secrets and spies. There was even talk of assassinations. Long forgotten monarchs murdered in their beds by jealous lords, children, brothers and even wives. Ariella shuddered. Tales of dark deeds always made her uncomfortable when she was alone in the library. She had always felt it was a place of such beauty and wonder that stories of evil didn't belong inside its inspiring walls.

She smiled again at her naivety as she let her gaze drift across the vastness of the library. The vaulted ceiling was a spectacular crisscross of frescoes painted by the finest artists in Dawnhaven. They told the stories of the island's history, its legends, the heroic victories and bitter failings. Above her was a particularly vivid image of a blood-red dragon spewing flames against a castle wall. She remembered the book that she had hurled at her brothers and retrieved it. It was bound in soft leather, dyed the same blood red as the dragon in the ceiling's fresco. In an elaborate gold script, its title read, "Dragon Breath: A comprehensive study of the effect of dragon breath by Theodore Vangaland".

Sounds like the type of book the twins would love. Those two would quite happily stroll up to a dragon and ask him to breathe on various objects while they recorded it. 'Sir Dragon, would you be so kind as to breathe fiery death on this haystack so I can observe the results?' Yes, that sounds exactly like my brothers.

The twins: Osias and Calixto, thunder and lightning, chaos given human form, twice. As much as she hated to admit it, she knew she would miss them. They brought light and colour, mixed with a good dose of disaster wherever they went. There had been many times over the last eight years when Ariella had needed light and colour in her life.

She slipped her hands into her pockets and drew her shoulders in close as the pain of the memories washed over her again. It was not the sharp pain of years ago, but a dull ache. Hakeem had told her that that pain too will pass, in time. As she thought of Hakeem, the fingers in each of her pockets closed around the two spheres. Each was no bigger than a glass marble that the children played with on the streets of Lightharbour.

Echo orbs.

A gift from Hakeem, eight years ago. He gave them to her here, in the library. He knew she would be there after she had heard the news. The news that changed Ariella forever. The news that her father was dead. She didn't believe it at first. How could he be dead? He was so strong, so brave, so adventurous. He was the ruler of Lightharbour, wise and fierce. How could he be gone?

Hakeem had found her in the far corner of the library, behind an old tapestry, curled up on the floor. She had been there for hours, weeping. Ariella remembered Hakeem's strength as he lifted her and carried her to one of the library's soft, cushioned benches. She remembered refusing to let go of his neck as she buried her head in the silk of his robes. She could scarcely believe that was eight years ago.

She spun the orbs through her fingers, still deep in her pockets. So much had changed and yet, so little.

A sharp tap, tap, broke into Ariella's thoughts. The sound came from one of the high windows in the library wall.

Tap, tap, tap.

Ariella narrowed her gaze on the window, trying to find the source of the noise. At first glance, it appeared the window contained nothing but the bright blue of the midsummer sky. Then there was a slight ripple of movement.

Tap, tap, tap.

The head of a tiny gargoyle peered over the edge of the window frame and locked eyes with Ariella. He was about the size of a pigeon, formed from the white stone that made up the majority of the buildings in Lightharbour. His face was carved into a hideous grin, with small, fox-like ears sticking upright from his bald head. The gargoyle leaned his head against the glass staring its stony eyes at Ariella. He lifted his right hand, and in it, he held a small bag made of luxurious blue velvet.

"Hakeem!" cried Ariella, recognising the tiny velvet bag.

She rushed over to the window where the gargoyle was perched, threw it open and leaned out. The tiny creature scampered down the sheer wall of the library like a gecko, its fingers holding tight to the stone. He dropped onto the windowsill beside her and held out the velvet bag. She took it and untied the delicate gold lace securing the top. As soon as the bag was loose, rich aromas spilt out, and Ariella took a long, deep breath.

"Chocolate," she whispered.

She leaned forward and kissed the tiny gargoyle on his cold white head. "Go and pass that on to Hakeem for me."

The gargoyle tilted his head to the side, nodded, then turned on his forked tail and was gone, skipping, jumping and climbing over the rooftops. She lost sight of him somewhere between the dome of the spice market and the spires of Archibald's Emporium of Exotic Animals. It always amazed her how Hakeem could get the gargoyles to run errands for him. She didn't know anyone else in Lightharbour whom the gargoyles obeyed like that.

The gargoyles of Lightharbour were not like ordinary gargoyles. They changed after the rebellion when Queen Lucia sacrificed herself and shattered the Burning Sceptre. She destroyed the shadow beasts and scattered the Light across Dawnhaven. Somehow, some of the

Light had found its way into the gargoyles, and, ever so slowly, they came to life. The initial shock of seeing stone carvings jumping across the city roofs settled down after a few months. Now they were accepted as just another aspect of the beautiful colour that makes up Lightharbour.

Ariella lifted out a piece of the chocolate. It was dark and silky, with small chunks of almonds buried throughout. Even on a day like today, the chocolate made her forget everything, just for a moment. She reached in for a second piece, but her fingers found a small roll of parchment bound with red silk. Her nimble fingers quickly untied the silk and unrolled the scroll. Written in Hakeem's beautiful calligraphy was a simple message.

"Be gracious with her."

Ariella's head dropped. Today's events came flooding back into her mind, and she sighed. This was not going to be an easy few hours. She looked out of the window over the great city state of Lightharbour. The white stone of the buildings shone in the bright sunlight.

How long will it be until I'm back here?

On the far side of the library, she heard the high doors swing open and the soft, steady footsteps of someone walking with purpose.

Okay, I need to get this over with.

Ariella took one last glance over the city, the place of her birth and her home, then she turned and walked to meet the footsteps.

The two ladies stood and faced each other in the silence of the library. Ariella was tall for her age, slender but strong. Her rich, chocolate brown hair fell past her shoulders. She tried to make herself taller than she was, her shoulders pushed back, and her chin lifted.

The silence continued; the seconds turned to minutes as the two held each other's gaze. Ariella was willing her emerald green eyes not to blink first. Typically, in situations such as this, she would come out the victor. She had a stubborn, competitive streak that had seldom seen her buckle. Most people would blink first and avert their eyes.

Most people. But not the lady before her: Queen Susanna, Lady of Lightharbour, House of the Eagle. She looked away from no one. Ariella lowered her eyes and shifted her feet. In a moment, she had gone from a proud, strong, stubborn, young woman, to a child, insecure and nervous. There was no one in the whole of Dawnhaven, no distant foreigner on any ship that had sailed into the harbour, no knight in the palace guard that could make her feel that way. No one, except her mother.

"Ariella," she began.

Ariella blinked. She recognised the soft, calm tone. She had been in court and heard her mother use that tone; it was reserved for 'special' circumstances. Once a visiting dignitary had, foolishly, assumed he could take advantage of the queen in a trade deal. Ariella had seen her disarm and humiliate some of the wealthiest merchants in Lightharbour with that voice. On one occasion she had to put the Captain of the Palace Guard in his place. He asserted that women should not be involved with matters of defence. That was a mistake. There was soon a new Captain of the Guard.

Ariella half lifted her head and tried to look into her mother's eyes. The same emerald green that she had inherited, and her mother had inherited from Ariella's grandmother, Queen Lucia, the last Queen of Dawnhaven. Her mother's face was calm, set, unreadable.

"Well?" asked the queen.

Numerous answers to that question came into Ariella's mind. None of them was helpful. Thankfully, she had learnt, the hard way, not to respond to her mother with sarcasm. Unfortunately for Ariella, she had no idea how to begin answering the question.

She started slowly. "I thought the announcement went rather well."

"Really?" said the queen, her voice moving dangerously away from soft to icy. "You think it went 'rather well'?"

"Um, well, it was nice. The banners looked nice, and I thought, the…"

"You thought?" the queen interrupted. Please tell me, what exactly did you think?"

What did you think I am trying to do?

As she started to answer, Ariella realised she had nothing to say that would help her situation.

"Did you consider including me in your plans? Did you not think that I may have a different perspective that might have benefited you in this process? Do you think that maybe bringing me in on your little secret before today might have been a good idea?"

The queen's voice was starting to rise now. She was losing some of her previous composure. Ariella began to shrink back.

"How could you possibly have thought this would go well?" The queen was shouting now. "You've made a fool of me, yourself, Lightharbour and the Guardians."

"The Guardians don't think they've been made a fool of!" Ariella shocked herself at her emotion as she answered her mother. "They think it's excellent. They chose me, they want me!"

"Well, they can't have you!" The queen took a step forward as she spoke, her eyes flashing dangerously.

"Why not?" yelled Ariella. She took a step towards her mother, her jaw tight. Her hands flew out of her pockets, fists clenched. She had never spoken to her like this before.

"You are the princess of Lightharbour, heir to the throne. You cannot go running off on adventures! Your city needs you here; your people need you here!"

For a moment, Ariella lost control. Even as the words left her lips, she regretted them.

"Father would've let me go!"

The effect was instant. The queen flinched like she had been struck. The intensity of the pain in her eyes took Ariella's breath away.

"I'm... I'm sorry. I'm sorry," she stammered.

For a moment, the queen stared at her eldest child, the torment of searing loss still visible in those piercing green eyes.

"You know nothing. You have no comprehension of what your father would want. You think of no one but yourself. You are a selfish child. You are not leaving tomorrow. You are not joining the Guardians. Your duty is to the throne, to Lightharbour and to me."

Her words hung in the chamber of the library and seemed to settle like dust around Ariella. She spoke quietly. Softly. Afterwards, she realised, for the first time in her life, that she had used the same tone as her mother.

"No."

"No?"

"No. I am leaving tomorrow, I am joining the Guardians, and there is nothing you can do to stop me except lock me in the dungeons."

At that, Ariella strode out of the room more confident and assured than ever. The high doors of the library closed behind her, and she ran. She hurried down the corridors of the palace, bursting through doors. Past servants and knights, many calling out 'Congratulations, Your Highness!' as she flew by. Up flights of stairs, she ran, around corners, through doors. She didn't stop until she was opposite a slim, oak entrance.

It led into a small, curved corridor on the far western tower, high up in the palace. She glanced over her shoulder and listened, trying to steady her heavy breathing. There was silence. She pushed open the door and looked inside. As usual, the corridor was empty. With a final glance around her, she stepped through the door and closed it silently behind her.

The light from the windows was soft and warm. Specks of dust fell through the shafts of light. Ariella took deep breaths and raised her hands to the white stone on the outer wall of the corridor. She felt for a moment until she found the tiny indentation, no larger than the tip of her finger. Into it, she placed the index finger of her left hand, and with her right, she felt along the wall again, this time, lower down. There it was, an identical mark, invisible to the eye. She placed her right index finger in the second indentation and pushed. A slim slab of the white stone swung outward from the corridor wall without a sound.

The gap in the wall was a fraction taller than Ariella in height but narrower than her shoulders. Beyond it was a small stone platform, and beyond that, nothing but the clear blue sky.

3

Echo Orbs

Ariella stepped lightly on to the platform and moved the stone into place behind her. She leaned back against the outside of the western tower and breathed. The platform was just wide enough for her to stand on, and from it led a series of other platforms forming hidden steps around the outside of the tower.

The warm sea breeze blew across her as she stood, delicately balancing, on the thin, white stone. The secret door that she had stepped through faced due west. All that lay before her was the Southern Sea, stretching far out to the horizon. Standing on this side of the tower meant she was hidden from the view of anyone in Lightharbour.

Being here on the outside of the palace always calmed her nerves. She took another deep breath, then skipped lightly up the stone steps that led her to the top of the tower. The tower was capped with a stone roof, domed but easy enough for Ariella to walk across. Surrounding it was a white stone wall that rose to her waist. From up here, she could see the whole city.

To the north was the port from which Lightharbour got its name, and its wealth. Ships arrived here from all over the world. They brought with them a dizzying range of spices and silks, gems and jewellery, weapons and wondrous animals. Ariella loved the port: the sights and smells, the different sailors from far off lands singing songs that caused her heart to soar. She loved to listen to their stories of adventures, tragedy, romance and treasure. Often, she thought of running, of leaving everything and sailing off into the sun, but something had always made her stay. Duty? Family? She did not know, she just knew that Dawnhaven was her home and where she was meant to be.

Away east lay the bulk of the massive city. Almost one million people called Lightharbour home, and that was only the official figure. Who knew how many more slipped unnoticed through its gates? It was by far the largest and most populous city in Dawnhaven.

To the south and west of the tower were the Eagle Cliffs, and beyond them, the Southern Sea. As she stood and watched, a pair of the giant sea eagles took off from their nest high on the cliffs. The birds were awe-inspiring, so powerful, so deadly and yet wonderfully graceful. Their bodies were the size of a small horse and their great wings spread out, vast and wide. Their silver feathers reflected the afternoon sun as they soared on the thermals, their keen eyes looking for tuna in the sea below.

Ariella sat on the stone wall and looked out across the city. She could see the main square where this morning's announcement had been made. The banners of her family, House of the Eagle, could be seen fluttering in the gentle breeze. Next to them flew the flags of the Guardians of Dawnhaven, the golden sun rising on the green earth.

She remembered her mother first telling her about the Guardians, the rebellion and the dividing of Dawnhaven into the five kingdoms. Since then the Guardians had been the protectors of the island. They were the thin line of unity that bound the kingdoms together. They reminded people of their collective past and their shared future.

Her mother would tell her stories of Vantor, the Lord Guardian, the greatest warrior of Dawnhaven and Master of the Light. How he was there in the final battle of the rebellion when Diatus' armies were destroyed. He was with Queen Lucia, Ariella's grandmother, when she paid the ultimate price to drive back the shadow beasts.

Ariella's favourite stories were always of Elsa Leaina, the Guardian's Master of Arms. Elsa, the Lioness, strong, fierce and graceful. She made her mother tell her tales of Elsa over and over again.

Maybe I'll finally get to meet her.

The reality of that sent her into a mild panic.

I might meet her! Do sojourners meet her during the first year of the Journey? Surely not, she's going to be way too busy with the fourth and fifth years. I'll not meet her for a while. Excellent, plenty of time before I make a total idiot of myself.

Ariella smiled and shook her head.

Get a grip Ari, you're not even on the Journey yet, and you're already planning your moment of great embarrassment in front of Elsa. First of all, you have to get out of the palace without your mother locking you in the dungeon.

She stuffed her hands deep into the pockets of her gown and drew her shoulders in close: her default posture when dealing with uncontrollable sadness. Unconsciously, her fingers felt for the echo orbs. The unconscious movement of them through her fingers usually calmed her down. But not today. The fingers in her left pocket quickly found the marble-sized orb and began passing it from one finger to the next. But her right fingers found nothing. She dug down into the deep corners of her pockets, slowly at first, but then frantically searching for her missing orb. She grabbed the inner lining of her pocket and pulled it inside out trying desperately to find her lost treasure.

Nothing.

Where is it?

She started searching the rooftop, pacing back and forth, trying to retrace her exact footsteps.

Nothing.

The corridor.

She jumped the low stone wall and ran down the steps to the hidden door. She paused for a moment with her ear to the stone. Silence. She quickly found the small holes on the outer wall, pulled open the door and slipped inside. Her eyes scanned the corridor, hoping to find a glimpse of the orb, praying it had rolled into the corner of the narrow passage.

Nothing.

Not good Ariella. Not good at all. Where is it? Where did you drop it?

Absentmindedly, she put her hands into the left pocket, her fingers closing on the remaining orb. She gasped. The orb was, ever so gently, humming. Someone's talking. Swiftly she pulled out the orb and placed it to her ear.

"I've lost her. What am I going to do?"

It was her mother's voice, but it sounded different. It was laced with a sense of deep sorrow, something Ariella had not heard before. She felt her throat tighten and tears spring in her eyes.

She's talking about me.

"She is not lost." It was Hakeem, his deep voice soft and melodic.

"How can you say that? She's going on the Journey. People die on the Journey! Even if she survives, she'll be a Guardian. She'll no longer be part of my House."

"She will always be your daughter. Being a Guardian will never change that."

There was a long pause. Ariella held the echo orb closer to her ear.

Where is it? Where did I drop it?

She tried to retrace the events of the last hour.

I felt it after I threw the dragon book at the twins. I'm sure it was in my pocket when the gargoyle brought Hakeem's gift. Where then? They've never fallen out on their own before.

Then she realised: it was the moment in the library when she had shouted at her mother. She remembered her hands flying from her pockets, fists clenched. She was so angry. Moments before she had been spinning the orb in her fingers.

The orb must've fallen when I pulled my hands out. It's still in the library.

"When did you know?" It was her mother again. There was no anger in her voice now, just sadness.

"Late last year, just as the selection began."

"How did you find out? The selection is secret, no one is supposed to know until today, until the announcement." The queen's voice cracked, and Ariella thought she heard the soft sound of her mother's tears.

"You didn't tell me." The queen spoke softly.

"No."

"Why?"

Hakeem sighed. Ariella felt for him. She knew when she went forward for selection that Hakeem was going to find out. She was sure that there was little that went on in Lightharbour he did not know about. It seemed to her that Hakeem was on first name terms with the whole city: nobles at court, traders in the markets and, especially, the sailors on the docks. Hakeem even had a way with the gargoyles, and the gargoyles seemed to be able to get anywhere.

"She is growing up my queen. She chooses her own path."

"A path away from Lightharbour, from her responsibilities, from me."

"Yes." Hakeem paused. "There is something different about Ariella. Something I cannot see, cannot predict. Whatever you say or do now, I do not believe that you can convince her to stay. She is going to leave for Trevena tomorrow."

"And then what?" Anger had returned to the queen's voice now.

"You have a city to rule. And the boys will need you more than ever. Soon Osias is going to realise that with Ariella as a Guardian, he is next in line to the throne. I think there may be some power struggles between your sons that will need your influence."

Ariella heard the queen try to suppress her laugh. She heard movement, then footsteps. Her mother's? Silence again. She held her breath, trying to hear the slightest sound from the library.

"What did I say?"

Ariella nearly jumped out of her skin. It was Hakeem's voice, loud and clear through the orb.

He must be holding it to his lips!

"Meet me in the garden, if you would be so kind, Your Highness." It was spoken as a request, but Ariella was already moving.

Oh joy, now I'm in trouble.

Ariella walked carefully through the palace, mindful to avoid as many people as possible. She found one of the many side doors that led out to the vast palace gardens. The sun had started to sink in the afternoon sky, but the garden was warm, and the honeybees flew lazily through the air seeking nectar. The fruit in the trees was beginning to grow after the spring blossom had fallen. Oranges, olives, pomegranates and pineapples all grew in the palace gardens. But Ariella's favourite was passion fruit. She craved it almost as much as the chocolate brought in on the trade ships.

She avoided the formal path of the central gardens, with its fountains, sculptures and topiary. Instead, she turned to the west and followed a smaller path heading to the edge of the garden. In the middle of the extended outer wall was a small gap. Through the opening was a stunning sun terrace perched precariously, overhanging the Eagle Cliffs. The view was spectacular. To the north and south, Ariella could see the massive sea cliffs stretching for miles. She could see the eyries of the nesting eagles and some of the magnificent birds soaring high in the clear blue sky.

To the west was the Southern Sea, calm as a millpond today, hardly a ripple on the surface. She loved the sea, extending for miles before her. It never ceased to amaze her how one day it looked like it would shatter like glass if you dipped your toe into it, yet on other days it could swallow the grandest ships in the navy, gone, smashed to pieces by the brutality of the swell.

This was Ariella's favourite place in the garden. Whether it was the view, the sense of freedom, the privacy or the closeness of the passion fruit vines, she did not know. Maybe all of them. When Hakeem said to meet her in the garden, she knew this was where he meant. He was already waiting for her, standing on the edge of the terrace. His eyes were fixed on an eagle flying over the sea. The massive bird was hunting an early supper for the chicks in the nest.

Hakeem turned at her approach, "Well young lady, you've caused quite a stir."

Ariella squirmed under Hakeem's heavy gaze, "Is she going to be okay?"

"She will be. In time." Hakeem kept his eyes on Ariella. She dropped hers to the white stone terrace. "Did you forget what I wrote in the note?"

"No. It's just, I got angry. Mother was so unreasonable, she was treating me like a child."

"Unreasonable?"

"Yes!" Ariella said that a little more forcibly than she intended.

Hakeem said nothing. He kept his intense brown eyes on her. She tried to meet them but had to keep looking away.

She was unreasonable, wasn't she? I don't know anymore. She was treating me like a child. She said I couldn't go, but I am going. It's all I've ever wanted. Surely, she can see that?

Ariella paused for a moment. Hakeem's eyes were searching her, looking for some response, "Maybe, I could have spoken to her before…"

"Before? Before it was announced to the whole of the city, you mean?"

"Yes." Her shoulders dropped, her chin rested on her chest.

"She loves you, Ariella. Much more than you realise. She was shocked by the announcement and angered by how it was done. Grace was needed. Did you treat her graciously?"

Ariella felt tears well in her eyes. She spoke just above a whisper, "I was angry. I told her father would've let me go."

It was Hakeem's turn for his shoulders to drop, "My dear, you are your father's daughter. You have a soul of adventure and people will follow you, but you have much to learn. We do not treat people with grace because they deserve it, we treat them with grace because it is the best for our own heart. Your heart is beautiful, Ariella. Guard it, guard it with everything you have." Hakeem paused. "And what have I told you about the echo orbs and spying on your mother?"

"It was an accident! It fell out when I was shouting at her. I was holding on to the orbs when we were arguing, and then I got so mad I pulled my hands out of my pockets and it fell out. I didn't notice, neither did she, we were so busy yelling at each other. I've never used it to spy on her, I promise." She realised she was pleading now, needing Hakeem to believe her.

Hakeem studied her, unspeaking. Ariella tried so hard to fight back the tears. She failed, and they came thick and fast. She never meant to say those things to her mother, never meant to hurt her, not really. Talking to her was just so uncomfortable. Hakeem pulled a beautiful, scarlet handkerchief from his chest pocket and dried her tears, "Don't cry. I believe you. No more tears today."

Hakeem spread his strong arms wide and Ariella dived into them. She buried her face in the luxurious silk scarf that wrapped around his head and several times around his neck. Nowhere in Dawnhaven produced silk like this. Hakeem told her it was from his birthplace, many miles across the sea. The silk was soft, a pale green emblazoned with a thousand golden flowers she didn't recognise.

Hakeem used to tell her stories of those faraway lands. When he was a young man Hakeem claimed he was a trader, although Ariella's father used to call him a pirate. Her father had always been vague about how he had met Hakeem. Ariella knew it was a long time ago but little else. Her father and Hakeem had been inseparable ever since Ariella was a child, constantly off on adventures and battling Ghost Raiders. When her father came to the throne of Lightharbour, Hakeem was the obvious choice as Chancellor, the monarch's most trusted advisor. After her father died, he had been a constant in her life. There were many times over the past years when she had needed him.

Hakeem let her go and smiled his big, generous smile. The many lines across his face creased deeper. His 'happy lines' he called them. He often told Ariella that they were a sign of a life well-lived, full of laughter, friends and adventures.

"You have packing to do. Tomorrow you make your way to Stonegard to start the Journey. It's going to be a long five years. Are you sure you can handle it? I don't think there'll be much chocolate to find in Trevena."

Ariella laughed and threw her arms around Hakeem. "You'll just have to send some gargoyles. I'm sure that'll cause a stir in Stonegard. I bet they've never seen a living gargoyle. Just think of the fun I could have with that!"

Hakeem laughed his deep, belly laugh, "Before you go, I have something for you, a small gift from my homeland."

He took out a small leather pouch with a delicate cord securing the top, untied it and tipped something into his hand. It was a smooth, crystal cube. In the centre of it, Ariella could see a soft, pale yellow glow.

"It's wonderful," she gasped. "What is it?"

"It's a sun cube. If you find yourself in darkness and you need the light of the sun, just crush a cube in your hand and let the light shine. It won't last forever, so use it well. Now go, child, you don't have long. You have an early start. Try to stay out of trouble, at least for the first year!"

Ariella stood on tiptoes, kissed Hakeem on his cheek and turned on her heel towards the gap in the garden wall.

"Ariella!" Hakeem called after her. "You've forgotten something."

Hakeem took his hand from his pocket and flicked a small marble shaped object from his thumb high in the air towards her. She caught it and smiled. Her echo orb.

"Do try not to leave it lying around the place. You could hear all sorts of things."

Hakeem smiled as he turned to watch the eagles soar in the late afternoon sun.

4

Leaving Home

Ariella had planned to rise early this morning, just not this early and not in this fashion. The sun was barely above the horizon, and already her emotions had swung wildly. On one extreme, missing her brothers madly and the other, madly wanting to stab them with a fork. She had woken just before dawn with a pang of sorrow realising that she was leaving today, possibly for good. She had started to climb out of bed when it felt like her room exploded. The door had burst open, swinging hard on its hinges and crashing back into the wall. In marched Osais, banging a saucepan with a wooden spoon. Following behind was Calixto, slamming two saucepan lids together as hard as he could.

"Get up! Get up! Come on you big sloth, rise and shine – it's a beautiful day!"

Osais ducked as a pillow went flying through the air towards his head.

"There's no need to be like that, dear sister!" chirped Calixto, still slamming the saucepan lids together. "We're just here to make sure you aren't late for your big day!"

"Get out!" screamed Ariella from under the covers where she had buried herself.

"Never!" Osais shouted back, grinning.

He dropped the saucepan and grabbed the covers by Ariella's feet. With one swift movement, he yanked them clean off the bed. Ariella was up on her feet and swinging a pillow at her brothers, driving them out of the room. She slammed the door shut behind them and leaned her back against it, trying to get her brain into action after the early morning assault.

Just think Ari, tomorrow morning you'll be able to wake up without the nervousness of an impending attack from Thunder and Lighting. It'll be a sweet, sweet day.

The rest of the morning was a blur. Packing, unpacking, then packing again. Hakeem came to see her just after breakfast. He had been direct with his advice on what to take and what to leave behind.

"Travel light, child," he instructed. "There'll be no romantic balls or state dinners to attend. The Journey is five years of intense training. The Guardians will give you the basic equipment and weapons you need to survive, so take only what you think you can't live without. But make sure you can carry it on your back."

Ariella finally pulled the strap on her backpack tight and closed the opening.

That's it. I'm done. If I need anything else, maybe I can pick it up in Stonegard.

She took a final look around, slung her pack over her shoulder and strode from the room. She continued down the palace hallway, past her brothers' bedroom and down the sweeping staircase. The place was so familiar to her. For fifteen years, this had been home. Now, it all felt different, as if she had left something of her past in her bedroom. She felt the excitement build up in her chest, and she quickened her pace, anxious now to get on the road. She was keen for a swift exit, no long goodbyes, no questions for which she didn't have answers.

She went through the rest of the palace, not stopping, her focus on the long trip to Stonegard. Just around the corner was the grand staircase above the magnificent entrance hall. She was almost running now, the anticipation growing. She sped around the final turn and was nearly floored. The noise erupted from the entrance hall below. Hundreds of people were shouting 'Goodbye, Farewell!' at the top of their voices. It seemed that the entire staff of the palace was there, as well as Hakeem and her brothers. And in the midst of it all, standing still, with a composed look on her face, her mother. Ariella tried to calm herself.

So much for a quick, quiet getaway.

I wonder who set this up? Hakeem? Maybe Thunder and Lightning as a final brotherly goodbye?

The only times she had walked down the grand staircase with a crowd to greet her were on occasions of state or lavish parties. For those, she would have been decked out in the most exquisite dresses of Lightharbour, silks and satins. Not today.

She looked down at the simple clothes she was wearing. Soft black leather riding boots with plain cotton trousers. A simple cotton shirt and a heavy jacket her father had given her for when he took her hunting. The jacket still smelled of the woods and fields, scents that always reminded her of him.

He would've let me go on the Journey. Wouldn't he?

She reached the bottom of the stairs to a multitude of bows and curtseys from the palace servants. Many of these had watched Ariella grow up and had served in the palace for years. There were some misty eyes around the room as people reminded each other of stories from her past. Osias and Calixto were grinning the same broad grin, their masses of curly, black hair looked even more unruly than usual.

"The real question today," began Calixto, "is what we're going to do with your room? Osais wants to turn it into an experimentation lab, but mother killed that idea."

"She was afraid I was going to burn down the palace," Osias said with genuine hurt in his voice.

Ariella smiled and threw her arms around both of their necks and pulled them roughly to her. She planted a massive kiss on each of their cheeks as they struggled against her.

"Get off!" they shouted together, but the crowd cheered in appreciation. Ariella kissed them again much to their disgust.

She finally let them go and turned to Hakeem, her wonderful Hakeem. He was the Chancellor, leader of the Council of Lightharbour, but he was so much more than that. He was her father's dearest friend and mother's most trusted advisor. She would miss him as much as she missed her family. She tried to control her tears, but her eyes filled up. She squeezed him as she closed her eyes and let the tears flow.

"Your father loved you so much, my dear child," said Hakeem. "He would have been so proud of you today."

"Yes, he would," answered the queen.

Ariella turned at her mother's voice and let go of Hakeem. It was the first time she had seen her since their argument in the library and overhearing her conversation on the echo orb. Queen Susanna looked her usual regal self, her long dark brown hair flowing down her back, braided with fine golden thread. She was taller than Ariella. The same slender build but carried with an air of unquestionable authority. She could silence whole rooms when she entered and end arguments with a tilt of her head. She was every inch the queen.

"He would have been immensely proud of you."

It was then Ariella noticed the slight redness around her eyes. It was something she had seen only a few times before. Her mother was a master of disguising what was happening behind those emerald eyes. But Ariella knew. Her mother had been crying. Right then, Ariella realised how much she loved her. She skipped the two steps towards her and embraced her as if she would never let go. Taken by surprise, the queen seemed uncertain at first. Then she embraced her daughter with equal zeal.

"I love you, Ariella."

She looked up at her mother. "I know I'll always be yours."

The queen kissed her softly on the forehead, then let her go.

Hakeem stepped forward, "It is time to leave, child."

"Not a child anymore," the queen corrected, "she's a sojourner."

The word stopped Ariella in her tracks. Sojourner. Suddenly it was all real. She turned and looked past the gathered crowd to the palace doors. They were standing open, inviting her. With a final smile at her mother, she turned towards the open doors. The crowd parted for her as she made her way into the bright morning sunlight.

Her horse was saddled and ready, the groom holding the reins and stroking the horse's forehead. She skilfully swung up into the saddle as her horse whinnied affectionately at her. He was a stunning bay, fifteen hands with a striking white star on his face. He had been a birthday gift from her mother three years ago, and Ariella jumped at every opportunity to ride him. She loved the freedom the horse gave her, either galloping through the surf beneath the Eagle Cliffs or hunting through the woods and fields that bordered Lightharbour. She had named him Crispin, a name she laughed at now.

Beside her were five more horses, four of them already had well-armed men mounted on them - the palace guards led by Captain Argon. Ariella had not had an easy relationship with the palace guards. Whenever she left the palace to go into the city, she was supposed to take an escort of the guards, but she hated it. She wanted to blend in and experience the city, to breathe in its wonder, so she had given her escort the slip a number of times. Her mother failed to see the funny side of it and would give her a lecture every time she did it. It never stopped her though; it was like she could not help herself.

Then Captain Argon got involved. The Captain of the Guards was a gruff, no-nonsense soldier who had little time for Ariella but took his job extremely seriously. He quickly identified that Ariella was the biggest safety risk in the royal household, so he had insisted on accompanying her personally whenever she left the palace. Ariella had tried many, many times to ditch him, but whatever plan she came up with she never managed to shake him off. All she wanted to do was to explore the city and have fun.

It's a little hard to do that with captain 'no fun' and his guards breathing down my neck.

"Your Highness," acknowledged the captain.

"Argon, do we need this many?"

The captain scowled, "I wanted an escort of twenty."

"Twenty!"

"That was my recommendation. The road to Stonegard is long, and there have been difficulties."

"You mean highwaymen, Argon."

"As I said, Your Highness, difficulties. The queen has made it clear that she is content with a close escort of five."

"Then you're one short, *Captain*."

He nodded in the direction of the guardhouse, over Ariella's shoulder. "He's on his way now. I needed him to finalise some details for the journey."

Ariella pirouetted her horse as the fifth guard approached. Her heart skipped, and her mouth went dry.

Oh no, not him. Why him?

The young guard strode towards the riders, his helm in his right hand, his left resting on the pommel of his longsword. Ariella sat up straighter in her saddle trying to catch his eye without *looking* like she was trying to catch his eye.

"Excellent. Now mount up, we have a long way to go today." Argon turned to Ariella. "Are you ready, Your Highness?"

"Of course," she replied curtly.

She was trying to sound like she was in control; unfortunately, she seemed spoiled.

Nice one, Ari, that was classy.

Frustrated with herself, she kicked her heels and spurred her horse forward at a canter, cutting across the palace courtyard. Her escort was taken by surprise but recovered quickly and was level with her by the time she was through the gates.

Her small escort led her through the crowded streets. Two behind, Captain Argon alongside and two in front, including the young guard. Ariella tried not to stare at him as he rode. He was a capable horseman, as were all the palace guards. His eyes swept the crowds back and forth, searching for anything out of place.

His name was Micah. He had only joined the palace guards last year. His father was a merchant who ran a small shop in Lightharbour that imported clockwork treasures from Khan. She had noticed him on his first day in the palace.

He was on sentry duty at the gates when she had left with her mother to buy presents for the twins. She remembered staring, without any subtlety, as they rode past. She nearly brought her horse to a halt in front of him. Thankfully her mother caught her reins and led the horse onwards. That would have been embarrassing, staring like a child in a sweet shop. She was not surprised when the next week's lessons with her tutors consisted of the intricacies of royal courtship. She learnt all about arranged marriages and the importance of succession.

I get the message, mother. I was only looking. But you're still looking, aren't you Ari?

She shook her head and tried to concentrate on something else. The crowds on the streets parted like water before the palace guards. They didn't draw any undue attention; they were a common sight on the roads of Lightharbour. The city was alive with noise. Everywhere she looked, there were people, carts and animals. Lightharbour was the principal trading port of Dawnhaven, and all around her, she could see people from the other kingdoms: nobles from Trevena decked in their finery; woodsmen from Darcian dressed in green with longbows slung across their backs; horse lords from the vast plains of Erestia with feathers strung through their hair and the Artificers of Khan, long-haired and bearded, their fur clothes making them stand out in the morning sun.

Intermingled with the people of Dawnhaven were travellers from across the Southern Sea. They were dark-skinned traders, their silks adding a splash of colour wherever they went. They brought with them exotic spices, plants and animals. The palace passion fruit vines that Ariella loved so much were imported years ago from one of these traders. Her favourite place to visit was Archibald's Emporium of Exotic Animals. Hakeem would take her there and show her the flamboyant parrots and mischievous spider monkeys. Ariella loved Lightharbour, the vibrancy, the smells, the mixing of so many cultures and customs.

The crowds grew as they approached the towering gates that stood open, dead in the centre of the high city walls. Built into the thick stone were whole houses and lines of shops. The gates were of oak, brought in from the Darcian Forest many years ago. They were weathered now, but still as strong as they had ever been. As they passed through, for a moment they were in shadow, then blazing sunshine.

All around them were gentle, rolling farms. The wheat and barley were growing well, green shoots emerging from the fertile soil. Surrounding Lightharbour were many farms like this. Not enough to sustain the entire city but enough to ward off starvation if a famine struck. It always seemed strange to Ariella that Lightharbour did not grow enough food to feed all its people. Such was the nature of Dawnhaven: five kingdoms, each independent yet forever linked. Each needed the other to survive, to flourish. It was what her grandfather, King Haldor, had always intended when the kingdom was divided more than twenty years ago.

They rode on through the day, stopping briefly for lunch. They rode long into the evening, spending the night in a comfortable inn on the roadside. Ariella guessed that word of her leaving had gone ahead of them as the innkeeper was expecting them. He went to great lengths to make sure that she was comfortable. Ariella smiled to herself.

Enjoy it while it lasts Ari, there's no way you're getting this treatment on the Journey.

It was an early start the next morning. The captain was particularly efficient at rousing his guards and Ariella, in preparation for the journey ahead. They would cross the border to Trevena later that day. Another day's riding would see them at Stonegard, just in time for the High Summer Festival and the start of the Journey.

The morning went by uneventfully. They passed through the Trevena border crossing without any issues. The border guards stood out in their bright red and orange uniform of the House of the Phoenix, royal house of King Tristan, Ariella's uncle. They waved them through with a simple nod of their heads.

There were other travellers on the road. Merchants and farmers were the most common. They passed by some travelling musicians who sprang into song when they saw the palace guards. It was a welcome break from the monotony of the ride. Unfortunately, they had soon overtaken them, and Ariella was left with the rhythm of Crispin's hooves and trying to not to stare at Micah.

Not long after lunch on that second day, they travelled through a small farming village. It was one of those idyllic settlements that Ariella imagined when she pictured Trevena. The houses were wooden framed with thatched roofs. The gardens were neatly tended, and flowers bloomed in the sunshine. There was a small inn, the Heifer's Rest, on the village green next to a duck pond.

It was not until the party had passed by the village green that a sense of uneasiness came over them. Argon, still riding next to Ariella, slowed the pace of his horse and stood in the stirrups. Looking from left to right, studying the scene, the other riders moved their horses around Ariella's, blocking her on all sides. They loosened their long swords in their scabbards.

"It's quiet," said the guard on Ariella's right.

Argon was silent for a moment, listening. "Lukas," he said to the guard riding next to Micah, "Ride on, slowly, point position."

The guard turned his horse and trotted fifty metres in front of the rest, then slowed his horse and walked forwards. The others formed a diamond around Ariella and followed Lukas. The tension was thick in the air, but the guards were calm, their eyes alert. Ariella realised that in the change of formation, the captain was riding in front of her. Micah was now on her right, so close she could reach out and touch him.

Will you please get a grip! He is here to guard you, and they are all ready to fight for you, and all you're thinking about is how close his arm is.

The sound of shouting, some way in the distance, interrupted her thoughts. Lukas held up his hand, and the party stopped. He bent his head, listening, then he waved them forward. The riders covered the fifty metres at speed.

"It's coming from the left, off the main road somewhere. Sounds like an argument over land, someone mentioned poison." Lukas informed them. "It's getting serious, I think they want to flog someone."

Argon took charge. "Okay, keep alert and let's get through this village. Get ready to run if we need to. Lukas, lead on."

"What?" Ariella questioned, staring at the Argon.

"We're leaving, Your Highness."

"Leaving? They're going to flog someone!"

"So, it would seem, but that is none of our concern today. We must remain focused on delivering you safely to Stonegard."

"None of our concern? We have to intervene!"

"Intervene?" Argon asked, trying to keep the frustration out of his voice.

"Yes!"

"No, Your Highness."

"No?" Ariella was stunned. No Captain of the Guard said "No" to her.

"No. My orders are simple, Your Highness. We are to get you to Stonegard in time for High Summer." He turned his horse away from her. The other riders gathered around Crispin.

"I'm the princess. I'm changing your orders."

Argon didn't even turn his head. "My orders come directly from the queen. We are taking you to Stonegard."

Ariella looked at the guards. None of them was watching her. The other riders were bunched in around Crispin, but she still had his reins. She gripped them tightly. The rider to her left paused as he turned his head to check the road behind them. It was a small gap, but it was all she needed. Pressing her heels into Crispin's side, she urged her mount through the gap towards the sounds of shouting.

5

Dead Fish and Rolling Pins

Ariella kicked Crispin into a gallop, and they flew across the field in the direction Lukas had indicated. Behind her, she could hear the shouts of the guards and the captain bellowing orders.

He'll get over it. I'm not letting them flog somebody over an argument.

There were a few scattered houses to either side of her as the grassy field sloped downwards. At the far end was a large farmhouse with several outbuildings. It sounded like the shouting was coming from the barn furthest away. Ariella pointed Crispin towards the barn and drove him on. She risked a glance over her shoulder. The guards were streaking after her and gaining ground. One of the guards was blowing hard on a small silver bugle.

Yeah, like I'm going to stop because you blew your little trumpet. Good luck with that.

She rounded the barn at full speed and right into a small mob of people. She had to pull Crispin up fast to stop her trampling over a particularly rotund lady with a fierce expression. She was facing the mob and whirling a heavy rolling pin around her head.

"Flog him!" she was shouting. "Flay the poisonous little imp! He's trying to kill us all!"

She was still whirling the rolling pin when she noticed Ariella. In all the noise, no one had heard her approach.

"Here's another one!" she screeched, pointing the rolling pin at Ariella. "They've come to kill our children!"

The mob went quiet for a moment as they tried to take in this new arrival. It appeared they were not used to fifteen-year-old girls galloping around their village on horseback. A barrel-chested beast of a man, with hands the size of loaves of bread, stepped forward.

"And who exactly do you think you are?" he asked, threateningly. He was just about to take another step towards her when Ariella's particularly unhappy escort charged around the corner of the barn, swords drawn.

Chaos erupted.

The guards tried to surround Ariella, but she was barging them out of the way with her horse. The captain was barking orders at his men while threatening the barrel-chested man and keeping a wary eye on the woman swinging the rolling pin. The barrel-chested man was shouting abuse at the captain and the rest of the guards. The rolling pin woman was advancing on the captain, convinced that she could take on the swords. All the while, one of the guards was blowing incessantly on his bugle.

Ariella finally lost it.

"Will you all shut up!" she yelled, standing high in her stirrups.

The effect was instantaneous. Everyone fell silent, much to her surprise. Even the bugle player stopped in mid blow, lips still around the end of the small horn.

Heck, they listened, that's a surprise. At least it shut up the fool on the bugle. If he plays one more note I'm going to trample it into the mud.

Argon pushed his horse forward in front of Ariella. "Your Highness, kindly leave this to the professionals."

"Please, Captain, can you and your men put away your swords?"

"Your Highness, I am sworn to protect you, and you are in danger."

"From a rolling pin, Captain, are you quite sure?"

The captain shot the lady with the rolling pin a fierce look and reluctantly motioned for his men to put away their swords.

He did as I said, that's a first. Now, let's figure out what's going on.

Ariella smiled at the large, fearsome lady. "Madam, if you would be so kind as to lower your rolling pin that would make the captain here much more relaxed."

Unused to being addressed in such a polite manner, the woman, somewhat against her will, found herself lowering the rolling pin and taking a step backwards. The barrel-chested man was still standing in front of Ariella and was still glaring.

"Now good sir, I am Princess Ariella of Lightharbour, House of the Eagle. Would you please let me know your name?"

Flustered, the man tried an awkward bow. Bowing was not something they did a lot in the village. Nor was meeting a princess and her guards.

"Your, err, ladyness, I am Robert of err...this farm and err...that house over there."

"Excellent," smiled Ariella, trying to reassure the man and keep the situation calm. "My escort and I were just passing through your village on the way to Stonegard. We noticed that you were upset about something. Is that right?"

"Damn right!" bellowed the rolling pin lady, finding her voice again. "This sewer rat," she waved her rolling pin towards somewhere near the back of the crowd, but Ariella couldn't make anyone out, "has been poisoning our fields and our river. If we hadn't caught him in time, he would've poisoned the lot of us. We're going to beat him, and there's nothing you can do about it!" she said, swinging her rolling pin again and staring at the captain.

"My good lady..." began Ariella.

"Don't you 'good lady' me! I'm no la-de-da *lady*, and this isn't Lightharbour, it's Trevena, so why don't you and you little soldiers sod off!" She took a step forward, pointing the rolling pin at Ariella.

The palace guards simultaneously drew their swords again and tried to surround Ariella.

"Put them away!" said Ariella, exasperatedly. "She's got a rolling pin, not a battle axe. Madam, we mean you no harm. We are only small in number and, as I said, we were on our way to Stonegard when..."

Ariella's voice dropped off as she heard a growing rumble coming from behind the barn. The noise grew louder and louder until bursting around the side of the barn came a troop of heavily armed palace guards, their banners displaying the House of the Eagle.

"What?" Ariella was spluttering. "What are you doing here?"

The lead rider ignored her and looked at Captain Argon who gave a series of hand movements. Immediately, the new guards surrounded the mob, spears lowered, creating a wall of steel with no way out.

"Help!" someone shouted.

"We're being invaded!" yelled another.

"We're all going to die!" came a high pitched voice.

"Captain, would you like to tell me, exactly, what is going on?" Ariella was trying to remain calm, but she could feel the anger building.

"My orders come from the queen and I am obeying them," he snapped.

"What orders?" she asked.

The captain shot Ariella an icy glare. "Our duty is the safety of the House of the Eagle, that includes you. I am ordered to do whatever is necessary to protect you from an imminent threat."

"Imminent threat? Is that what you're calling it? A threat from an unarmed farmer named Robert and a militant milkmaid with a rolling pin! Have they got you and your men terrified, Captain?"

"She was threatening you, Your Highness."

"With a rolling pin! This was what the bugle was about, wasn't it? You were signalling them!" She glared back at the bugle player who seemed to shrink even further into his saddle.

Ariella turned her attention to the scene in front of her. The villagers had quickly turned from a baying mob to a quivering mass. All except the rolling pin lady. She was still swinging the pin and threatening soldiers.

"Everyone put away your weapons!" Ariella shouted.

The guards hesitated, looking back and forth between the crowd, the captain and the princess.

"Now!" she yelled.

Reluctantly, Argon gave a curt nod. The guards raised their spears and put away their swords, but they kept their horses surrounding the villagers.

"Now, everyone back away, slowly." Ariella stared down any of the guards that dared to look at her. Eventually, they all moved several paces away from the villagers.

"Captain, would you mind explaining to me why there are now another fifty palace guards standing with us in this field?"

"I do not take orders from or justify my actions to you, Your Highness. My orders are directly from the queen." He did not appreciate the tone Ariella was using.

"Queen's orders? That was what you meant by 'finalising some details' when we were back at the palace, was it? They've been following us since then, haven't they? I thought you said that you wanted an escort of twenty. Why are there fifty of them?"

The captain didn't answer. He glared at Ariella, his displeasure evident.

"This is ridiculous. What did she expect to happen to me?"

"If I may be so bold, Your Highness, I believe she foresaw a situation like this."

Ariella spun around, wondering who had spoken. She blinked hard, her mouth dry. It was Micah, his deep, brown eyes locked with hers. There was no hint of a smile; he was serious.

"That's what you think, is it?"

Damn, he's gorgeous, I could stare into those eyes all day. What? Get a grip, Ari!

"Okay let's see if we can sort this mess out then. Captain, withdraw your men to the other side of the barn."

"No,"

"No?"

"No," the captain said again. "I will not neglect my duty and leave you unattended."

"No, of course not, I'm in danger. After all, she does have a rolling pin."

The captain seemed about to argue but relented. "Micah, stay with the princess. Do not leave her side. The rest of you, with me." The captain turned his horse and trotted to the other side of the barn, thirty yards away but out of sight. Micah moved his horse, so it was almost touching Ariella's. His eyes were fixed on the rolling pin wielding lady at the front of the crowd.

Well, that turned out wonderfully.

Ariella was suddenly extremely conscious that her hair must be a mess after the gallop across the field. She tried to run her hands through it, and flick it across her shoulder away from Micah, revealing her better side. At least that's what she hoped she was doing. She was concentrating so hard on making herself look good that she missed the hush that fell on the group. She tried several more times to get her hair to do what she wanted when, at last, she noticed the silence. She jolted her hand back to her side and looked around. Everyone was staring at her with a bemused look on their face. Robert the farmer, the rolling pin lady, the crowd behind her, and, of course, Micah.

She coughed loudly, "Right," she said, "shall we get started?" She cast a sideways look at Micah who had gone back to watching the rolling pin lady.

Well, that was about as embarrassing as it could get. Top job Ari, outstanding work.

She turned her attention to the villagers in front of her and found Robert, the barrel-chested farmer.

"Robert, would you be so kind as to tell me what's been going on?"

"Well, your ladyness, it's been a bit of a long tale, you see." He cleared his throat loudly and then launched into his story. "The fields have been looking weak this year, not just my fields, but all of them: Trevor's farm down the lane and old Paddy's place on the other side of the river. Looking weak they all have been. No one knew why. The sun's been shining, rain's been pouring, the soil is good. We were all a bit clueless. Then yesterday morning, little Daniel was fishing in the river when he saw the fish, your ladyness." He paused, clearly upset.

"Go on," Ariella urged.

"They're dead, your ladyness, all of them. Just lying there in the river, belly up, dead, completely dead. I checked them with a stick. All the fish were dead."

"She gets the picture, Robert, get on with it so we can punish him," the rolling pin lady snapped, tapping her pin against her open hand.

Ariella ignored her, "Keep going, Robert."

"The river was dark, the water I mean, it looked dark, it was creepy with all them fish lying belly up an' all. Well, then it got horrible. Old Paddy was out in his field this morning checking on his wheat, and that's when he saw it." His face turned white and he hesitated. A solemn silence hung heavily on the crowd. Even the rolling pin lady stopped still.

"It's like they're, well, bleeding."

"Bleeding? What is bleeding?"

"The wheat, your ladyness, the roots of wheat were bleeding. It was thick, sticky blood, so dark it was almost black. It was the freakiest thing I've ever seen in my life. When Paddy found it, he came screaming across the fields like he'd seen a ghost. Then we all started pulling up the plants in our fields. It's the same everywhere in the village: wheat, barley, turnips, spuds, even the roots of Esme's marigolds were bleeding." He nodded towards the rolling pin lady. She gave a loud sniff and wiped her teary eyes at the thought of her bleeding marigolds.

A tall, gangly man with a long wispy grey beard stepped forward from the crowd. He held out a long green shoot of wheat, freshly pulled from the field. Ariella dropped down from her saddle, Micah mirroring her movements, hand ever on the pommel of his sword.

She stepped forward, her eyes fixed on the roots. What should have been fresh, healthy roots were tangled and matted. Matted with something that looked exactly like dark, dried blood.

Ariella reached out to take the shoot, but Micah was quicker. Stepping forward before she could touch it, he took it in his gloved hand. He lifted it close to Ariella, allowing her to examine it. She leant in to look at it, but the smell made her gag.

"What is that smell?"

"Blood," Micah spoke grimly, eyes narrowed, turning the shoot over in his fingers. "It smells exactly like blood."

"But how? Plants don't bleed, not wheat, turnips or marigolds. It's got to be a trick, right?" She realised how uncertain she sounded as she looked up at Micah trying to get some reassurance.

"No, Your Highness, they don't, but," he paused, looking over to Robert. "You said this is all over the village?"

"Yes, every field we've checked."

"See! I told you, poisonous little imp, let's flog him and put a stop to this!" Esme was wielding her rolling pin again.

There was a murmur of consent from the crowd.

"Bring him here," called Esme, desperate to see justice done.

The crowd began to part and two burly men, who looked like farmhands, walked forward. Between them, arms pinned behind his back, was a boy, roughly the same age as Ariella, with hair as white as the driven snow.

Ariella leaned towards Micah and whispered, "Quickly, go and get the captain." He looked at her, his face serious, and nodded. The two men half marched, half dragged the boy to where Ariella was standing with Robert and Esme.

"This is him, didn't I tell you? Poisoner! Look at that hair, unnatural it is, he's an evil little grunt!"

The boy lifted his head and gave Esme a filthy look. His white hair was matted with dirt while blood dripped from a gash just above his left ear. His face was drawn and dirty, a few bruises were starting to swell up. But despite all this, Ariella recognised him instantly.

"Oh, no."

She hadn't meant to say it out loud. As soon as she spoke, the boy flicked his head towards her, the recognition showing immediately in his face.

He grinned.

"Hello, Ariella, fancy meeting you here and under such wonderful circumstances."

The two men holding the boy shook him when he spoke and shoved his head forward. Esme and Robert gasped and looked at Ariella.

"You know him?" Stunned, Robert was looking back and forth between the boy and Ariella.

"I told you she was one of them!" Esme's rolling pin was swinging again "They're here to finish us all off. They want us dead, and our children!"

The crowd was furious now. Some of the men were flexing their muscles and slamming fists into open palms. Ariella took a step back and stumbled. She bumped right into the returning Micah, who caught her quickly. She looked up at him, hoping to see those brown eyes looking down on her. Micah was looking ahead, eyes on the crowd. He returned her to her feet simply, professionally. Ariella flushed.

Well, that was awkward and wonderful all at the same time, not had many moments I can say that about.

The captain stepped in front of them, facing down the crowd. His sword remained in its sheath, but his cold, hard stare was enough to keep them back for the time being.

"We are not here with this young tramp. We have no idea who he is or what he is doing." The captain's tone was threatening, and he touched his sword hilt as he spoke.

Ariella coughed lightly, "Captain, that is not entirely true."

"Your Highness?" It was the captain's turn to look shocked. "You know this boy?"

"Well, sort of. He was at the Announcement, he's one of the ten. He's a sojourner too."

"This one? A sojourner? Have the Guardians let their standards slip?" The captain was incredulous.

Esme was spluttering. "This one can't be a Guardian, he's a poisoner I tell you! We caught him by the river looking suspicious, he was all shifty, keeping to the shadows and trying not to be seen."

The boy laughed at that. "Of course I was trying not to be seen, I was trespassing! I was trying to water my horse without getting set upon by you village idiots!"

"Did you find the poison when you searched him?" It was Micah, asking calmly, but deliberately.

"Of course not," Esme snapped. "He hid it, didn't he?"

"Did he? Where? You've found his horse, I assume? No poison anywhere around?"

"Err, no." Esme was starting to look unsure of herself, so Micah pushed his advantage.

"Robert, you mentioned that the fields have been looking weak for a while now, and you found the fish dead yesterday morning?"

"Yes, that's right."

"Well, that settles it," smiled Micah.

"It settles nothing!" she was pointing her rolling pin at Micah now.

"This boy was with us two days ago in Lightharbour. He could not have got here yesterday morning. Robert said whatever has been ruining your crops has been going on for a few months. There is no way the boy was involved."

The villagers looked uncertain now, a few of them nodding at Micah's logic.

"Well, he was still trespassing! We can put him in the stocks." Esme was getting desperate.

"Oh, shut up Esme," muttered Robert motioning to the two men holding the boy and they dumped him, unceremoniously, on the ground. The villagers drifted away as the boy slowly got to his feet, rubbing life back into his arms.

"Thanks for that," he nodded at Micah who returned it without a smile. "Now, where have they put my horse?" He started to walk away.

"Wait!" Ariella called after him.

"What's up, Ari?"

Micah looked startled, "Her name is Princess Ariella."

"Nope, not anymore," the boy met the Micah's stare without flinching. "She's a sojourner now. There are no titles in the Guardians, no hierarchy; we are all the same." He turned to look at Ariella, "She better get used to it. Now, where is that stupid horse?"

The boy turned and walked away. Micah and Ariella made their way back to the rest of the guards and their horses.

"I'm glad I recognised him," said Ariella, "Or that could've ended badly. It was the hair, it stands out a mile. The problem is I can't remember his name. There were nine others at the Announcement, and I was, err, preoccupied. I can't remember any of their names."

They turned their horses and trotted back up the gentle slope towards the main road through the village.

"Micah, lead on," Argon ordered.

43

He nodded and kicked his horse into a canter. As he rode past Ariella, he spoke so quietly she almost missed it.

"My name is Eleazar."

6

Butterflies at Night

Ariella did not think she would like Trevena. She was used to the bustle of Lightharbour, the noise and smells. Lightharbour was an assault on the senses; everywhere you looked there was something new to take in. The countryside of Trevena was as far removed from that as Ariella could imagine.

Trevena was renowned as the garden of Dawnhaven. It seemed that everywhere she looked something was growing. They passed wheat and barley next to fields of corn. There was a dizzying array of vegetables being grown and, off to the south, away in the distance, they caught a glimpse of the great vineyards. All of the wine of Dawnhaven was grown in Southern Trevena.

One of Ariella's tutors spent a whole week describing to her different types of soil, drainage and grape varieties. She used to doze off in those lessons until she slipped a glass of her mother's wine from the table one day. She could remember the ruby red liquid splashing in the crystal as she took a sip. It seemed beautiful to her, heavy with fruit and fabulous aroma. She could still remember the taste. She managed only a sip before her mother caught her and whisked the glass away. From then on, she paid more attention to her tutors when they taught about wine.

As they passed that last day riding along the roads of Trevena, she found herself growing to like the countryside there. The people seemed calmer here than in Lightharbour; the pace of life was slower, more peaceful.

Peaceful? We're not adding to the peace with fifty-five palace guards trotting by. What am I thinking? I can't ride into Stonegard like this, I'll look a total idiot.

She called out to the captain, riding a little way ahead of her. "How long until we arrive in Stonegard, Captain?"

The captain did not turn around. "We'll be there before sunset, Your Highness, all being well."

The sun was high in the sky. She guessed it was just past midday.

She called back to him. "Do you think we could send some of these Guards back to Lightharbour? I'd rather not ride into Stonegard with a small army at my back. My uncle might get suspicious. He'll think I'm trying to capture the city."

The captain pulled up his horse and looked up and down at the ranks of riders. He seemed to be weighing up his options.

"Come on, we'll be safe now. I promise not to go riding off on my own or do anything else stupid."

The captain's eyes narrowed as he stared long and hard at Ariella. "Please, Captain?"

"Okay, Your Highness, we're close enough to Stonegard to be safe now. I'll get the fifty to stay behind us, out of sight - but within earshot of the bugle."

The captain halted the column then turned his horse and trotted down the line to the leader of the fifty. After a brief conversation, the horsemen peeled off to the side of the road and dismounted. The original five riders arranged themselves in formation around Ariella.

Next stop, Stonegard and the Journey. You better be ready, Ari, this is going to be an exciting year.

The setting sun cast a warm glow on the countryside as the riders approached the city walls of Stonegard, the great capital of Trevena. In the years before the breaking when Dawnhaven was one kingdom, Trevena had been the capital of the whole island. It was built by some distant relative of Ariella's whose name she could never recall.

She could remember coming here as a child and loving the tall towers with bright orange and red pennants fluttering in the breeze. It always felt like a proper castle to her, not like the palace at Lightharbour. This castle had battlements and arrow slits for the archers. There was a deep moat with a long drawbridge and portcullis.

The guards here looked so different from their Lightharbour equivalents. Ariella's guards wore either stiffened leather or chainmail under their uniforms. The walls of Stonegard were lined with guards in shining plate mail that reflected the last rays of sunlight into the faces of the riders. Two thick grey stone walls surrounded a massive central keep. The moat was deep and still, the water an inky blue. When she was here as a child, she had always tried to spot the golden fish that would swim lazily under the drawbridge.

The road was heavy with traffic today as preparations were being made for the High Summer Festival. There were carts carrying salted beef and wild boar. Huge Shire horses were pulling giant trailers laden with barrels of wine from the southern vineyards. They passed wagons stacked high with crates filled with all manner of fireworks brought in from Khan.

Micah was waiting for them amid the passing carts and horses. "Looks like the preparations are in full swing. The innkeeper at the Friendly Phoenix is expecting us, Your Highness. All arrangements for your arrival have been made."

"The Friendly Phoenix?" came a voice from the crowd.

The small party turned to see Eleazar leaning on a large cart filled with barrels of salted beef, marked with the emblem of Wolftop, capital of Erestia.

"Really?" The captain scowled. "Are you following us, boy? I'd advise against it, I don't like being followed."

"My dear Argon, this a free city and I am at liberty to spend my last night of freedom wherever I choose."

"And how can someone like you afford the Friendly Phoenix?"

"Someone like me? I have no idea what you're driving at, Argon. I'm a simple young man spending his hard-earned coin on the finer things of life one last time." With that, he turned, winked at Ariella and led his horse off into the crowd, whistling happily.

The innkeeper at the Friendly Phoenix wonderfully matched the name of his inn. His hair was bright orange and his suit was scarlet. He seemed to shine in the candlelight as he showed Ariella to her room.

"It is such a pleasure to welcome royalty to my humble inn," he said. "Most royal guests stay in the Keep." Ariella was momentarily uncomfortable.

"I'm not here as a guest of my uncle. I'm here for High Summer," she paused, "and the Journey."

The Innkeeper's eyes grew wide, but he was too respectful to say anything. He smiled a caring smile and left her in her room. "Finest room in the inn, and therefore the finest room in Stonegard," the innkeeper had told her. "Except the royal rooms in the Keep, of course," he added with a bow.

The room was excellent, opulent even, but all it served to do was make Ariella think of home. It was the first time since she had left Lightharbour that she had missed the palace and her family.

It's a bit late for all that, Ari. High Summer tomorrow and then the Journey. Anything could happen.

She turned in early, after trying to eat the supper that Captain Argon had arranged for her. She was so nervous about the next day that she could hardly take a bite. Sleep eluded her for hours as she tossed back and forth in the bed. She dozed for a while and then woke again. The blankets were too hot, then she was too cold. Too many pillows, then not enough.

Will you get a grip?

She was getting frustrated with herself. Her stomach started rumbling, which made sleeping even harder.

I wonder if there's any supper left over? I'm sure there'll be someone on duty downstairs who'll let me raid the kitchen.

She threw on some clothes and tiptoed to the door. It opened silently, and she stepped out onto the thick carpet of the hallway and froze.

Standing in the shadows in the centre of the long corridor was a figure. Dressed entirely in tight black clothes with a black hood drawn up over their head, they blended seamlessly into the darkness. Ariella squinted as she made out the form. Their back was toward her, stooped as if listening.

Ariella was rooted to the spot.

Who the hell is that? And more to the point, what do they want?

The silhouette was going slowly from door to door, moving away from Ariella. It paused at each door for a few moments and then moved to the next.

It looks like they're listening. But for what? Breathing? These doors are thick. How good can their hearing be?

The figure checked two more doors, then stopped longer than usual at the second to last door along the hallway. Ariella watched as they adjusted their hood with a gloved hand exposing their ear. Silently they pressed it against the door and waited. Ariella held her breath, still watching.

The hooded figure pulled away, readjusted their hood and stood to full height. They were shorter than Ariella with a slim frame. Their hand slipped into the pocket of the black cloak and pulled out something tiny, no bigger than a hairpin. They moved their hands towards the door.

It's a lock pick! That's a thief. Now, what do I do?

She realised she had no weapons and was pretty sure she couldn't take this hooded thief in a fight. The intruder withdrew the lock pick and placed it back in their pocket. Then, ever so slowly, put their hand on the door handle and turned it.

Okay, Ari, any bright ideas?

She only had one. She took a deep breath, and she screamed. A full-blooded, top of the lungs, someone is ripping my arms off, type of scream. The effect was instantaneous. The hooded figure spun around to face Ariella. Their face was covered with a mask. Only their eyes could be seen. But those eyes. Blue. Ice cold blue. Even in the half-light of the hallway, those eyes left a mark on Ariella.

She gasped.

It's a woman.

Ariella heard the captain's thunderous voice and the sound of running feet. Doors were banging open, and there was the unmistakable sound of swords being drawn from their sheaths. It seemed that the whole inn had awoken.

The hooded figure blinked once and then...flash. It was like a blur. Ariella hardly saw it but she felt a burning sensation in her left shoulder.

Micah, the captain and the other guards came charging up the stairs as the thief dived through the open window at the far end of the corridor. Micah flew after them with the other guards following as Argon ran to Ariella's side.

"Princess Ariella! What's happened?" His face was grave.

The pain in her shoulder was now almost unbearable. She started to slump to the floor, but the captain caught her and laid her down gently, his brow furrowed.

"The woman," Ariella pointed feebly in the direction of the window. "She's a thief."

He reached out his hand to her shoulder. She felt a sharp pain, then darkness washed over her. The last thing she remembered was the captain holding a small thin dart, the tip red with her blood and the other end shaped into a pair of delicate, colourful butterfly wings.

7

Sojourner

Ariella woke to the sound of muffled voices from the far side of the room. The low light of sunrise was streaming through a gap in her curtains, specks of dust gently floating in the air.

She lay awake for a moment, trying to piece together what had just happened. She remembered the hooded figure trying to break into the room along the hallway. In her mind, she could still see the cold blue eyes and the flash of the woman's hand as she sent the tiny dart flying towards her. She remembered the captain, Micah and the other guards rushing to the sound of her scream. And the butterfly dart. She remembered how pretty she thought it looked as the captain pulled it from her shoulder.

She lifted her hand to the point where the dart had hit her. There was a small hole in her shirt, but no pain. She pushed her finger through the hole onto her skin. Still no pain. She jabbed her finger again, hard into her flesh. Nothing.

From the far side of her room, she heard a muffled conversation. She sat up quickly, and the voices stopped. "Your Highness?" It was the captain, a look of concern on his face. "How are you?"

"I'm fine. Strangely." Ariella's finger was still on her shoulder, trying to find the mark left by the dart. "What happened? There's no mark, no pain at all."

"Yes. Your Highness, may I introduce Karlov Featherfall." The captain motioned to the man standing beside him. Karlov was younger than the captain, around Micah's age.

His blonde hair was cut short, his eyes were severe but young. He was frowning, a mixture of concern and annoyance.

"Is there any pain in your shoulder Ariella?" Karlov asked. The question was direct, almost blunt.

Ariella was still a little groggy, "Who are you?"

Karlov didn't answer.

Who is this guy? What's he doing in my room?

The captain coughed. Then she saw it. A round metal disc pinned on the left side of Karlov's chest, right over his heart. A small golden circle with a sliver of deep green emerald. The dawning sun rising over a field of green.

"You're a Guardian!"

"And you're a sojourner." He moved towards her bed. "I asked 'Is there any pain in your shoulder?'"

"No, none at all. I don't understand."

Karlov raised his hand and closed his eyes. Ariella didn't notice it at first, but ever so slowly, a pale green light began to radiate from Karlov's hand. It formed an aura that seemed to silently pulse. He placed his hand on Ariella's shoulder, right over where the dart had entered. She felt a gentle warmth and then it was gone.

Karlov closed his hand and turned to the captain. "The High Summer Festival begins in an hour, she needs to be ready."

The captain nodded, and Karlov left the room without looking back at Ariella.

"Captain, will you please tell me what happened?"

"Forgive me, Your Highness, but there is no time. You heard Karlov, in an hour you have to be in the city square. You need to get dressed."

And with that, he too was gone, leaving Ariella alone in her room.

That's just great, what happened last night? Who was the woman in the hood, and what did she stick me with? How did Karlov end up in my room with the captain? And he's a Guardian. I hope I don't see him today. I don't think he likes me.

She gave her head a shake and jumped from the bed, dressing quickly. Looking around the room, she found her backpack and the old hunting jacket.

She checked the echo orbs were still deep in her pockets, then stepped out into the hallway. Micah and another guard were waiting for her. Their faces were alert, and they both had their hands resting on the hilts of their swords.

"Are you ready to go, Your Highness?" Micah asked her.

"Yes," but she paused, her hand on her shoulder, eyes towards the window at the end of the hallway. Through it, she could see the rooftops of Stonegard and the blue summer sky.

"Did you get her?"

"Her, Your Highness?"

"Yes, the woman in the hood."

Micah shook his head. "Unfortunately, not. He," he corrected himself, "sorry, she was gone by the time I got to the window."

Ariella wasn't surprised. There was something about the way the hooded woman moved, the way she so easily attacked Ariella.

She wasn't a novice, she had done that many, many times before. She had an escape route planned. There was no chance Micah could've got to her.

The other guard shifted and looked up at Micah, who nodded in response.

"Your Highness, it's time. We have to go."

She led them down the stairs and found Captain Argon and the other guards waiting for them. They left the Friendly Phoenix in a tight group, the captain taking no chances. Ariella was enclosed within the guards as they moved through the crowd.

It seemed everyone in the city was on the way to the main square. The start of the Journey was the highlight of the High Summer Festival and no one wanted to miss it. The city square was awash with colour: bright red and orange pennants of Trevena mixed with the gold and green of the Guardians.

At the far end of the square was a stage erected against the inside of the inner wall. It was empty at the moment, but Ariella knew that in a short while she would be up there with the forty-nine other sojourners, ten from each kingdom ready to begin their five year Journey. The first year would be here in Trevena, then Khan, Darcian, and the fourth year in her own Lightharbour before finishing in Erestia. She had never travelled outside of Lightharbour and Trevena but travelling to the other kingdoms was something Ariella was most looking forward to. She had read about the massive mountains of Khan, the dense forests of Darcian and vast Erestian plains. Reading was one thing, now she would actually be able to go and see them for herself.

The captain led the small group through the crowded square over to the far side, near the stage. There was a small roped off area in front of a large oak door set in the inner wall. Outside the door were two guards, a man and a woman, who also wore green and gold discs.

They watched the small group as they approached, their faces expressionless. As the group got to the rope, the woman stepped forward.

"This area is sealed. Sojourners only." Her tone was official. She looked past the captain, her eyes on Ariella.

The captain pulled a scroll from inside his jacket and handed it to the woman. She turned it over in her hand, examining the wax seal. She nodded, broke the seal and unrolled the scroll.

She looked up, her eyes again on Ariella. "Ariella Lightharbour?"

Ariella nodded, her mouth too dry to speak. She suddenly felt weak with nerves, the pit of her stomach churning.

"We have never trained a princess before."

Ariella dropped her gaze and stared at her toes. "When you step past this rope, you are no longer a princess. Are you ready for that?" There was an almost disbelieving tone in the woman's voice.

She doesn't think I can do it.

The nervousness she had felt moments before turned to stubborn pride. Ariella met the woman's gaze and stepped past the captain. "I'm ready, and I can handle myself," she said.

The woman nodded and half-smiled. "We'll see. My name is Lalea Onderskat. Welcome to the Guardians." She removed the rope barrier and stepped aside, allowing Ariella to approach the door in the wall.

She hesitated and turned to look at the guards. Captain Argon's face was like granite.

"Princess Ariella, I have discharged my duty. You are now under the authority of the Guardians." He turned on his heel, began walking away, then stopped. He half turned and met Ariella's eyes. "Good luck, Your Highness," he said, then he was gone.

The rest of the guards followed Argon. Micah was the last to go. He was watching her, a smile on his face.

What is that for? Is he happy to be rid of me? No, it's more like, pride. He's proud of me!

Ariella's first instinct was to run and throw her arms around him. Lalea must have noticed the look in Ariella's eyes. She laid a firm hand on her shoulder and steered her back towards the door.

"Let's go, Ariella. You're the last to arrive."

The second guard opened the door for her and she stepped through. She blinked as she went from the bright sunlight into the gloom of the large waiting room within the inner wall.

The waiting hall was vast. There were no windows. The light was provided by a series of burning torches fixed along two long walls. The room was sparse; there was no furniture and, as far as Ariella could tell, there was only the door she came through. Scattered throughout the large room were small groups of young men and women, the sojourners.

"You made it!" Eleazar strolled towards Ariella. "I thought you'd changed your mind and run off back to your palace in Lightharbour."

Ariella gave him a frosty look. "I'm happy to disappoint you."

"Oh, Your Highness, you misunderstand me. I'm thrilled to be spending my Journey with such an esteemed person as yourself." He bowed, mockingly, and grinned at Ariella, thoroughly enjoying himself.

She had a sudden urge to smash her fist into Eleazar's sarcastic mouth. "I should've left you with Esme and her rolling pin."

"But, Your Highness, think of all the fun we would have missed out on over the next five years together."

Ariella swore under her breath and clenched her fist. The blast of trumpets echoing through the walls of the waiting room interrupted her.

The sojourners froze. It was time.

Lalea stepped into the middle of the room and raised her voice. "Welcome to the Journey. You will now be formed into your Knots. Each Knot will have a boy and a girl from each of the five kingdoms, ten in total. Your Knot will be your new family for the five years of the Journey. When your name is called, follow me." She unrolled a piece of paper and read out ten names in quick succession. Without waiting for any acknowledgement, she walked from the room, out towards the stage.

There was a moment of hesitation, and then ten people hurried to follow her.

A hush fell in the room and then bubbles of excited conversation sprung up amongst the remaining sojourners. Ariella side stepped Eleazar before he could start again and walked to the far side of the room. More trumpets were sounded from outside, sounds of cheering and clapping. Ariella began to feel nauseous, her insides churning.

Keep it together Ari, you're not a child anymore.

A moment later, Lalea walked purposefully to the middle of the room again. It was the same routine, ten names, ten people left for the stage. More trumpets, more cheering.

Only thirty of us left.

She scanned the room and spotted Eleazar's white hair amongst a group that Ariella thought she recognised. They must be the others from Lightharbour. She tried to remember some of them, but the day of the Announcement had not been good for her. She had been so consumed with her own problems that she couldn't think of any of their names.

In what seemed like moments, Lalea was back in the room with another ten names. Ariella was listening as they were read, names she didn't recognise. Five names, six names, seven names, then she heard it

"Eleazar Heredis."

She held her breath.

Please not me, please not me.

Lalea lifted her head from the paper and looked straight at her. "Ariella Lightharbour."

Ariella tried hard not to react as she followed the others from the room. Eleazar stepped in next to her. "Isn't this fantastic?" He laughed, sarcastically, "You get to spend the next five years with me!"

Ignoring him, Ariella stepped into the sunlight, the sound of trumpets and cheering crowds filling her ears.

At the far end of the stage were the twenty sojourners that had gone before them. Dead centre of the stage Ariella spotted her uncle, King Tristan, ruler of Trevena. She had a good relationship with him. He was her mother's oldest brother and always had a stern look on his face and serious air about him. Ariella used to try and make him laugh when she was younger. Sometimes it would take her hours, but eventually she'd get a smile.

As she climbed the steps to the stage, she tried to catch his eye, to get a smile or a nod, some form of acknowledgement that might calm her nerves. The King was inspecting each of the sojourners as they stepped on to the stage. Ariella watched his eyes as they went from one face to the next. She saw his eyes move to Eleazar, just in front of her, then on to her. She smiled a big, friendly smile. The king blinked, frowned and looked away.

Great, he's angry with me too.

She barely noticed that the others had stopped and lined up on the stage. The crowd was still cheering as the king raised his hand for silence. Lalea addressed the crowd with a voice that carried to the very back of the square.

"People of Dawnhaven, I present to you Indio Gryphonfriend and Phoebe Montecorde from the Khan mountains; Jaron Asheart and Theia Silvestris from the Darcian forest; Joachim Wolflord and Esther Carissimi from the plains of Erestia; Felix Fortis and Eugenie Rexsalve from the kingdom of Trevena; Eleazar Heredis and Ariella Lightharbour from the city of Lightharbour."

The crowd cheered wildly. Some of the sojourners waved. One, Ariella thought it was Eugenie, curtsied. Ariella just stood there, the conflicting emotions of anger, nervousness and annoyance getting the better of her.

Lalea continued. "Sojourners, this is your Knot, these are your brothers and sisters. For the next five years, you will live together, eat together, learn together and fight together." More cheering from the crowd.

Will they please stop cheering? I need to get off this stage.

"I present to you your Knot leader." Lalea turned and indicated with her left hand. Ariella looked where she was pointing.

"Karlov Featherfall."

Karlov walked from the back of the stage, his face was hard.

Seriously? I get Eleazar and now him? This day keeps getting worse.

The intimidating Guardian from the Friendly Phoenix was appraising each of his new charges. He did not look impressed. He locked eyes with each of the young sojourners in turn. Then shook his head.

"I am your Knot leader for the next five years. I am not your mother, your father or your best friend. I have no interest in you liking me. It is my job to turn you into Guardians, and Guardians you will become, or you will die trying. Now, follow me," he commanded.

The sojourners' faces went pale as they followed Karlov to the side of the stage. She managed to stand behind the others so that she was concealed from the crowd. She composed herself, taking deep breaths and pushing away the mix of emotions that she was feeling. She saw Lalea returning with the next Knot and saw her uncle raise his hand again to silence the boisterous crowd. Lalea was reading out the names when Ariella noticed three figures standing in the shadows behind her uncle. She gasped. Loudly. Karlov flicked around and gave a look that made Ariella drop her head.

"Nice move, princess," Eleazar whispered.

"Get lost," Ariella was in no mood to play games. She raised her head slightly, her eyes fixed on the three figures at the back of the stage.

Standing in the middle was a tall man with broad, muscular shoulders. His grey hair and neatly trimmed beard were flecked with the black of his youth. He stood motionless, eyes alert, missing nothing and yet calm, almost peaceful.

She had never laid eyes on him before, but she knew who he was: Vantor, Lord Guardian. She had heard countless stories of his exploits, daring deeds and stunning triumphs. Looking at the man standing before her, the aura he exuded, Ariella believed them all. A flicker of movement from behind Vantor caught her attention. A second man was causing tiny bursts of blue light to spark from his fingertips. He looked bored. Vantor looked down at the man and gave him a reproachful look. The man rolled his eyes and let a final spark dance across the back of his hand and disappear into the sky. The man was somewhere around his mid-forties with a shaved head and intricate tattoos. The markings started on his left cheek and wound down his neck and under his shirt. His bare arms were covered with similar dark marks, the patterns intricate and beautiful. He carried a short wooden staff with a glass prism enclosed in a metal claw at the top. As Ariella was studying him, the man turned his head and locked eyes with her. He smiled a mischievous smile. She gasped as she saw sparks of blue light fly across his eyes. In an instant, they were gone. He chuckled and looked away, absent-mindedly letting the blue sparks dance across his fingers again.

"That's Malum Asinum." The quiet voice came from just over her shoulder. She half-turned. The boy who spoke was the smallest on the platform.

His hair was wispy and blew across his face in the gentle breeze. "He's the Master of the Prism. Scares the beejebies out of me."

"What's a beejebie?"

The boy gave her a confused look. "Not sure. It was something my nanny used to say to me when I was growing up. Everything scared the beejebies out of her. Spiders, wasps, thunder, cows, black cats, big dogs, small dogs."

"Cows?"

"Oh, yes. Terrifying things cows. I think it's the way they look at you." The boy shuddered. "I'm Felix. Felix Fortis. My father is a baron.

I heard you're a princess, is that right? Does that mean you're related to King Tristan?"

Ariella smiled politely, nodded and turned back to the three figures in the shadow. The person beyond Vantor and Malum was deep in the shade of the inner wall, their face obscured. A brief lull settled over the square as Lalea went to gather the final Knot for their presentation. The three figures seemed to lean into each other and speak quietly. Malum let out a short burst of laughter that carried to where Ariella was standing as he took a few steps forward, looking at the crowd. As he moved further out of the shadows, so did his companion and, not for the first time that day, Ariella's mouth went dry, and her stomach churned. It was Elsa Leaina, the Lioness, the Guardians' Master of Arms.

Oh no, she's here. Let's try hard not to do anything stupid.

Elsa was the one that Ariella had always dreamed about meeting. During those hours alone in the library imagining adventures, it was Elsa who was her companion.

Now she's here, a stone's throw from me. I could run over there and say 'Hi'. Yeah, Ari, you could, and then you'd be thrown off the stage for being a crazy stalker.

A blast of trumpets snapped Ariella back into the moment. The final Knot had been introduced, and the king had come to the front of the stage.

He turned sideways so he could address the assembled sojourners and the crowd.

"Sojourners, welcome to Trevena."

The crowd roared their greeting in an echo of their king's. "For the next twelve months, you will spend your days here in our beautiful kingdom, the Garden of Dawnhaven. The year ahead will be challenging. It will be dangerous. You will have to face your fears, overcome your insecurities and deal with your prejudices."

Ariella heard someone down the line from her snort in derision at that comment. Karlov heard it too. She saw his face flinch, but he did not turn to look.

"When my father broke Dawnhaven into the Five Kingdoms, he gathered the wisest from each land for a council. Together they birthed the idea of the Guardians. For twenty years the Guardians have defended our island and unified our kingdoms. They are the vein of gold that runs through Dawnhaven; they are our heartbeat, our soul. Today you start a journey that will see you counted among their number. Remember this day and mark it, for you will never be the same." He nodded to Lord Vantor and stepped aside. Vantor strode to the front of the stage, and a hush fell over the crowd. He studied the line of young men and women before him.

"It is time," he said. His voice was calm and low but somehow seemed to fill the air. Ariella felt her hands begin to shake.

"Today you take your oath, today and every day. They are simple words, yet are the call of the Guardians. Many times, over the next five years, you will have cause to question, doubt, even rebel against these words. Stay strong, allow the Light to lead you. These words are our core, our life. Today and every day." Lord Vantor paused, and Elsa stepped up beside him.

As Elsa spoke, her voice rose and fell like a melody, it was mesmerizing. "Sojourners repeat the oath after me:"

> *We are the light in the darkness*
> *The shining steel and burning flame*
> *We are the breaking of Dawn*
> *We give ourselves for the good of Dawnhaven.*
> *We pledge to use our steel and the Light for the protection of this island.*
> *We forsake our kingdoms, our names and our thrones.*
> *This day and every day.*

From somewhere off to their right, a band struck up a raucous tune, and the crowd went wild again. From behind Ariella came a quiet whimper. "Oh no, what have I done?" Felix had gone white as a sheet, and his hands were shaking. "I don't think I can do this."

"It's a little late, Felix," Eleazar whispered to him. "It's going to be okay."

"Really? You think so?"

"Course it is." He gave Ariella a wink. "After all, we've got a princess with us."

That thought seemed to lift Felix's spirits.

"That's right, she's a princess. It can't be that bad, can it?"

Lalea started to lead the Knots from the stage.

"Follow me," Karlov commanded. No one argued or delayed. They fell in step with him and followed him down from the stage and away from the waiting room. Karlov led them towards a gate set in the wall on the north side of the main square. There were several

Guardians on sentry duty. They nodded to Karlov as he passed through.

They came to a large compound with walls on three sides and the principal city inner wall completing an almost perfect square. There were five towers, one on each corner, and the fifth, and most significant, in the middle of the inner wall. The towers appeared to be slim, elegant and extremely tall. They were the highest towers in all of Stonegard. Off to the right and left were two large stone buildings the same height as the inner wall. Dead ahead of them was the grandest of the buildings, not extravagant, but of a higher class than the other two.

Karlov stopped and motioned for the group to gather around him. He handed each of them a wooden ring, two inches across. It had a horizontal bar through the centre, dividing the top half from the bottom. Behind the bar, a pin was attached. A second bar fanned out from the middle to the edge of the ring. Ariella looked around and saw everyone else was as confused as she.

"This is your pin," Karlov began. "The pins are like a ranking system. We use them so that we can immediately identify which stage of the Journey you're in. As first year sojourners your pin will have one ray, symbolising your first year. Next year, you receive a pin with two rays, the year after, three rays and so on until your badge is complete at the end of your fifth year. When you have completed your training, you receive a new badge," he signalled to the badge pinned to his chest -the green lower half and five gold bars sectioning the top half, like rays of the sun. "This is the pin you'll receive at your graduation. The dawn over the haven."

Ariella ran her fingers over the smooth wood. It was sturdy, durable.

"That's the pretty bit over and done with," he continued. "Now begins the serious work. This year is going to be the single hardest thing you have done in your life. That is, until next year." He laughed to himself, amused by his humour. "Look around you. This compound will be your home for the next twelve months. The nine others next to you will be your brothers and sisters. You are a Knot. Anyone know why we call it a Knot?" There was silence. Karlov scowled. "It's called a Knot because the tighter you become, the stronger you become. There are two of you from each of the five kingdoms.

You don't know each other, you may not like the look of each other, but by the end of this year you will grow to lean on each other, trust each other and who knows? Maybe even love each other." Karlov laughed again. "That's about enough of that. You've got ten minutes until lunch is served in the mess hall. Get to your rooms, dump your gear and get to lunch. Any questions?"

There was silence.

"Excellent." Karlov pointed to the nearest tower. "That is tower one, our tower. The mess hall is in the basement. Sleeping quarters are on the floors above that. Get to it!"

"Excuse me?" It was the tall blonde girl. She spoke to Karlov in a way that Ariella was sure she had addressed many servants in her life.

Karlov ignored her.

"I said, "Excuse me?" Her voice got louder.

"Name?" Karlov's voice was low, almost a growl.

The girl looked suddenly flustered.

"I am Eugenie Rexsalve."

"Well, Eugenie Rexsalve, you will address me as Sir or Sir Karlov. Is that clear?"

Eugenie went red. "Yes...Sir."

"Excellent. You had a question?"

"You said 'sleeping quarters'?"

"Your point is?"

"Girls and boys? Together?" Her voice went up an octave.

"Of all the problems you're going to face this year, Eugenie Rexsalve, you're focusing on sleeping arrangements?" Karlov sighed and rolled his eyes. "It is going to be a long year. Relax, Eugenie, there are separate quarters for boys and girls. Now go, you've only got eight minutes, and if you're late, they'll take your food to the orphanage."

That was enough. The Knot broke into a run towards their tower.

8

The Knot

The Knot ran across the courtyard and burst through the tower doors sending them banging back on their hinges.

The tall, muscular Erestian was in the lead. He hesitated for a moment in the entrance chamber before spotting the wide spiral staircase on his right and hurtling up it. The other nine sprinted after him, the delicious smells wafting up from the basement stairs spurring them on.

The stairs were wide enough for three people to take at once and led to a spacious landing with a lounge area and windows out onto the compound. They dropped their bags against the curved landing wall and took off down the stairs guided by the smells from the kitchen below.

The dining room was circular with a massive oval table in the middle large enough to seat twenty people around it. There was a fireplace at the far end surrounded by clusters of snug looking armchairs. Despite being underground, the room was bright and airy with a comfortable feel.

The beautiful smell that had drawn Ariella and the others had come from a table laden with food: all manner of roasted meats, steaming vegetables smothered in butter and heaps of every sort of potato - roasted, mashed and baked. The boys were already seated and tucking into the mountains of food. At the far end of the oval table sat Karlov tearing off chunks of meat from a large chicken leg. The girls descended on the food without a word.

After a while, Karlov broke the silence.

"Listen up, everyone." He paused as the sounds of eating died away.

"Straight after lunch, we're off to the Quartermaster to get your gear, then to the Master of Arms for weapons. After that, I get to see why you got selected to come on the Journey. Impress me." He pushed back his chair and left the table, pausing at the staircase. "Meet me outside when you're done." A mischievous smile spread across his face. "You've got one minute."

We're meeting the Master of Arms. Elsa is the Master of Arms! I'm about to meet Elsa, the Lioness of the Guardians. I think I'm going to be sick.

There was a moment of stillness then brief pandemonium as the last mouthfuls of food were shovelled in and bread rolls concealed in pockets for later. Then a mad dash back up the stairs and out the doors. Karlov was already outside, standing in the courtyard talking to another Guardian. The Knot gathered together, but Karlov ignored them as he and his companion set off for the gates.

Ariella watched as Karlov left them and looked past him to see where he was going. Standing at the gate, arms folded, waiting for Karlov, was Micah.

What's he doing here? Has he come to see me? Maybe he wants to say goodbye properly?

She started to blush and took a few steps away from the Knot towards Micah. He and Karlov had their heads close together, they seemed to be talking intently. As she approached, they stopped talking and looked in her direction, their faces dark and tense. Karlov turned back to Micah, shook his hand then started walking back towards Ariella.

She tried to catch Micah's eye, but he had already begun walking away.

"Everything okay?" she asked.

Karlov stopped and stared at her, waiting.

"Sorry, Sir. Is everything okay, Sir?"

Karlov still had a dark look on his face. "Get back with your Knot Ariella." He strode past her to where the Knot was gathered, Ariella following behind.

What's Micah told him that's made him go off like that?

She looked back towards the gate to see if Micah had come back, but there was no sign of him.

"Follow me," barked Karlov. The Knot followed without a word.

Karlov led them across the courtyard to the building on the right and the first of several doors along the ground floor. The wooden door had a large letter Q marked in its centre. One of the other Knots was leaving, and each of the sojourners carried a large sack. Inside was a large tiled area. At the far end was a huge stone counter, and behind it was a Guardian with a bored expression.

"You're lat, Karlov."

Karlov ignored him, speaking to the Knot. "This is the Quartermaster's. Here you will get your clothes for the next twelve months. The clothes are designed for functionality and specifically for working in Trevena." He eyed Eugenie. "They are not designed for fashion, so nobody mentions anything about how they don't match your eye colour, hair colour or anything else. Is that clear?" The Knot nodded as one. "Then get to it. Meet me outside when you're done." Karlov slammed the door when he left.

The red-haired boy from Khan, Indio Gryphonfriend, broke the silence. "Someone forgot to drink their happy juice at lunch."

"I wonder what's put him in a foul mood." It was the boy from Darcian, Jaron Asheart. He was taller than Ariella with short, chestnut hair and bright blue eyes.

He looked over at Ariella. "Did he say anything to you?"

She shook her head. "He just told me to get back to the Knot."

Indio chipped in. "Do you know who he was talking to at the gate?"

"Yeah, his name is Micah. He's a palace guard from Lightharbour. He was here escorting me."

"I'd like to get to know that guard. Did you see him?" Eugenie said to know no one in particular. "He's gorgeous."

Ariella felt a wave of jealousy wash over her. Unfortunately, Theia saw it in her face.

"Look!" she pointed, "Ariella doesn't like that, Eugenie. I think she has eyes on her guard." The two girls laughed together as Ariella's jealousy turned to anger and her fists clenched. Before she could react, she felt a gentle hand on her shoulder. She turned and saw Phoebe shake her head with a kind look.

"Ooo, the giant's got involved now," taunted Theia. "Maybe she likes your guard too."

Eugenie laughed. "Her? Don't be ridiculous. Look at her. She's a freak."

Indio and Jaron bristled at that comment.

"Shut up, Eugenie," said Indio.

"Or what?" Eugenie's eyes narrowed as she stared at Indio. The tension threatened to bubble over.

"When you've quite finished!" It was the bored-looking Guardian behind the counter. "First day and you're ready to attack each other. It's going to be a long year."

Phoebe's hand was still on Ariella's shoulder, and she walked them both to the counter, turning their backs on the others.

The Guardian looked up at Phoebe, unfazed by her size. He walked through the doorway behind the counter and came back moments later with a large sack tied at the top with thick string.

"This should do for you." He handed her the sack and then sized up Ariella before disappearing again, coming back with a similar sack. "Next!" he called.

Within a few minutes, all ten had their sacks and were standing out in the courtyard again with Karlov, who still was not smiling.

"This way and keep up."

Karlov led them through the second door in the long stone building. A pair of cross swords were marked on the door. Indio smiled. It was another large room, similar to the previous one, but this one had no counter.

This room had racks. Lots of racks. Racks on every wall and many more self-standing racks filled the floor. On each of them were weapons of every shape, size and description: longbows, short bows and crossbows. Curved scimitars and thin rapiers were lined up alongside giant broadswords. Maces and morning stars hung opposite all manner of axes, daggers and knives. Joachim, the tall Erestian, cracked his knuckles and smiled. It was the first time Ariella had seen any emotion from him.

Indio slapped Jaron on the back and grinned. "This is more like it." He had just started moving towards a rack filled with battle axes when the door at the end of the room opened and in walked Lalea.

"Step back," she commanded Indio.

She's not Elsa. We only get the assistant.

Stepping into the middle of the room, she addressed the Knot. "As you know, I am Lalea Onderskat, and I serve as Assistant Master of Arms. Before we begin, let me go through the rules."

Indio rolled his eyes as Jaron pulled him back from the axes.

"Rule number one: First year sojourners are not allowed weapons inside the compound unless they're in training." She locked eyes with each of the ten as she spoke. "Rule two: Weapons are to be collected before training and returned following training. Rule three: Regardless of previous experience, you will learn to use each of the weapons in this room."

She let her words sink in before she continued. "Karlov, it's over to you."

He nodded. "Right. Everyone grab a weapon. Your own choice, and let's see if you can handle it."

Indio let out a whoop of joy, winked at Jaron and dived straight for the axe rack. Within moments he was swinging a substantial double-bladed battle axe through the air. Jaron stepped past him towards the bows where Theia had already picked out a stunning looking longbow and was testing the string.

Ariella stood back, watching the others.

Joachim moved over to the curved cavalry sabres and was examining them closely. Eugenie was looking through the array of long swords while Phoebe shuffled over to the axe rack by Indio.

A movement to her side caught her attention. Her jaw dropped as she watched Esther practising with a long-bladed spear, spinning it through her hands and behind her back like a seasoned warrior. She noticed Ariella watching her, and stopped, embarrassed.

"That was amazing!" said Ariella.

Esther blushed, "Thank you," she replied, replacing the spear.

"What about you, princess, not joining in?" Eleazar's voice startled her. She spun around and watched him as he flicked a dagger into the air and caught it by its tip.

"Go and bug someone else."

"But why? It's so much fun bugging you." Eleazar laughed as he made the dagger dance through his fingers.

Ariella walked away from him towards the vast rack of swords. Felix was there as well. He seemed flustered.

"Are you all right?" she asked.

"What? Oh, yes, well, no, not really. I've never been that good at the weapons side of things. I tend to get myself all mixed up, if you know what I mean."

Ariella nodded, not having a clue what he meant but thought it was easier just to agree with him.

She scanned the rack of swords until she found what she was looking for - a light, thin, long-bladed rapier. It was the type that her father and Hakeem had taught her how to use.

Karlov raised his voice. "Time's up. Grab your weapons and come with me. Let's see if you can fight."

She grabbed the rapier and followed the others out into the courtyard.

9

Weapons and Light

Karlov was not waiting for them.

He was already walking toward an open space to the right of the main entrance gate. It was marked by a low rope line, two feet off the ground.

"This is the training area." Karlov gestured. "We only use the weapons in this area. Everybody get that?" There was a murmur of consent. "Great. Now get yourself warmed up and then we'll take a look at you."

Inside the training area were various targets and dummies to practise on. Large, circular marks were positioned against the far wall to allow the archers to take aim. Scattered around were simple scarecrows stuffed with straw, perfect for practising a sword thrust.

Ariella set to work on one of the dummies, going through the practice steps she had been taught. Every day back in the palace, Hakeem had made her practise. "Little and often," he had said. The rapier felt good in her hand. It swung effortlessly through the still afternoon air. She was soon lost in the pre-set moves that she had learnt. A loud clanging of metal snapped her concentration. She looked over to see Felix hastily retrieving his sword, which appeared to have rebounded off one of the practice dummies and gone skidding across the courtyard.

Theia and Eugenie were watching and sniggering at Felix's mishap.

"Some family this Knot is," Jaron spoke softly. Ariella had not noticed him and Indio approach. They were both dripping with sweat from their exertions.

"That's enough." Karlov waved them over to the edge of the training area where he was standing. "Ariella, let's see what they taught you in Lightharbour."

Indio gave her a thumbs-up as she walked past.

Karlov stood facing her with a long sword, poised.

Remember. Remember everything Hakeem taught you. Defence, guard, parry, move, footwork. And breathe, don't forget to breathe!

She exhaled sharply, realising that she'd been holding her breath. Theia sniggered.

Don't worry about her. Focus. Focus on him and not getting hit with that sword.

She lowered the tip of her rapier, right foot forward as she had been taught, her left hand outstretched behind her to help her balance. The classic stance of a fencer.

Karlov copied her, adopting her stance. He smiled and lunged, driving his sword at her chest. Ariella parried and stepped backwards as Karlov came again. They sparred skilfully together, exchanging blows, neither gaining the advantage.

Indio gave Jaron a wide grin. "She's good." He called over to Theia. "Don't you think so, Theia. She's good, isn't she?" Theia ignored him as he and Jaron laughed.

The duel in the arena was getting quicker and quicker, the two fencers moving at a blur. Strike after strike was exchanged and each time the blow was parried.

Karlov withdrew a step and nodded in respect. "Excellent Ariella. You've been trained well, and you've learnt well. Orthodox, organised and diligent. You've been a fine student of the rules of fencing."

He lifted his blade, stepped forward and thrust. As each time before Ariella blocked his strike, but this time Karlov bent his sword arm, twisted his body and slammed the open palm of his left hand into Ariella's sternum. She cried out in pain as the wind was blasted from her lungs and she dropped to her knees, gasping for air.

Karlov reached down and pulled her to her feet and gave her a long hard look. "We don't do orthodox fighting here; it's not a playground. The world we live in doesn't play by the rules, Ariella. It's mean and dirty. There are ghosts that will tear your heart out in a moment if you let them. We are Guardians. We are all that stands between Dawnhaven and the shadows. We don't play by the rules. Got it?"

Ariella nodded.

"Good. Now, get out."

She walked back over to Indio and Jaron.

Theia called over as Eugenie laughed.

"Did you see that Indio? Wasn't she so good?"

Indio's face went red. "Come on, Jaron, let's go, we can take those two."

Jaron rolled his eyes, shook his head and pointed at Phoebe, who was easing herself into the training area.

"I want to see this."

Phoebe carried a long sword almost identical to Karlov's. She moved with grace and handled the sword as if she had done it for years. Karlov looked wary as he approached her. He took an opening swing with his sword, aiming at Phoebe's side. The tall girl barely moved. She blocked the incoming strike with her sword and instantly swung a massive fist into the side of Karlov's head sending him spinning to the floor.

The Knot let out a gasp as Karlov lay face down on the stone. Phoebe did not move; her face was expressionless. After a moment, Karlov pushed himself up and back onto his feet, an ugly welt developing over his eye.

"Gosh!" said Indio.

Nervously the Knot watched and waited, trying to figure out how Karlov would react. The Knot leader rolled his shoulders and flexed his back. Phoebe still had not moved. He walked towards her stopping only when they were close enough to touch.

"Phoebe Montecorde, that is the best strike I have ever seen from a first year sojourner." His face broke into a smile and he raised his sword and bowed. "I salute you. You get served first at dinner tonight." Phoebe gave him a half smile and retreated beyond the rope.

Ariella caught her eye. "Phoebe, that was amazing. Where did you learn that?"

She shrugged her shoulders but did not reply.

"Did your father teach you?" As Ariella asked the question, she saw a moment of pain in Phoebe's eyes as she shook her head.

"Well, I think you're brilliant."

Phoebe gave her the same half smile she gave Karlov but said nothing.

Karlov looked over at the waiting sojourners. "Felix, let's get this over with, shall we?"

Ariella looked over at Felix, and her heart sank. He was terrified. His hands were shaking so badly he could hardly hold his sword.

Indio, Jaron and Ariella exchanged looks trying to think of some way to help him.

Indio whispered, "This is going to be painful. How did he make it past the test?"

Eugenie and Theia started sniggering again as Felix tripped on the rope and dropped his sword.

Before anyone could respond, Esther had walked past them and put her hand on Felix's arm. She did not say anything; she just smiled. Felix looked at her, swallowed and picked up his sword. The shaking in his hands had stopped.

"Wow!" said Indio.

"Wow indeed," echoed Ariella.

Jaron nodded. "It's amazing what happens when the right girl smiles at you."

Their optimism was short lived.

Felix was less nervous, but he still could not wield a sword. It was only desperation that fended off Karlov's first few blows, and he was lucky in deflecting the next. Again, Karlov pressed his attack, raining down blow after blow until Felix was driven to his knees trying to defend himself. Karlov struck hard and Felix's sword was knocked to the ground.

To Ariella's horror, Karlov didn't stop. He raised his sword over the defenceless Felix.

She screamed as the blade came down. "No!"

But the blade never reached its target.

A blue Light flashed from Felix's hand, the brightness causing Ariella to close her eyes. When she opened them again, her mouth dropped open. Felix was still on his knees, but just above his head was Karlov's sword, stopped dead in the middle of the shimmering blue Light.

10

A Bloody Nose

The Knot stood in stunned silence, eyes wide and mouths open. Karlov let go of the hilt of his sword, and it stayed where it was, suspended in mid-air, encased in the blue Light emanating from Felix's hands.

Jaron looked over at Indio. "That answers your question."
Indio's face was blank. "About how he got here. He didn't swing a sword at a dummy, he can already use his Light."

"It shut those two up," said Ariella looking over at Eugenie and Theia.

"Excellent," said Indio, "that's made my day. Top job, Felix, you legend!"

Felix was still down on his knees with a stunned look on his face. Indio's shout startled him and the Light faded away, the sword dropping to the stone courtyard with a long clang.

"How is that possible?" asked Ariella. "It's supposed to take at least a year of training before you can pull off something like that."

Jaron shrugged. "No idea. Maybe some people are gifted differently."

Meanwhile, Felix had recovered from the shock of stopping Karlov's sword as it rushed towards his head. He jumped to his feet and backed away.

Felix was sweating. "You...you...you could've killed me!"
"But I didn't," Karlov replied. "You stopped me."
"But you were trying to kill me!"
"I was trying to get a reaction."

Indio laughed at that. "He certainly got a reaction from you, Felix." Felix glanced over, and Indio spoke under his breath, "He looks like a startled rabbit."

"I nearly died!" Felix shouted. "You're a lunatic!"

"Welcome to the Guardians. This is not the first time that's happened, is it Felix?" Karlov asked.

Felix shook his head.

"In stressful situations?"

"Yes," Felix responded. "I get in stressful situations quite a lot. It, sort of, just happens. I don't make it happen, it does it by itself."

Karlov laughed and turned to the rest of the Knot. "Who's next?"

After an hour of putting them through their paces the new recruits were tired. "That'll do for starters," said Karlov. "Hand in your weapons, get back to your rooms, change into your new gear and then meet me in the mess hall."

The Knot dispersed. Theia and Eugenie went together, whispering and exchanging muffled laughs. Ariella fell in next to Felix with Indio and Jaron close behind.

"That was impressive," said Ariella, smiling at the still trembling Felix.

"I'll say," chipped in Indio. "The way that sword stopped dead in the air, I thought it was going to cave your head in. I was picturing splatters of brain and blood all over the stones."

Felix turned white as Jaron thumped Indio's arm.

"Don't worry," said Jaron. "Karlov was only trying to get something out of you. He must've known what you could do, or at least he'd heard what you could do."

Ariella nodded. "That's right. Karlov is here to help us, not hurt us."

"At least not this year anyway," answered Indio. "He'll save that for year two and three if we're not making the grade." Felix shot him a nervous look as Jaron thumped him again.

They were the last to reach their tower, so Ariella said goodbye to the boys and walked into her room. She could feel the tension hanging in the air. Theia and Eugenie were each sitting on a bed under a large window looking out towards the outer wall of Stonegard. They were both smirking. Esther was sitting on the middle bed, knees drawn up to her chest. She looked angry. Over on the right was Phoebe changing into the gear that the quartermaster had given her. The dark green uniform squeezed her tight and was unflattering. She seemed absent, lost in her own world, oblivious to the others in the room.

"Hi," said Ariella.

She was greeted by silence. Theia and Eugenie stood up and started to change, ignoring the other three. Ariella tried to catch Esther's gaze to see if she could get any sign of what had just happened. Their eyes met momentarily and Ariella attempted to convey a silent question. "What's going on?" but Esther gave a quick shake of her head and busied herself with her gear.

The only remaining bed was between Esther and Phoebe, so Ariella dumped her bag on it and started pulling out the clothes.

"Hey," Theia nudged Eugenie. "I don't think making her sleep over there has helped. I can still smell her."

"Well there's not much more we can do," said Eugenie.

"She could sleep on the landing," Theia suggested with a shrug of her shoulders.

Phoebe did not say anything.

Ariella was not even sure she had heard them. She was in her own world. Esther was ignoring them as well, changing quickly into her Guardian uniform.

Ariella guessed what had caused the tension in the room when she came in a moment ago.

"If you've got a problem Theia, why don't you find somewhere else to stay? I think we passed a pig farm on the outskirts of the city. You should feel right at home there."

Theia and Eugenie turned towards Ariella and took a step forward, bristling. Esther darted between them and ran from the room, slamming the door behind her.

"Who's going to make me? You?" Theia sneered. "I saw you out there today, all pretty and fancy with your tiny sword. I bet you've never even been in a real fight."

Ariella looked uncertain.

She's right. Pillow fights with Osias and Calixto don't count.

What am I doing here?

Eugenie noticed the look on her face and pointed. "You're right Theia! She's a polished little princess with no idea about the real world. What a joke! I think that you and the freak here," she nodded towards Phoebe, "should both go and sleep outside. The stench is unbearable."

"Don't call her that." The word 'freak' had set something off in Ariella. She wasn't sure what it was, but she knew that she couldn't let anyone call one of her Knot a 'freak'.

Eugenie laughed, "She is a freak!"

Ariella lost control. She was never quite sure what happened next, but she would always remember the feel of the bone of Eugenie's nose breaking as she slammed her fist into it. A thin arc of blood sprayed out from either side, some of it finding Theia's cheek.

Eugenie screamed. Theia stepped back, her hands raised, as Ariella turned on her.

"I said, 'Don't call her that.'" Her fists were still clenched.

Eugenie was down on her knees, sobbing loudly and trying to stem the flow of blood. Ariella raised her fists again looking to take down Theia when her arms were pinned to her sides, and she was lifted from the floor. Phoebe carried Ariella gently away from Theia and back to her bed. She stood her down but kept her arms pinned, waiting for Ariella's breathing to relax, all the while saying nothing.

Just as Ariella had calmed down Lalea hurried into the room with Esther at her heels. She quickly assessed the situation.

"Esther, you and Phoebe are already changed, go downstairs and wait for Karlov." Phoebe hesitated and looked from Lalea to Ariella. "Go now," said Lalea, "I'll take care of this." She turned to the three remaining girls. "Theia, take your clothes and get changed in the bathroom." Theia went without arguing, giving Ariella a nervous glance.

When Theia had left, Lalea closed the door and knelt beside Eugenie.

"It's broken!" she wailed, her voice nasal from the injury.

"Yes," agreed Lalea without any emotion in her voice. As she stretched out her hand, a faint green glow spread from her fingers, barely touching Eugenie's face.

After a moment, Eugenie stopped sobbing, and the green Light faded away. Lalea stood and helped Eugenie to her feet.

"Let's take a look at you," said Lalea. "Perfect. You have such a pretty nose, it would help you a lot to stop sticking it up in the air. I may not be around next time to mend it."

Eugenie's eyes widened, and she glanced at Ariella, backing away.

"Theia is changing in the bathroom, why don't you join her?" Lalea picked up Eugenie's clothes and handed them to her, guiding her to the door, closing it behind her. The two were left alone in the room. Lalea was silently studying Ariella as if deciding what to do.

Well, that was a smart move, Ari, really well done, you should be proud of yourself. I wonder if anyone has been kicked off the Journey on the first day? I bet that'll be some kind of record.

Ariella shifted uneasily, desperate for the silence to be broken but not wanting to say anything else dumb.

"Ariella, that was foolish." Her voice was kind but intense. "If you cannot control your emotions, you will not survive the Journey. The people who die here are not the worst sojourners, the least skilled or the least able. The ones who die are those who make poor decisions in dangerous situations like you did today. If you do that out in the field, you are a danger to yourself and your Knot." She leaned in and gripped Ariella's shoulders. "Do not let that happen, Ariella. Learn to control your emotions, whatever it takes." Lalea squeezed her and let her go, her face relaxing. "Now, get changed, you've got to meet Karlov."

Lalea left the room, leaving Ariella alone.

Smart Ari, real smart. You can't spend the next five years punching everyone who hacks you off.

She sighed and began stripping off her clothes. Habitually she checked her pockets, finding the echo orbs. She paused. An idea began to form.

Well, it's not spying on your mother. I promised Hakeem I wouldn't spy on her but he didn't say anything about spying on other people. Besides, if I leave one of them with my gear and take one with me then technically it won't be spying. It would be an accident.

She quickly gathered the clothes the quartermaster had given her and got dressed. The soft green leather felt comfortable and allowed her to move freely without it getting in the way. She packed her old clothes in her pack and placed one of the echo orbs on the top, pulling down the straps securely and stowing it under her bed.

That should do it.

She closed the door behind her and went down the stairs into the mess hall. She was the last to arrive. The others were seated around the table, and Karlov was nowhere to be seen. She sat in a spare chair beside Indio and Jaron.

"What's been going on?" whispered Jaron. "The girls were freaked out."

Ariella looked around the room.

Esther was sitting across from them, chewing nervously on the tips of her hair. Phoebe was next to her and had a faraway look in her eyes again. Theia and Eugenie were sat close together at the far end of the table, not talking, but looking uncomfortable. Every few minutes, Eugenie would check her nose, nudging it back and forth with her fingertips and trying to avoid looking at Ariella.

"I got a bit carried away," said Ariella.

Indio joined in the conversation. "Carried away how?"

"I sort of hit Eugenie."

"Excellent!" said Indio, too loudly.

Everyone in the room froze and looked at Indio. Before anyone could say anything, Karlov marched into the room and at his heels was Malum Asinum. That got everyone's attention. They sat bolt upright, every eye focused on the Guardian's Master of the Prism.

"What on earth is he doing here?" whispered Indio.

Malum walked to the end of the table with Karlov.

"In case any of you don't know, this is Malum Asinum. He has kindly agreed to spend some time with us this afternoon to explain to you how the Light will feature in your first year of the Journey."

Malum nodded to Karlov as he idly traced one of his facial tattoos with his index finger. He focused on Indio.

"And that, young Indio, is what I am doing here." He smiled at Indio's startled look. "Yes. My ears are that good."

Malum began pacing around the table, swinging his wooden staff, the glass prism catching the light and casting rainbows across the walls.

"The Light has always existed. As far back as the songs and legends of Dawnhaven go there have been tales of the Light. It was centred in the Blazing Sceptre carried by the kings and queens of this island. They used it to battle great foes and to heal grievous wounds. It was the symbol of all that was good about our land. That was before Prince Diatus, who, jealous of his twin brother's throne, led the rebellion against King Haldor and Queen Lucia.

Diatus landed his armies on the coast of Trevena and marched on Stonegard. His troops were a vast horde of Ghost Raiders and Faron mercenaries from the Eastern Islands. They were ferocious and bloodthirsty, burning and destroying everything in their path. But they were ill-disciplined. They were no match for our armies. We met them head on, broke their advance and began driving them back to the sea. Then, at the moment of his defeat, Diatus showed the extent of his power and his hatred. He unleashed the Shadows."

He paused to watch the sojourners and study their faces.

"Where the beasts came from or how he controlled them, we can only guess. The Shadows too. Our blades did not affect them. In one move, Diatus had turned the tide of battle, and hope seemed lost. Our armies were driven back, unable to resist the Shadows as they began to surround us. They came on relentlessly, seeking King Haldor, driven on by Diatus's hatred of his twin.

In the final stand, when the Shadows threatened to overwhelm us, Queen Lucia ran to the point of the fiercest fighting and shattered the Blazing Sceptre. She knew the power contained in the Sceptre would engulf the Shadows. She also knew it would cost her own life. She was the bravest person I ever knew."

Ariella's eyes widened.

That's my grandmother. He was there when she died.

She had never heard anyone who was at the battle tell the story.

Malum continued, "The breaking of the Sceptre unleashed a torrent of blinding Light that overwhelmed every Shadow on the battlefield. The remainder of Diatus's armies, knowing they were defeated, fled to their ships, leaving their beaten prince to face the wrath of his brother. Queen Lucia gave her life for Dawnhaven, her family and her king."

For a moment, he held Ariella's gaze, his eyes filled with intense sadness.

"The breaking of the Sceptre affected Dawnhaven in a way she could never have anticipated. Up until that point, the Light was always focused on one spot, one place: the sceptre. Upon the shattering, the Light was cast across the island, filling every person. Now everyone on the island has a connection to the Light."

"After the rebellion, King Haldor, mourning the loss of his wife and the treachery of his twin, broke Dawnhaven into the five kingdoms. The power of the island would no longer be focused on one person, one city or one throne. The king knew that to maintain unity, the kingdoms had to rely on each other, and they needed a common ally, a force for good that would rise above the loyalty of any one kingdom. They required a focus that would be a symbol for all that was good about our land.

That is why he formed the Guardians, defenders of Dawnhaven and wielders of the Light."

He stopped his pacing and lowered his staff, pointing at each of the Knot in turn. "Each of you has been selected by your people to serve as Guardians. To give up your loyalty to one kingdom and to instead give your allegiance to Dawnhaven. It is my job to train you to be carriers of the Light. To use it for the good of all. We start tomorrow. You will meet me at nine in the training area, and we will discover just what Light dwells within you."

He nodded to Karlov and left the room. The Knot sat in silence for a moment then broke into excited conversations.

"Hey!" Karlov interrupted and the room fell silent. "That's your lot for the first day. Get some rest, have breakfast early, and don't be late for Malum. He's not pretty when sojourners are late."

"He's not pretty anyway," muttered Indio. Jaron rolled his eyes.

11

The Sun Prism

The next morning Ariella woke slowly.

The blankets on her bed seemed unusually heavy, and she wasn't feeling compelled to fight them. She heard stirring from across the room and opened one eye. Phoebe was up and getting ready for the day while the other girls were still sound asleep. The aroma of cooking bacon and fresh bread drifting through the compound captured her attention and gave her the will she needed to roll out of bed.

The other girls began to wake up as Ariella started to dress. No one spoke. The frostiness from the day before was still evident. Theia drew back the curtains above her bed and the bright morning light shone in.

"Oh heck," she muttered, "it's late."

The girls dressed quickly and went to the mess hall. A picture of carnage greeted them. Seated around the large table were Karlov and four of the boys, reclining on their chairs, rubbing their stomachs and taking it in turns to belch loudly. In the middle of the table were scattered crusts of bread, bacon rinds and a pile of empty dishes.

Karlov laughed, "You girls will have to be quicker than that! Malum is expecting you all in the courtyard in ten minutes, so do eat up."

Theia was furious, "What's the deal? Eating all the food before we get a chance at it too."

Indio and Jaron looked sheepish and Eleazar paused with the last piece of bacon on his fork. Joachim stood up, towering over Theia. He puffed out his chest and belched in her face, "You were late."

Theia's jaw clenched as she looked to Karlov. "Well, you were," Karlov replied, shrugging his shoulders.

"I think there's some porridge left," smiled Indio.

Eugenie was incensed "Porridge? Porridge? Do I look like I eat porridge?"

"Of course not, Eugenie," said Eleazar, his face a picture of sincerity. "There are a great many things that you do look like; however, an eater of porridge is not one of them."

Eugenie frowned, trying to figure out if she had just been insulted. Ariella slumped into the chair opposite Jaron and helped herself to some porridge, trying not to look disappointed.

"Sorry, Ari," mumbled Indio. "Didn't think about...you know..."

"Anyone else?" she offered with a smile.

"Yep," answered Jaron "That's about it. Sorry."

"It's okay," Ariella sighed, tucking into the porridge.

Theia muttered something inaudible and sat with Eugenie, both debating whether or not to try the porridge.

A piercing screech filled the air, causing the unprepared sojourners to cover their ears in a desperate attempt to block out the noise.

"What is that?!" exclaimed Esther.

"No idea," Eleazar replied as the Knot rushed upstairs to the entrance hall. Karlov followed at his own pace, glancing around the room, laughing at everyone's startled faces.

"Felix!" yelled Karlov. "Shut up!"

The screeching stopped.

Everyone looked at Karlov questioningly. He just shrugged his shoulders.

Ten minutes later they were outside with Karlov and a bored-looking Malum Asinum, Master of the Prism.

"Only nine, Karlov?" asked Malum.

Felix came bursting through the door of the tower and sprinted over to the training area, hair still soaking wet. He stood beside Indio, who promptly whispered, "What was that all about? You know, the screeching?"

"I sing in the shower," confessed a sheepish Felix.

"Singing, or strangling cats?" enquired Indio innocently.

"That's everyone," said Karlov.

"Good," nodded Malum. "Today things get interesting."

"I'm bored already," whispered Indio.

Malum flicked his fingers and blue sparks flew. Indio cried out as his fringe caught fire. The nine stared dumbfounded at Indio as he desperately whacked his forehead, trying to extinguish the flames.

Malum laughed as the sojourners fell silent and edged backwards. "Now, where were we? Ah yes."

"Today you will find out which colour of Light dwells within you. Each citizen of Dawnhaven possesses a colour of Light inside of them to a greater or lesser degree. You can never control the Light, but as Guardians, you will be taught to wield it and work in harmony with it."

Malum spun his staff as he spoke, the crystal prism refracting rainbows across the courtyard.

"Light is made up of three primary colours: red, green and blue. Each person has one of those colours of the Light within. Today we find out which one is in you."

Malum signalled to the fifth and largest tower in the compound. The top of the tower was flat, with a defensive wall around its edge. Ariella could see the silhouettes of two Guardians behind the wall on sentry duty. On top of the wall was a thick metal rod, the head covered by a heavy black cloth, tied around the rod.

"That is the sun prism," explained Malum. "It's made from the same crystal as the Blazing Sceptre that the kings and queens of Dawnhaven used to carry. It is extremely rare and truly unique. There is only one known source of the crystal, a deep mine somewhere in the Khan mountains."

Indio raised his hand.

"No Indio, I don't know the exact location."

Indio sighed, and lowered his hand as Malum continued. "In a moment we will remove the cloth and the morning sun will shine through the Prism onto each of you. As that happens, the Light inside of you will be drawn out, revealing your colour. Understood?"

There was a collective silence.

Malum rolled his eyes. "Follow me," he commanded as he led the Knot towards the fifth tower. He stopped and pointed to markings in the courtyard that Ariella hadn't noticed before. From the base of the fifth tower came two thin lines of crystal sunk into the stones of the courtyard. They extended about one hundred yards from the tower in a perfect arc. At the top of the arc were ten circles, each about the size of a large dinner plate. The circles were a yellow crystal with a green line through the middle: the symbol of the Guardians.

The ten sojourners hesitated just outside the arc. Ariella watched the faces of the others.

Excellent, they're all as terrified as me.

Malum pointed to the circles.

"Everyone take a circle. Make sure your feet are fully on the crystal. We don't want any accidents now, do we?"

What does that mean? Accidents? As if we're not nervous enough already.

"Where you stand is crucial," Malum explained. "You need to be within the boundaries of the crystal when the sun prism blazes. Stepping outside the crystal's protection would put you under the full power of the prism's Light and that, well, that wouldn't be ideal."

"Wouldn't be ideal, how Sir?" Eleazar asked.

"Well, no one, besides Lord Vantor of course, has survived stepping off the crystal into the Light of the sun prism."

Felix paled.

"Nothing to worry about, just stay on the crystal. The sunlight will flow through the sun prism and fill this area with intense white Light, but you'll see your colour, the colour that is inside of you."

Malum gave a signal, and one of the sentries untied the cloth and let it fall. Ariella gasped. On top of the rod was a massive crystal the size of a watermelon. The sun's rays were refracting through it, flooding the courtyard with every colour of the rainbow.

The crystal arc they were standing in was suddenly filled with a blazing white Light. Ariella shut her eyes in pain. She tried to open them again, but the brightness was so severe it hurt her to look.

Around her, she could hear the voices of the other sojourners.

"It's stunning," said Jaron.

"Beautiful," whispered Esther

Ariella tried to focus her eyes again, but the pain grew. She started to feel sick and her legs were getting weaker. Even with her eyes closed, she could feel the searing white Light.

What's wrong with me? Why can't I look?

She felt herself starting to sway, her knees buckling.

Stay on the crystal, stay on the crystal!

"Ari? What's wrong?" she heard the concern in Jaron's voice.

I have no idea. I think I'm going to be sick.

She started to go light-headed as her strength left her. She felt herself falling backwards, unable to stop.

"Shut it down!" Malum yelled. "Shut it down now!"

As she hit the floor, the white Light died and the pain eased. She heard footsteps all around her and many whispers. Someone knelt beside her and felt her forehead.

"Ariella?" It was Karlov. "Can you hear me?"

She blinked and opened her eyes. "What just happened?" she groaned.

No one answered.

Malum stood beside Karlov. "Can you stand?" he asked.

She nodded, "I think so." The pain had all but gone, and she could focus again. She got to her feet gingerly.

This is so embarrassing. Of course, you're the only one who collapses, Ari. What a shambles! You couldn't even handle a bit of Light. Some Guardian you're going to make.

"Karlov, we're done here," said Malum. "Take them inside."

Karlov led the sojourners into their tower and down to the mess hall. Jaron stepped in beside Ariella.

"How are you feeling?"

"Better," she replied. "All I saw was a blinding white Light. I couldn't even open my eyes."

"You didn't see the colours?"

She shook her head.

"Oh Ari, it was incredible," said Jaron. "The Lights were the most stunning I've ever seen."

"What happened?"

"As they pulled the cloth off the sun prism the whole courtyard lit up. It was like a massive rainbow filling the place. But as the white Light fell on the arc, the crystals we were standing on burst into columns of Light. Mine was green, it was mind-blowing."

Jaron had a misty look in his eye.

He's going to cry. How good was it?

Why did I collapse?

"What about me," she asked, "what colour was I?"

Jaron avoided her eyes. "Um, err, you, err, you were kind of…"

"Kind of what?"

"Kind of everything and nothing. Your Light kept flickering and changing colours."

Everything and nothing? What does that mean? What am I? Malum said everyone had one colour, can't mine make up its mind?

Lost in thought, she didn't notice Malum come into the mess hall and close the door. On the table he unrolled a large scroll. The scroll showed a diagram of three interlocking circles of red, green and blue. Where the three circles overlapped, the colours changed. The centre, where all three circles met, was pure white.

"The three different colours of Light reveal to us the core of a person," began Malum. "It shows their instincts when encountering challenges and reveals their strengths. It does not restrict the use of your Light; it merely reveals how you are most comfortable using it. The Light is not magic. There are no incantations like those the Ghost Raiders use. The Light is not something you control, it is something that you work with, and as your ability increases, it is something that can guide you. Each of you will use the Light in your own unique way. The Light responds to you as an individual. It is not something that you can bend to your will, but you will learn to work in harmony with it. Now, I'd like to ask all the reds to stand."

What about me? When do I stand? What colour of Light was I?
Ariella raised her hand.

"Excuse me, sir, before we do this, could you explain what happened out there? What colour of Light..."

Before she could finish her question, Malum cut her off.
"Not now Ariella, we will discuss it later."
"But I need..."
"I said not now."
"But..."
"Do not argue with me sojourner. This is not the royal palace," Malum growled.

Theia sniggered as Ariella slumped in her chair.
What an idiot. He thinks I'm asking because I'm some spoiled princess.

Why won't he talk now? What's wrong with me? Is the Light in everyone else but me? Have I failed even before I've started?

"Now, as I was saying," continued Malum, "could the reds please stand?"

Theia, Indio and Joachim stood up.

"The natural impulse of red Light is to advance, to attack, to gain ground. It is aggressive and impulsive. Red Light wielders tend to be ambitious and competitive. They prefer action to planning, heart responses over rational thinking. As with all three colours, we seek to help red Light users curb the weaknesses of their personalities while maximising their strengths. You may sit."

"Can those of the blue Light please stand."
Eleazar stood up with Phoebe, Eugenie and Felix.

"The blue Light is, in many ways, the balance of red. Whereas those of the red Light prefer to attack, the natural response of blue Light users is to defend. They are the protectors, the ones who shield those around them. They tend to be diligent planners: cautious in their approach, unwilling to take risks. They serve as a wonderful balance to the red Light users. Part of your training on the Journey will be learning to work together and appreciate the strengths of each other's Light."

Indio laughed, "Sounds like blue Light users are good for staying at home and guarding my lunch while the reds go and get things done."

Malum flicked his fingers up, green sparks flew, and Indio's already singed fringe caught alight once again.

"Hey!" Indio groaned as he tried to put out the flames on his head for the second time that day.

Jaron and Eleazar stifled their laughs.

"Finally, can those of the green Light please stand?" asked Malum.

Esther and Jaron stood.

"Green Light is all about growth," said Malum. "Life and vitality are found in green Light. They tend to be the most carefree of Light users."

Indio burst out laughing.

"Karlov?!" He laughed. "Carefree? Has there been a mistake?"

Green sparks flew from Karlov's hand and Indio's fringe started smouldering. Eleazar grabbed a cushion from the nearest armchair and beat him with it, a desperate attempt to extinguish the flames.

"Yes," answered Malum, "carefree." He smiled as the flames on Indio's head went out, but Eleazar continued to repeatedly whack him with the cushion. "Green Light carriers are our best healers. They generally lack the forcefulness of reds and the careful planning of blues. They are loyal friends and provide a much-needed balance to the other two colours."

"That covers it then," said Malum. "Today was just the beginning. Identifying your Light doesn't teach you how to use it. For that, you must study, listen and practise. It's going to be a steep learning curve."

"All right everyone," said Karlov, "get yourselves some lunch and then it's out into the training area this afternoon."

That's it? What about me? What about someone whose Light can't figure itself out?

Indio and Eleazar stood up with a muttered, "I'm hungry" and "You're always hungry."

Ariella stood and headed towards Malum.

Time to get some answers.

But before she got to him, Karlov stepped in front of her. "That's enough for today. Go get some food."

"But..."

"That's enough for today."

And with that, he turned and left with Malum. She looked at the rest of her Knot waiting around for lunch to be served. Each of them with a clear colour.

They all fit, they belong here. But what about me? The girl of no colour at all.

12

Thunderheads

For three months, the daily routine of the Knot remained unchanged: wake up, breakfast, weapons training, lunch, Light training, dinner. The only variation was in the evening where Karlov drilled them in whatever discipline they were faring badly. Although monotonous, their skills were growing. By the end of those months, each of the Knot could handle several of Lalea's weapons.

Ariella had finally grasped the longbow and, although not anywhere near Jaron or Theia's ability, she could hit the target at a decent range. She still favoured the light rapier that she used back in Lightharbour, but there was an edge to her fighting now. She no longer practised for fun; she fought to win.

During the last combat session, she had deflected Eleazar's spinning knives before feigning injury. She had then tripped him and slammed the hilt of her rapier into the back of his head, flooring him. Eleazar groaned, blinking, trying to get rid of the bright stars he saw from the impact.

Karlov applauded her, "You've finally learnt to fight dirty. I love it!"

Indio had, at last, settled on a battle axe small enough that he could wield effectively, and Jaron had taken strides in his ability to use a longsword. Even Felix could now use a weapon without endangering himself and those around him. After several mishaps requiring Karlov's healing skills, the Knot leader had made him choose a mace, rather than a sword as his primary weapon.

"Less chance of accidents," was all Karlov said as he handed Felix the mace.

Training in the use of the Light had not gone as well. Malum was patient, but they were slow learners. Karlov started to intensify their sessions and brought Malum into their mornings to put them through their paces with weapons and their Light. Most of them could draw out the Light in themselves to some degree. They could form small glowing balls that could light up a room. Felix could even throw his, although this didn't please everyone. He got carried away one day and was a little casual with his aim. A ball of blue Light exploded just beyond Theia, singeing the tip of her ponytail and causing her to leap in fright.

"Idiot!" she screamed, gripping her burnt hair and advancing on Felix, who was back-pedalling.

Indio and Eleazar didn't help calm the situation. They had both collapsed into each other with howls of laughter as they mimicked Theia's startled expression.

"I'll snap your fingers if you ever pull a stunt like that again," she growled.

"Chill out, will you?" said Jaron, "Where's your sense of humour?"

"That's what it is to you, isn't it?" she shot back, "a great big joke. You behave like kids and you make me sick."

"Careful," laughed Indio. "If you're sick on the floor, Karlov will have you scrubbing the stones with your toothbrush."

Theia's face grew menacing.

"That's enough guys, leave her alone," said Ariella, stepping in front of the boys.

Theia lifted her chin and stared into Ariella's green eyes. "I don't need your help, princess," she spat.

Turning on her heel, she strode away

"What a smashing person she is, such a delicate soul, don't you think?" asked Eleazar.

"Definitely," nodded Indio.

"That's enough," called Malum. "Get back to your training."

"Come on," sighed Jaron, "Let's get this session finished."

"Hey, check me out," said Indio as he spun a small red ball of Light over in his hand.

"Not bad," nodded Eleazar, "Can you throw it?"

"Easy as pie," he said and flung his hand out, but the ball of Light simply leapt a few feet straight up and exploded.

"Not again," he moaned as he frantically banged his hair trying to extinguish the flames.

Eleazar and Jaron leapt at the chance to whack Indio's head and rained down slap after slap, long after the flames had been extinguished.

"Get off!" yelled Indio.

"I think it's out," said Eleazar, a serious look on his face

"No kidding," said Indio, "You two nearly knocked me unconscious."

"Just trying to help," smiled Jaron. "That's what friends are for."

"Well, let's see if you guys can do any better," said Indio, "I'll stand back, and only laugh a little bit."

Eleazar frowned and furrowed his brow as he formed a pulsating blue ball of Light in his hand.

"Not bad," smiled Indio. "Now give it a throw."

Eleazar gave him a nervous look and threw his hand out. The ball of Light wobbled in the air for a moment and then dropped to the floor, imploding with a hiss.

"Ha!" laughed Indio, "top job."

"At least I have all my hair," said Eleazar

Indio shut up as Jaron created a green Light ball. His was calmly pulsating in a gentle rhythm.

"That's beautiful," said Ariella.

Jaron smiled at her, but his concentration was lost, and the ball started to deflate like someone had stuck a pin in a balloon.

"No, no, no," said Jaron, trying to grasp the ball, but he only succeeded in squeezing it into nothing.

"Sorry," said Ariella, "I'll shut up next time."

"Your turn, Ari," said Eleazar, "Let's see what you've got."

Her mouth suddenly went dry.

"It's okay, I think that's us done for the day. Don't want to overdo it, do we?" she said.

"You're kidding," said Indio.

"Come on, Ari," urged Jaron.

"Don't be such a princess," goaded Eleazar.

"All right," she snapped, "just to shut you lot up."

She swallowed, took a deep breath and tried to clear her mind.

You can do this. It's in you, remember? That's what Malum said. Yeah, but what colour do you think will come today? I wish you would just make up your mind. Are you talking to the Light now, Ari? Yep, I guess you are.

She opened her hand and a soft red Light began to form into a small ball. But just as it got to the size of an orange, it flickered, crackled and collapsed.

"You can do this," said Jaron.

Shutting her eyes, she opened her hand again, willing the Light to form.

"Nice colour," said Indio.

Opening her eyes, she gasped. The ball of Light was blue. Before she could react, it flickered and disintegrated again. No one said anything. Ariella shook her shoulders, opened and closed her fists, then opened her left hand, closing her eyes again. For a few moments, there was silence, then she felt the warm glow in her hand. She opened her eyes. The ball of Light was red again.

"Will you make up your mind!" she yelled, startling the boys and the rest of the Knot. All eyes were on her as the ball of Light dispersed.

"That will do for today," called Malum. "We'll have another session tomorrow."

Tomorrow was not better, nor the next day. Ariella's Light could not settle. The others were progressing well, all except Joachim. His red Light only emerged when he lost his temper, which was common, but he lacked any control over it. He kept his distance from the others in the Knot.

"I wonder what his problem is?" asked Ariella after a particularly expressive fit of rage from Joachim. It ended up with him throwing his hands in the air, causing his red Light to explode out of his hands and shatter a window high up in one of the towers.

"We've no clue," replied Jaron. "We've tried to include him, to get him to talk, but he just grunts. He's not interested in anything but food and the next session of weapons training."

Indio nodded, "He's a pain in the arse. The other night Eleazar was juggling with apples. He didn't realize that one of the apples was Joachim's and it turns out Joachim doesn't like people juggling with his apples. I thought he was going to kill him. He's nuts."

"Killing Eleazar? Maybe he's not so bad after all," said Ariella.

"Ele's not so bad, Ari, you should give him a break," replied Jaron.

"Give him a break? After what he's done to me! I'll give him a break. I'll even let him pick which arm I break. I'm a generous girl."

"Come on, Ari, admittedly the rat in your pillowcase was pretty harsh," said Indio. "But I laughed when he swapped the cream on your strawberries for mayonnaise."

"Did you, Indio? That's great to know. I'll tuck that thought away for another day."

Indio was suddenly nervous. "Did I say laugh? It wasn't a proper laugh, it was more of a snort or a cough than a laugh. And you know what? Once I'd thought about it, I realised it wasn't funny and that Ele should be punished for it."

"Nice back-pedalling, Indio, real slick," said Jaron.

Before Indio could protest any more, an intense blue Light flared in the training area, causing them to shield their eyes. Karlov had the Knot fighting in pairs to develop their team skills. Theia and Eugenie were attacking Esther and Felix. The girls had both targeted Esther, trying to take her out of the fight before they focused on Felix. They had her pinned back with their swords while Esther was desperately holding them off with her spear. Felix had tried to come to her aid, but his hand-to-hand combat skills were no match for Eugenie. She nonchalantly disarmed him before smashing him to the floor and turning her attention once again to Esther. Esther's defence grew more and more desperate and, eventually, she buckled under the onslaught, her spear knocked to the floor. But before the final blow could land, Felix reacted.

The blue flare had exploded out of his outstretched hand and formed a wall of Light in front of the frightened Esther. Just as Felix's Light had held Karlov's sword on their first day, it now held Theia and Eugenie, their faces fixed in shock.

"What on earth?" said Indio.

"Felix, hold it there," said Ariella as she approached the Light holding the two girls.

Eleazar picked up a small pebble from the courtyard and tossed it into the Light. It bounced off with a soft thud. Ariella drew her sword and poked it at the Light. It was like hitting a wall.

"Wow," said Eleazar. "That's amazing!"

Indio went and stood in front of the frozen Theia and Eugenie and began waving with a big grin on his face. "I think we should keep them like this; it's an improvement."

"That's enough," called Karlov. "Let them out, Felix."

Felix dropped his arm, dispelling the Light and the startled girls collapsed to the floor. Eugenie looked embarrassed, but Theia was protesting loudly.

"That's it for today. Go and hand your weapons into Lalea and grab some lunch," said Karlov.

As they approached Lalea's weapons store, the Assistant Master of Arms was walking out to meet them.

"Keep the weapons," Lalea called. "You're going to need them."

She pulled Karlov to one side, and they whispered together for a few minutes.

"Keep our weapons? This sounds like it's going to be fun," smiled Indio, swinging his axe.

Ariella rolled her eyes, but she couldn't stop grinning.

At last, a break from continuous training. Maybe Indio's right, this might be fun.

"Gather round everyone," called Karlov. "We've been given a job to do, our first, so let's make sure we nail it."

He gave the Knot a long hard look before continuing. "There's an orchard an hour's ride from here that's got a particularly bad case of Thunderhead infestation."

Felix groaned, Eugenie laughed, the rest of the Knot looked confused.

"Thunderheads," muttered Joachim, "what are they?"

"He speaks," whispered Eleazar.

Indio tried to stifle his laugh.

Karlov ignored them. "Thunderheads are unique to Trevena; it's the soil here they love, apparently. They are about the size of a small dog, but don't be fooled. They are heavily armoured balls of murderous destruction. They live in colonies buried underground all over the countryside of Trevena. Normally the colonies are small, but occasionally they reach infestation stage and then they can destroy whole farms. Luckily for you lot we have a full-on infestation to deal with, so you get to test out the skills you've learnt over the last three months."

Joachim cracked his knuckles and Esther winced.

"Report to the stables for your horses and meet me back here in ten minutes." The Knot hesitated. "Go!" yelled Karlov.

Ten minutes later, the Knot was assembled on horseback in the middle of the courtyard.

"Single file," commanded Karlov. "Stay close, let's move."

93

He nudged his horse into a trot out of the gates and into the streets of Stonegard, the Knot following behind. A few minutes later they were amongst the fields of Trevena, an autumn breeze blowing in their faces.

Ariella breathed deeply.

It feels amazing to be out of the city; it's been too long.

Karlov led them at a brisk pace. The fields of wheat and barley gave way to all manner of fruit orchards, a hundred different varieties of apples, pears and plums. After a few hours riding Karlov held up his hand and the column of riders halted.

Jaron moved his horse up next to Ariella's. "What's he doing?" he asked, looking at Karlov.

"I'm not sure," she replied.

Felix was riding the horse in front of them and turned in the saddle. "He's listening."

"For what?" Jaron and Ariella asked in unison.

Before Felix could answer, Karlov kicked his horse into a canter, and the column was moving. They only rode for a few minutes before Karlov stopped again.

"Felix," called Jaron, "what's he listening for?"

Felix turned to Jaron. His face had gone white again. "Thunder."

"Thunder?" said Ariella looking up at the clear blue sky. "Why's he listening for thunder?"

Then they heard it. A dull, low rumble of thunder.

"Felix," asked Ariella, growing nervous. "Why can I hear thunder when there's not a cloud in the sky?"

"They're not called Thunderheads without good reason. Their heads are covered with thick, heavy armour, and they attack by charging those heads into things."

"Things?" asked Jaron.

Felix shrugged: "trees, barns, walls, animals, wagons, even people. You know, things."

Ahead of them, Karlov stood high in his stirrups and motioned for the Knot to gather around him.

"Listen up everyone, this may keep you from getting hurt today." The Knot looked startled as more peals of thunder rolled around them. "The Thunderheads here have reached infestation stage. That means there is no controlling them, no capturing them. They are essentially insane. That means we take them out, and we do it fast. The Thunderheads are weak in the sides and the rear. Do not try to take them on headfirst; you will lose and losing to a Thunderhead means broken bones. Is that clear?"

The Knot nodded.

"Excellent. Stay together, fight as a team, just like I've been teaching you. Any questions? No? Good. Secure the horses here; they'll not help us in there." Karlov motioned to a large apple orchard off to the side of the road.

The Knot fanned out and approached the first line of trees as more thunder echoed around them. They drew their weapons, Jaron and Theia notching arrows to their bows. Eleazar nervously spun his long knives in his hands. Indio practised a few swings with his axe and grinned. Ariella drew her rapier; the cold metal felt reassuring in her hand.

The thunder grew louder and more frequent as they advanced through the trees. Up ahead they saw a tall apple tree shake violently and heard the thuds as piles of apples fell to the earth. The tree shook, again and again, each time accompanied by a peal of thunder. Then there was a massive crack, and the trunk exploded at its base, sending splinters flying in every direction. The tall tree tumbled to the ground and lay still. The advancing Knot hesitated and exchanged anxious glances.

"Keep moving," commanded Karlov positioned in the middle of the line.

Ariella was near one end of the line on Karlov's left, with Phoebe on her outside and Indio, Jaron and Eleazar on the inside. The other five were on the far side of Karlov. Ariella was scanning the trees in front of her trying to catch a glimpse of whatever had shattered the apple tree.

Suddenly there was a blur of movement just in front of them, a mighty crash of thunder and a nearby tree shook violently. Then Ariella saw it: a small creature, no higher than her knee, with four stumpy legs, wide feet and a short, stocky tail. The body was thick and round, a blurred mixture of browns and greens with a few flashes of yellow. She could just make out its head, with a jagged mouth and small black eyes. All over the front of its body were thick, armoured scales notched and ridged. It shook itself, backed away a few meters from the tree and then leapt forward with frightening speed.

CRASH!

The tree shuddered but remained upright.

The Thunderhead shook itself, backed away and charged.

CRASH!

"What are you waiting for?" yelled Karlov at the five on his left. "Take it out!"

Jaron let fly with his arrow. It struck the Thunderhead as it was backing away from the tree. The arrow slammed into the thick armour on its head and was deflected high and away by the armoured plates. The Thunderhead did not even flinch.

Eleazar glanced at Jaron. "This is going to be harder than it looks."

The Thunderhead charged again and slammed into the tree, sending splinters of wood flying in every direction.

"Oww!" cried Indio as a splinter dug into his thigh. "That's it, I'm mad!"

He leapt towards the creature as it shook itself at the base of the tree, recovering from the impact. He swung his great axe down on the creature's head.

SMACK!

The axe rebounded off the great armoured plates and was thrown from Indio's hands, landing just a few meters from Ariella.

"Hey!" she cried, "are you trying to kill me?"

The Thunderhead studied Indio with its tiny black eyes and began backing away.

"Indio, get out of the way!" Jaron yelled, dumping his bow and drawing his sword.

Indio realized what was happening. He turned and started running for his axe, but the Thunderhead had already begun its charge. Indio was sprinting across the floor of the orchard towards his axe, too slowly. The Thunderhead was accelerating and gaining him on him fast. There was no way he'd get to his axe in time.

Jaron and Ariella dived into the creature's path, trying to distract it from Indio. Eleazar threw one of his long knives. It struck the side of the creature's head, and there it stayed, embedded in the armoured scale. The creature didn't even break its stride.

"Oh, heck," muttered Eleazar.

The Thunderhead was at full speed, moments away from impact with Indio, Jaron and Ariella. Ariella closed her eyes ready for the crunch, but it never came. Swiftly, without a sound, Phoebe had intercepted the onrushing creature. She slammed her great sword down on its unprotected back, killing it instantly.

"And that, my young sojourners, is how you deal with a Thunderhead," said a smiling Karlov. "Excellent work, Phoebe. One down, probably a few hundred left. Indio, pick up your axe and try not to drop it again, okay?"

Indio, breathing heavily, retrieved his axe. "Thanks, Phoebe. I owe you."

Phoebe nodded but remained silent, her face a picture of calm determination. Eleazar recovered his knife from the Thunderhead, and the Knot continued through the orchard towards the ever-increasing sound of thunder. The further into the trees they moved, the greater the devastation. Smashed and shattered apple trees lay strewn across the soft green grass that covered the orchard floor. Everywhere they looked were charging Thunderheads. They seemed to be in a rage, crashing into each other and ricocheting off trees. It was carnage.

"Stay together, pick them off one at a time. Remember, aim for the sides and rear. Let's go," commanded Karlov.

Ariella and the four others with her edged towards the scene of destruction. It was mayhem. The Thunderheads were continuously charging through the orchard attacking anything in front of them. Thankfully, they were too distracted to notice Ariella and the others arrive. The noise of their thunderous impact was deafening. The sojourners had to shout just to be heard.

"Hit them when they're dazed," yelled Ariella. "Use the trees as cover."

The others nodded and split off in pairs with Jaron hanging back with his longbow he'd retrieved from the ground. Indio and Eleazar took up a position a few paces behind a large apple tree towards which a Thunderhead was charging.

CRASH!

Before the creature could recover from the impact, they were upon it, Eleazar's knives finding the gaps in its armour. Phoebe and Ariella continued using their tactic, taking out the Thunderheads before they could recover from a charge. Jaron used his bow to good effect, standing in between the two pairs and hitting the Thunderheads in their weak rear.

"Keep going!" called Karlov. "With luck, we may save some of this orchard."

They continued to move ahead, taking down the Thunderheads as they went.

"Look!" shouted Jaron, pointing up ahead.

A hundred yards or so ahead of them was an old stone farmhouse with a thatched roof. There were two small gable windows with pretty flower boxes and a painted red front door. Under normal circumstances, it would have been idyllic. Not today. Today it was surrounded by a seething mass of Thunderheads launching themselves relentlessly at the stone walls.

A girl's scream pierced the air.

"There's someone in there!" shouted Ariella above the incessant sound of thunder. "Quickly!"

The five of them broke into a run, dodging the charging Thunderheads. Jaron's arrows whistled over them, removing any from their path that he could. The walls were shaking under the mass of attacks. The girl screamed again. Indio and Phoebe were in the lead and smashed into the rear of the mass of creatures around the farmhouse, sword and battle axe carving through the Thunderheads. Ariella and Eleazar followed behind, darting in and out, cutting through the lightly armoured rear of the creatures.

Masses of dust and small pieces of stone were falling from the wall.

"We've got to get her out," said Ariella. "The whole place is coming down. Phoebe, Indio, carve us a path to the door."

The four of them started to push through the mass of Thunderheads. Jaron was still outside the ring, raining down arrow after arrow. A huge piece of stone tumbled out of the wall just behind the small group, crushing several Thunderheads underneath it.

"Too many," said Eleazar, breathing heavily from the exertion. "We're not going to get to the door in time."

The gable window on the first floor flew open and they heard the girl scream again. She was being held by an older girl that looked like her sister. They had a look of terror in their eyes.

"They're going to have to jump," called Jaron. "If the house comes down while they're still inside, it'll all be over."

"They can't jump from there! The fall will kill them," replied Ariella.

Indio spoke up, "Not if Phoebe catches them."

Ariella looked at her giant companion. She was still swinging her greatsword, fighting desperately to get to the front door.

It might work, or she might drop them.

They're dead either way, Ari. Let's give them a fighting chance.

"What do you think, Phoebe?"

Phoebe did not say anything. She paused, looked at the two girls in the window, looked back at Ariella and nodded.

"All right guys, let's make her some space."

Jaron concentrated his fire on the Thunderheads around Phoebe as the others cleared out as many as they could.

Ariella called up to the two girls.

"You're going to have to jump!"

The girls looked even more terrified.

"We can't get to the door, you'll have to jump!"

They're scared out of their wits, Ari. Reassure them, comfort them!

She pointed to Phoebe "This is my friend Phoebe. She's the strongest girl I've ever met. She's amazing, she'll catch you, trust me!"

There was a massive groan as the far corner of the house collapsed under the Thunderhead barrage.

"Now!" yelled Ariella. "The house is coming down, you've got to jump!" The house gave another groan as the whole building shuddered.

"We've got to move," said Eleazar, "the whole place is coming down."

"Not yet," said Ariella, "we can do this."

The smaller girl had stopped screaming and was now sobbing, her head buried in her sister's neck.

"Please!" called Ariella. "Jump!"

The older sister took a terrified look back into the house, shut her eyes, held her sister tightly in her arms and jumped out of the window.

She screamed as she fell and continued to scream for a few more seconds before she realized that Phoebe was holding her in her powerful arms.

"Phoebe, you keep impressing me," smiled Eleazar as he slapped her shoulder. "Now, run!"

The four of them and the two girls Phoebe was still carrying ran towards Jaron. Behind them, the old farmhouse gave a final moan before collapsing forwards in a massive cloud of dust.

13

A Leap of Faith

The collapsing farmhouse had taken out most of the Thunderheads and sent the rest scurrying away. As the dust settled, there was a moment of calm. Phoebe was still holding the two girls, the fear easing away from their faces. The youngest must have been around five years old, the eldest a little older. They looked tiny.

Ariella smiled at the eldest. "Hi, my name's Ariella. What's yours?"

"Amy," she replied. "This is my sister Sophie."

"Pleased to meet you, Amy. Were you the only two in the house?"

Amy nodded. "Mummy and Daddy went out to check on the trees when they heard the thunder. I don't know where they are now." Her eyes welled up with tears.

A sudden scream filled the air, startling the sojourners. On the far side of the ruined farmhouse were Karlov and the rest of the Knot.

With them were a man and woman dressed in farm clothes. It was the woman who was screaming, great tears rolling down her cheeks.

"Mummy!" cried Amy and dropped from Phoebe's arms with her sister. They ran around the ruins of their home and flung themselves at their parents. Amy quickly retold the story of their escape. When she spoke of Phoebe catching them, her eyes went wide with delight. Ariella smiled at Phoebe, who smiled back.

She smiled. There's some emotion there after all.

Karlov brought them back to matters at hand. "Great work, you lot. Well done. We've cleared the Thunderheads out from this side of the orchard and from looking around here we seem to have broken the back of them. We just need to do a final sweep to make sure we've cleaned them all out."

Esther spoke up, "Where's Joachim? Is he not with you?"

Jaron shook his head. "Last time we saw him he was with you."

"I lost sight of him when it all kicked off," said Eugenie. "Maybe he got scared and ran up a tree."

"I don't think that sounds like Joachim," said Ariella.

"Really?" sneered Theia, "and you know so much, don't you?"

"Knock it off, Theia," snapped Jaron.

Karlov took charge. "Theia, Eugenie, Felix, Esther, you come with me, and we'll sweep to the right of the farmhouse away from the road. The rest of you go left and shout when you find him."

Ariella headed off again with the other four searching for their lost companion. Occasionally, they bumped into a deranged Thunderhead that needed dealing with, but otherwise the orchards were empty. After ten minutes of searching, they heard the distinct clap of thunder from up ahead. Then another, and another.

"Come on," said Ariella, breaking into a sprint.

The five came charging through the trees and burst into a large clearing to a scene of chaos. On the far side, in the centre of a pile of dead Thunderheads, was Joachim, swinging a sabre with one hand and an old tree branch in the other. He was desperately trying to keep at bay a growing number of Thunderheads who had taken an intense dislike to him.

"I might've known," said Ariella. "Jaron, would you go and shout for Karlov? We'll go to help him."

Jaron nodded and took off through the trees shouting for Karlov. The remaining four ran into the clearing, weapons drawn. The fighting around Joachim was growing in intensity. Wave after wave of Thunderheads were charging at him. It was all he could do to jump, dodge or deflect his way out of trouble. But his luck would not hold. Just out of Joachim's field of vision, a nasty looking Thunderhead with a huge scar down its side had backed away and aimed at the isolated Guardian.

"Joachim!" called Ariella, "to your right!"

But it was too late. The charging ball of fury took Joachim unawares and smashed headlong into his leg. The usual thunderclap was replaced instead by a sickening snap as Joachim's leg gave way, and he collapsed on the ground. Before the Thunderhead could retreat,

Indio was on it, smashing his axe down on its back. The others cut through the remaining Thunderheads forming a defensive ring around Joachim as he tried to climb back to his feet. The creatures just kept on coming.

"What did you do to them, Joachim?" said Eleazar "They seem intent on finishing you off."

Joachim said nothing but spat on the ground as he tried to stand.

"We've got to get him out of here," said Ariella. "This clearing is too exposed.They're going to surround us, and that's not going to be pretty. Indio go help Joachim. See if we can move him."

Indio ran to Joachim's side and tried to help him up.

"Get off me!" he yelled. "I can do it. I don't need you losers."

"Joachim, stop being an idiot!" yelled Ariella, desperately defending herself from the charging Thunderheads.

"Let's ditch him, Ari," called Indio, "and see how he manages on his own."

Eleazar nodded in agreement.

"No way. We don't leave any of our Knot. He's one of us."

"But he hates us," said Indio

"We should be used to it. Theia and Eugenie hate us too and they're still our Knot," replied Ariella. "We're not leaving him."

"Well, we need a plan," said Eleazar. "Even with Phoebe, we can't hold them off forever."

Phoebe was swinging her greatsword in a huge arc, forcing the Thunderheads back and preventing them from making a clear charge at the fallen Joachim. On and on they came, hurling themselves at the sojourners, driven on by their rage. The Knot's defence grew ever more desperate as they started to buckle under the onslaught.

"We've got to run, Ari," shouted Eleazar. "They'll take us all out if we stay here." He looked for an opening in the ranks of Thunderheads - an escape route. There was none; they were surrounded. "Killed on our first mission," he muttered. "That's embarrassing."

Suddenly he heard a sharp whistle from his right and ducked instinctively as an arrow flew from the trees, then another. Two Thunderheads fell to the ground. Indio let out a cheer as Karlov and the others burst from the trees.

"Excellent timing," sighed Eleazar.

Jaron and Theia were raining arrows down on the Thunderheads as Eugenie, Felix and Esther drove into the rear, scattering them. The last few were picked off easily as Karlov strode into the circle with a furious look on his face. He walked across to Joachim, lying on the ground grimacing in pain.

"What exactly did you think you were doing?" he shouted. "Thought you could clear the whole lot on your own? How did that work out for you?"

Joachim pulled himself to his feet, his eyes blazing with anger. "I don't need you! I don't need any of you!"

Karlov was mad. "You are a sojourner and this is your Knot. I don't care if you don't like it. Get used to it!"

"No chance. I never asked for this; I never wanted this! You can all throw yourself off a cliff for all I care, you and all the other Guardians!"

Karlov held Joachim's unwavering gaze, then his face softened as he looked to the other nine.

"Don't need any of them? Let's see how you get back to your horse without them."

With that, Karlov turned on his heel and walked out of the clearing towards the horses. There was stunned silence. Nobody moved. A few cast unpleasant looks at Joachim as he sank back to the ground, unable to stand. Nobody said anything.

Esther walked across to her fellow Erestian and studied his leg. "It's broken, Joachim. You're not getting back to your horse without help."

"Get away from me," he snarled.

Esther shook her head and walked away as Joachim continued to try to get to his feet.

Jaron edged up to Ariella. "What do you reckon? We leave him?"

She shook her head. "We don't leave people, even when they are idiots."

She looked around at the Knot. Theia and Eugenie were apart from the rest, apparently uninterested in Joachim. Esther and Felix stood next to each other, both upset by the situation. Eleazar was comparing weapons with Indio. Ariella sighed.

"Jaron, would you go and find a tree branch we could use as a crutch?" He nodded and slipped into the trees.

Ariella started walking towards Joachim and beckoned for Felix to join her. Joachim was lying on his back, trying to catch his breath after attempting to stand on his shattered leg. Ariella's shadow fell across him and he opened his eyes.

"You can get lost too."

"Joachim, stop being a jerk. We're not leaving without you, and the sooner you can get that through your thick head, the better." She pulled Felix closer. "What do you think, Felix? You're the best user of the Light we've got. I've seen Lalea and Karlov heal using their Light. Fancy a crack at it?"

Joachim was angry now. "Get that spineless, pathetic freak away from me!"

Ariella tapped his broken leg with her foot and he howled in pain. "Sorry, Joachim, I slipped. Now, be a good boy and shut up for a moment."

Felix swallowed and went pale.

"I've no idea how you do what you do, Felix, but it seems natural to you so just let it flow." Ariella smiled, trying to reassure him.

Felix hesitated, but just then Esther came and put her hand on Felix's arm, smiled at him and nodded. "You can do this, Felix. I know you can."

Some of the colour returned to Felix's cheeks, and he knelt beside Joachim. He took a deep breath, shut his eyes and opened his hands above the mangled leg. For a moment nothing seemed to be happening. Then, ever so slowly, Felix's distinct blue Light seemed to be oozing from his fingers and rolling onto Joachim's leg. The tall Erestian boy sat up, his eyes wide and mouth hanging open. The rest of the Knot gathered around, watching and waiting. Theia and Eugenie came over to see what would happen.

After a few minutes, Felix closed his hands and opened his eyes. He looked up at Ariella. "I'm not sure if that did anything, but it's the best I could do."

Ariella glanced over at Phoebe. "Could you help him up?"

Before Joachim could resist, Phoebe had tucked her arms under Joachim's and lifted him to his feet. He winced in pain but was able to put some pressure on his broken leg.

"Well," Ariella asked, "how is it?"

Joachim hesitated for a moment checking out his previously shattered leg. "It's not perfect," he muttered. "There's still a pain when I lean on it."

"But?" pushed Ariella.

"It's not broken," he replied through gritted teeth.

"Anything you want to say?"

He gave Ariella a filthy look then glanced at Felix. "Thank you." He said reluctantly.

By this time Jaron had returned with a branch he had fashioned into a makeshift crutch and he tossed it to Joachim who grunted his thanks.

"You're welcome," smiled Jaron.

"Come on," said Ariella, "let's get back to Karlov and find our way out of here."

The Knot made their way through the orchard towards where they had left the horses.

"I'm starving," moaned Indio. "I don't suppose anyone has any food with them?"

"Here," called Jaron as he reached up and pulled an apple from a nearby tree and threw it over to him. The apple was a delicious looking yellow-green and Indio took a huge bite.

"Arrggh!" he cried as he spat the apple from his mouth, dropping the rest to the ground. "What kind of apple is that?"

"Indio," said Eleazar, "what's that on your chin?"

Indio wiped his face with the back of his hand, "It's just the apple juice."

Ariella came over, "It doesn't look like apple juice."

Indio turned his hand over and looked at it. Where he expected to see the sticky juice from an apple, he saw a dark, thick, red liquid.

"It's blood," said Indio checking his face and mouth, "but it's not my blood."

"Then whose blood is it?" asked Jaron.

Eleazar had picked up the apple Indio had dropped. "Look."

The hole in the apple where Indio had taken a bite was dripping the same dark, thick, red liquid.

"Are you kidding me?" said Indio. "The apple is bleeding? What the heck is going on? Is someone playing a trick 'cos it's pretty grim."

Eleazar went to another tree and pulled off an apple. He sliced it in half, letting it drop to the floor. The same thick blood trickled out on to the green grass. The young sojourners exchanged nervous glances. They all went to a different tree and tried more apples. Everywhere was the same. The apples were bleeding.

Nearby was one of the trees smashed down by the Thunderheads. Indio took his axe to the bark around the fallen tree trunk. The same sticky blood oozed from the bark. The blood was being carried up the trunk of the tree.

"This is nuts," he said, wiping the blood off the blade of his axe. "I've never heard of trees bleeding before."

"We have," said Eleazar, "haven't we, Ari?"

She nodded.

"Is this a Lightharbour thing?" asked Jaron.

"No," said Ariella. "It was the day before we arrived in Stonegard. We were on the outskirts of Trevena when we passed through a village in an uproar. Their crops all had the same thing, even the flowers had it. They were all dying."

"You were there too?" Indio asked Eleazar.

He nodded, "It was the day she saved my life."

That comment caught Ariella off guard.

"You saved his life?" asked Jaron with a big grin on his face.

"Well, I, sort of, I suppose so. Maybe."

"She went all 'princess' and shouted at her guards," said Eleazar. "It was a sight to see. Of course, I already had an escape plan worked out but thanks to the princess I didn't have to use it."

Jaron laughed, "That's why you're so horrible to her!"

Eleazar blushed and nodded, "I don't like being in debt to people, and I find it difficult to say thank you."

Jaron laughed harder and Indio joined in. Eleazer threw one of the blood-soaked apples at Indio and caught him square on the nose. The bloody pulp sprayed as Indo recoiled, trying to wipe the mess out of his eyes. Eleazer scooped down to grab another apple while Jaron started to back-pedal, holding his hands out in surrender.

"Easy, Ele, back up, we're sorry!" called Jaron,

"Come on," said Eleazar testily. "Let's show these apples to Karlov and see if he knows what's going on."

The three boys walked on, leaving Ariella behind, speechless.

He's horrible to me because he doesn't know how to say thank you! Is that supposed to be funny?

"Hey!" she yelled after him. "Here's an idea, instead of putting rats in my pillowcase you could just say thank you!"

Eleazar didn't turn around or stop walking, he simply lifted his arm in a wave.

That's it? A wave. No apology. He's an idiot, I don't care how thankful he is!

The four of them caught up with the rest of the Knot as they met Karlov waiting by the horses. They wasted no time filling him in on the details of Felix healing Joachim's leg and the bleeding apples. Karlov walked a few paces back into the orchard and picked an apple from a tree, slicing it open with his knife. His face dropped when the same red liquid splashed over his blade.

He took another apple in both hands. Ariella saw his gentle green Light form a sphere around his hands, pulsing like a heartbeat. Karlov closed his eyes, allowing the Light to do its work, the Knot standing in silence. After a few minutes, he opened his eyes, took out his knife and sliced the apple. He looked disappointed as the blood dripped onto the green grass. He pulled a few more apples from the trees and stuffed them in his saddlebag.

"Let's get back to Stonegard. Every mile we're going to check the crops on each side of the road. I want to know how widespread this thing is."

The Knot did as they were commanded. Every mile they paused and checked apple trees, plum trees and pear trees. As the farms changed, they checked wheat, barley, maize, turnips, carrots and potatoes. All along the route it was the same. The countryside was bleeding.

14

The Unseen Visitor

By the time they arrived back at Stonegard, the sun had almost set and the twin Dawnhaven moons were visible in the early evening sky. Normally the traffic around the gates at this time would be quiet, but on this particular evening it was pandemonium. There were people everywhere shouting, crying, jostling with each other and arguing with the brightly coloured Trevena soldiers.

Karlov hadn't smiled since he had sliced open the bloody apple, and the scenes before them didn't help his mood.

"Felix, you and Theia go and find out what's going on," he ordered. The rest of the Knot waited outside the main gates trying to keep out of the way of the masses of people flooding into the city.

They returned after half an hour with worried looks on their faces.

"Well?" barked Karlov, in no mood for pleasantries.

"It's everywhere," said Felix, his eyes wide. "There are people here from every county in Trevena. Plants are bleeding everywhere. The crops are ruined; everything is soaked in blood. What's going on Karlov? What's happening?"

Karlov did not answer.

"I spoke to some people from Darcian," said Theia. "They're saying the poison is from Khan." She gave Indio and Phoebe a malicious glance as she spoke. "They're saying their crops have been poisoned by the river. They reckon every farm in Trevena uses the Willowbank to irrigate their crops; they think the poison is in the river. They're telling tales of dead fish turned blood red, bleeding from their gills. It can only be Khan. They have poisoned the river as it runs out of the mountains."

"That sounds like something Khan would do," sneered Eugenie.

"Shut your face, Eugenie!" shouted Indio, his hand moving to his axe.

"That's enough," snapped Karlov. "Let's get back to the compound. Move!" He kicked his horse into a trot, forcing his way through the crowded streets, the others following behind.

The Guardian compound was only slightly less manic than the streets. Different Knots were rushing everywhere, gathering weapons, collecting supplies. It seemed that more Guardians from across Trevena had arrived.

"This is not good," murmured Jaron.

Eleazar nodded in agreement.

Karlov dismounted. "Stable your horses, hand in your weapons then get some food in your bellies. I've got a feeling it's going to be a busy few days." With that, he disappeared into the central building in the compound, one the Knot had yet to enter.

"Come on," said Indio. "I'm starving."

They stabled the horses and dumped their weapons as fast as they could, the promise of good food spurring them on. Jaron was the quickest and first to reach their tower.

"Hey," he called as the others approached, "someone has left us a present."

On the very centre of the tower's door was pinned a stunning purple butterfly, its delicate wings outstretched.

"Yeah," said Indio, swinging open the door. "Very impressive. Now can I get my dinner?"

Ariella paused, studying the butterfly.

That looks familiar. It's almost like the one on top of the pin that the thief threw at me.

She absent mindedly rubbed the place where the pin had struck her and was about to step inside when she saw the look on Eleazar's face. He had gone deathly pale and was scanning the tops of the wall all around the compound.

"Eleazar?" she asked, "are you okay?"

"Yes, I'm fine," he said abruptly and stepped past her into the tower and up the stairs, ignoring the smells of food coming from the mess hall.

What's going on with him? What's the deal with butterflies?

The rest of the Knot pushed past Ariella as she stood in the doorway, and the smell of roast pheasant made her forget about butterflies.

After dinner, she was curled up in one of the mess hall armchairs when Karlov came down the stairs. It was soon apparent that the meetings he had been in had done nothing to ease his mood.

"Get some rest. We have a long ride in the morning."

"What's the plan, Sir?" Ariella asked.

"Lord Vantor has ordered every Guardian in Trevena to go and scout out the countryside. We need to find out if it's as widespread as people are saying. We've been tasked to track the Willowbank all the way down to Lake Evermere and bring back water samples."

"Excuse me, Sir," said Theia, politely. "Should we not all be riding north to stop those barbarians from Khan poisoning the rest of Dawnhaven?" Eugenie nodded in agreement, casting a withering look at Phoebe and Indio.

"That does it," snarled Indio, jumping up from his seat and sending his chair crashing to the floor. He made to leap across the table to tackle the grinning Theia, but, before he could move, Phoebe had thrown one of her long arms across his chest and was holding him back.

"Let me go! I'm going to smash her face in!"

"What did I tell you?" said the gloating Theia. "Barbarians."

"Theia, I'm not in the mood for your garbage, so shut up or you'll be scrubbing the toilets with your toothbrush." Karlov meant it. "Everyone get some rest and be ready to ride at first light."

Ariella and Jaron stepped in front of Indio blocking his view of Theia. Ariella smiled up at Phoebe as she held onto Indio.

"Thanks, Phoebe," she said.

"Come on, Indio, let's get out of here," said Jaron as Phoebe eased her grip.

Ariella looked around the mess hall. The girls were drifting upstairs. Felix had said something about practising some more in the training ground, and Joachim was tucking into his third helping of dinner.

"Did Eleazar not come down?" she asked.

Indio and Jaron shook their heads. "I didn't see him after we came in through the front door," said Jaron.

"Something's not right," said Ariella. "I saw him go upstairs. He looked upset."

"I'd be upset if I missed dinner," said Indio.

"Not exactly what I meant." Something in Eleazar's eyes had unsettled Ariella, but she couldn't put her finger on it.

"Do you want us to go check on him?" said Jaron, noticing the look on Ariella's face.

"Yeah," smiled Indio, "I could tell him all about the dinner he missed. That'll cheer him up."

"Sweet Indio, I'm sure he'd love that," said Ariella.

The three of them left the mess hall and made their way past the girls' landing up to the boys' room. The door was closed. No one was around.

"Maybe he went to bed early," suggested Ariella.

The two boys looked at her as if she had said something stupid.

"Fat chance," said Indio, shoving open the bedroom door and yelling, "Hey Ele, you missed dinner!"

The three strode into the room and stopped dead in their tracks. They saw Eleazar sitting on his bed, a resigned look on his face. He was watching the left-hand window obscured by the open door. A moment later, all the lights went out, and the room was filled with unnatural darkness so deep you could not see your hand in front of your face.

"Ele!" yelled Jaron.

Indio rushed forward into the centre of the room and shouted in pain as he whacked his toe against a bedpost.

"Find some light!" yelled Jaron.

Ariella reached into her jacket pocket and grasped her pouch of sun cubes, blindly untying the cord. She pulled one out and crushed it in her hand. Instantly a warm glow broke out and flooded the room, driving back the thick blackness. Indio was jumping up and down on one foot clutching his toe, while Jaron was trying to get his bearings in the now brightly lit room. Eleazar had not moved. He was sitting motionless on his bed, staring out of the open window.

Ariella and Jaron ran to the window, searching for someone or something that had caused the darkness in the room. The courtyard below was still buzzing with activity. There was nothing out of the ordinary.

"What is going on, Ele?" said Indio, sitting on a bed, clutching his foot.

Eleazar still said nothing.

Jaron returned from the window and sat down next to him. "Ele," he began gently, "Do you know what that blackness was?"

"It was creepy as heck, that's what it was," said Indio. "I've been in some dark caves in my life but nothing like that. Speaking of creepy, what shifted it? The darkness blocked all the light from the window."

Ariella opened her hand and showed them the crushed crystal. "It's a sun cube," she said, "a gift from an old friend." The light began to fade away, leaving only the little daylight that was left from the open window.

"Excellent gift," smiled Jaron. "Thank your friend for us."

He turned back to Eleazar. "You want to tell us what that was about?"

Eleazar blinked, breaking his long stare out of the open window. He glanced at Ariella. "It was an old friend."

"Jaron," whispered Ariella, fear creeping into her voice, "look!"

She pointed to a spot on the wall a palm's width above Eleazar's head. Imbedded in the stone wall was a long, slender dart. It was metal, the bright surface reflecting the flickering candles. At the end of the needle was a beautiful, delicate butterfly.

"What are you doing in here?" growled Joachim startling everyone in the room.

"We invited her, so get over it," said Indio, limping in front of Joachim, shielding Ariella and the needle from his view.

"Don't worry, I'm leaving," said Ariella, patting Eleazar on the shoulder and with her other hand snatching the needle from the wall and hiding it in her pocket. "See you in the morning, at first light."

"Oh joy," groaned Indio, collapsing back on his bed.

Ariella skipped down the stairs, past her room and down again towards the mess hall. The food had been cleared away and the fire was still burning in the hearth. She dropped into one of the armchairs, checked to make sure no one was around and pulled out the needle. It was about the length of her hand, light but strong. The end had been fashioned into a pair of butterfly wings.

This is exactly like the one the captain pulled out of my shoulder. The question is: what's it doing stuck in the wall above Eleazar's head? Was whoever threw it trying to hit him? Was it a warning? Is it the same person that attacked me? If it is the same person that attacked me, were they actually after Eleazar in the Friendly Phoenix and I just stumbled across them? What did he mean by 'an old friend'? Does he know who threw it? He looked so passive like he knew something was going to happen. Steady Ari, you're going to drive yourself nuts with

112

all the questions. One thing's for certain: Eleazar knows more than he is letting on. I think I'll just have to go and drag it out of him. I'm sure Indio and Jaron will help. We just have to find somewhere quiet.

She was just about to climb out of the armchair when she felt a soft hum in her pocket - the echo orb. She pulled it out and held it to her ear.

".... it's like I was telling you Theia, Khan can't be trusted. Ever since the splitting of the kingdoms, Khan has only cared about itself. First, they poison Trevena, then Darcian will be next, just you wait and see."

That's Eugenie, the stirring cow!

Theia agreed, "They're barbarians, filthy freaks."

"My Father always says you can't trust the mountains. We have to watch them, Theia. Karlov's on their side, of course. He's from Khan."

Ariella heard the sound of the bedroom door opening through the echo orb. Theia and Eugenie fell silent.

Great, that's just what we need. Eugenie spreading that kind of garbage around, like Theia needs any help to be a witch.

She pushed herself out of the soft chair and made her way up the stairs.

Indio's going to explode when I tell him this. I better make sure Phoebe's around to stop him re-breaking Eugenie's perfect nose. At least it'll distract Eleazar, and maybe we can get him talking.

As she approached her landing, she found the staircase up to the boys' floor blocked by Lalea and Karlov talking in whispers.

"Ah, there you are," said Lalea. "The other girls are in the room. You can join them and get some rest. You've got a busy few days ahead of you." Lalea spoke in such a way that you found yourself doing exactly what she asked before you even realised.

Ariella's hand was on her bedroom door when she remembered that she was trying to get to see Eleazar and the others tonight. She hesitated and looked around. Karlov and Lalea were still blocking the stairs, watching her.

"Bedtime, Ariella," she said in a tone that allowed no room for arguments.

Ariella sighed.

It'll be a long ride tomorrow. I'll be able to speak to them then.

"Goodnight," she said and slipped into her room.

The Knot was up and ready before the first light of dawn. The mood Karlov was in yesterday meant no one wanted to be late. The streets of Stonegard were quiet as they left through the main gate, picking up the southern road that took them along the eastern edge of the Willowbank River. Karlov had given the Knot five small wooden boxes to carry. Each of the boxes contained a dozen small glass tubes with cork stoppers.

"The trip to Lake Evermere is over two hundred miles and will take us the best part of a week. We're going to take samples along the Willowbank. Malum wants to run tests on them," explained Karlov.

"What kind of tests?" asked Felix.

"I have no idea," he growled. "Do you want to go and knock on Malum's door and ask him?"

Felix shut up and avoided Karlov's gaze.

"Didn't think so. Let's move."

The journey was long, slow and thoroughly boring. Eleazar made a point of avoiding Ariella, so there was no time to talk about the butterfly dart or 'old friends'. During one of the night stops, camping by the Willowbank, Ariella, Indio and Jaron were sent off together to gather wood for the cooking fire. When they had collected a few bundles and were far enough away from the others, she filled them in on the conversation she overheard between Eugenie and Theia. She left out the details of the echo orbs. That would be her secret.

"That scheming, vicious, vindictive harpy," roared Indio.

"Shhh," said Ariella, slapping Indio on the arm.

"Sorry, Ari," he mumbled. "They make me mad."

"I know, we'll just keep an eye on them okay?"

"You don't think there's any truth in it, do you?" Jaron asked.

"Don't you start," snapped Indio. "Of course, there's no truth in it. Queen Abalyne loves Dawnhaven. She would never do anything to hurt it. The Elders of Everfrost feel the same. My uncle adores the Guardians, he would never allow anything like that."

"Your uncle?" enquired Jaron.

"Aye, my uncle. Ketil Gryphonfriend, commander of the Gryphon Cavalry and General of the Armies of Khan," said Indio proudly, puffing out his chest. "I've lived with him ever since my parents were killed." Indio's normally joyful demeanour changed and his eyes filled with sadness.

"I'm sorry, Indio," said Jaron. "I didn't know."

Ariella put her hand over Indio's. "I know how you feel. My father was killed too, about eight years ago."

Indio looked up at her, and spoke softly, "I don't remember my parents, not really. Just fuzzy images."

"How did they die?" Jaron asked.

"They were in the army, on patrol way up in the Northern fishing villages. They hunt whales and seals up there. Tough people, hard as nails. There had been reports of Ghost Raiders coming in as the ice melted. They caught a group of them attacking one of the villages. The fighting was intense." His eyes welled up. "They died together, defending people weaker than themselves, defending Dawnhaven." His sadness turned to anger. "That's why people like that witch Eugenie hack me off. They don't know what they're talking about."

"My father was killed by Ghost Raiders too," said Ariella softly.

"Really?" said Jaron, "I thought your father was a king. What was he doing fighting Ghost Raiders?"

Ariella smiled sadly. "My father was a sailor at heart. He didn't love diplomacy or politics, but he had to do it. He hated sending other people to defend the kingdom while he was stuck in the palace. He would use any excuse to go and fight alongside them. He died like your parents, Indio, defending a fishing village, people weaker than himself. Defending Dawnhaven."

Speaking about her father brought on a wave of emotions, and she wasn't ready for the intensity. Within moments tears were rolling freely down her cheeks.

The three sat in silence, allowing the grief to pass. After a while, Jaron began to sing softly, his voice deep and rich. There were words to the song, but Ariella couldn't make them out; instead, she was captivated by the sorrow of the melody. Fresh tears flowed as she sat and listened. As Jaron neared the end of the song, its tone changed, from deep sadness to a steadfast hope. Ariella had never heard anything like it before. She felt changed, like the sorrow of her father's death had lifted.

"That was beautiful," she whispered, blinking away the last of her tears.

"Crikey, Jaron, I've never heard anything like that. I've heard the best singers in Khan sing for the queen in the Great Hall of Everfrost and none of them can hold a candle to that. It was amazing." Indio's eyes were wide in wonder. "What was it?"

Jaron blushed and dropped his gaze at their comments. "It's called the Ranger's Farewell. It's the song we sing when a ranger passes from this life to the next."

"When I pass from this life to whatever is next, I want you to come and sing that for me." The look in Indio's eye told Jaron he wasn't joking.

"Sure Indio, I'll come to sing for you, just not anytime soon, okay?"

"Deal," laughed Indio.

A far off shout interrupted them.

"Oi! You lazy idiots! Where's our firewood, I'm starving!"

"Joachim," the three of them said in unison.

"What a jerk," muttered Indio, "shall we ignore him and stay here for a bit?"

"We could do," said Ariella, "but that means dinner will be late."

Indio's face fell, "Great point, Ari. Well made." He called back. "Keep your pants on! We're coming!"

They grabbed up the firewood they had collected and jogged back towards the camp.

15

The Blood Curse

The mood in the Knot was sombre. Conversations were short, and the banter had ceased. The eyes of the young sojourners were wide with the weight of the tragedy unfolding around them. As they had travelled down the eastern side of the Willowbank, they had encountered bloodied crops, decaying fish and a despairing people. The river was devastated. The water had been tinged red. All along its length the Knot found dead fish, their bloated bellies turned up to the sky, thick dark blood spilling from their gills.

Inland, it seemed that no farm or crop had escaped the poison. The wheat and barley fields of northern Trevena gave way to the vineyards and olive groves of the south. But they too had been laid waste by the Blood Curse - the name people had given to the poison they saw all around them. Rich green olives had been tinged red with the poison they contained. Grapes hung heavy on the vines, but they too had fallen victim. No crop was spared. Along the roadside they found mounds of fruit, lemons and oranges that had been piled up and left to rot, their bloodied pulps staining the earth red.

"This is awful," said Esther, riding alongside Ariella. "I've never seen anything like this." The Erestian girl looked horrified, unable to tear her eyes away from the rotting, blood-filled fruit.

It was a thoroughly depressing sight, but worse still was the plight of the people. Trevena and, indeed, all of Dawnhaven relied on the crops here to sustain them through the winter months. The people along the road were acutely aware of what a failed harvest meant for them and the kingdom. Hopelessness was evident in their eyes.

The rumblings against Khan were growing louder with every day. It seemed more and more people were anxious to point the finger at the mountain kingdom. Nor were the Guardians spared the people's anger.

"Some Guardians you are," spat a worn-out looking woman as she trudged along the road, her baby strapped to her back. "Supposed to protect us, that's right, isn't it?" she looked accusingly at Ariella as they rode past. "Some protection!" she shouted after them as they carried on down the road.

The woman's words shocked Ariella. "They're blaming us," she said, glancing over at Karlov. His face was as grim as ever, but at her words, she saw a flash of pain.

"Yes," he muttered, "they're blaming us."

"Why?" asked Esther.

"Because we can't stop it," said Eleazar darkly.

Karlov glared at him but didn't reply. He kicked his horse on, away out in front of the Knot, lost in his thoughts.

By the end of the week, they had collected nearly sixty water samples for Malum's tests. In front of them lay the end of their journey. Lake Evermere was the holiday destination of Trevena's wealthy. Its crystal waters expanded out of the Willowbank and stretched away south as far as the eye could see. The shoreline was dotted with private estates, vineyards, picturesque towns and villages. It should have been a welcome sight for the sojourners at the end of their long trip, but instead it marked the lowest point.

Evermere was dying.

They had hoped the vastness of the Lake had protected it. That perhaps the poison had become diluted and therefore ineffective.

They were wrong.

As they approached the lake, they came across a small fishing village, similar to dozens of others spread around the shore. There was a small stone jetty and moored alongside it were several fishing boats.

One of the boats was in the process of lifting its net onto the jetty. Three of the crew members were moving skilfully, manoeuvring the net and lowering it down. A small group of villagers had gathered around, waiting expectantly as the fish were brought in.

"They're dead," whispered Jaron.

Ariella and Indio followed Jaron's gaze.

"They look alive to me," said Indio, as the fishermen dumped the fish onto the wet stones.

"Watch," he replied, not taking his eyes off the net.

Ariella gasped as the net was pulled away and the pile of fish lay still, lifeless. Creeping out from around the mound was an ever-increasing pool of thick, red blood.

The heads of the fisherman hung low. One of them kicked a fish that had escaped the mound, and it flopped back into the lake. The crowd started to shuffle away in despair.

Some of the villagers spotted the Knot. Their faces turned angry and they started muttering amongst themselves.

"This is not good," said Eleazar nervously.

Karlov had the same thought. "Move out. Joachim, take the lead."

The Knot turned their horses and began edging away.

"Seen enough?"

Ariella twisted in her saddle and saw one of the fishermen, the one who had kicked the fish back into the lake, coming towards them.

"What's the matter? Nothing to say?" his lip was curled in anger, the crowd moving up behind him.

"Call yourselves Guardians? You've guarded nothing but yourselves and those savages up in the mountains. They've poisoned our river, our lake, our fields and you do nothing!" The man was shouting now, his anger rising.

Karlov turned his horse to meet him. "We are doing everything we can, Sir, I assure you."

"I'm no Sir," he spat. "I'm not some fat nobleman born with a silver spoon. I work for my living, and so do these people here." He waved his hand to the crowd behind him, who were growing restless. "You let our living die around us. Meanwhile, you've been protecting those animals in Khan."

"Easy, Indio," whispered Ariella as she moved her horse next to him, putting her hand on his arm. She could feel his muscles tense. She signalled to Jaron with her eyes. He nodded and moved his horse to Indio's other side. The last thing this situation needed was an explosive Indio.

Karlov was still trying to calm the fisherman when a small stone came whistling from the back of the crowd and landed right on the nose of Felix's horse. The horse reared in pain and surprise, then bolted out of the village, Felix clinging desperately to its neck. Esther and Eleazar spun their horses and took off after him.

Another stone came spinning from the mob and caught Joachim on the side of the head. Ariella winced when she heard the thump as the stone connected with his skull. Joachim wobbled in his saddle and roared in pain and surprise, drawing his sword.

"Put it away!" demanded Karlov, pushing his horse in front of Joachim.

More stones were flung from the crowd. People and horses started yelping as the stones landed amongst the Knot. Joachim's face was fixed in a menacing growl, his hand tightly gripped around his curved sword.

"Back off, Joachim," commanded Karlov, getting into Joachim's face. The tall Erestian ducked as another stone came flying towards him. He didn't sheath his sword.

"Ariella lead them out of here!" called Karlov.

Ariella spun her horse and sprung into a gallop as more stones rained around them. The others followed her, pushing their horses hard. Karlov and Joachim were the last to leave. Karlov had to grab the reins of Joachim's horse and pull him away from the crowd.

The Knot regrouped a mile outside the village. Esther and Eleazar had helped Felix get control of his horse, although Felix looked more terrified than the animal. Apart from a few cuts and bruises, the Knot was unharmed but shaken up.

"They attacked us," gasped Felix. "Us! We're Guardians." He was shaking his head.

"Why do they blame us?" asked Esther.

Karlov sighed. "Because we're Guardians. We give ourselves for the good of Dawnhaven. We pledge to use our steel and our Light for the protection of this island. We forsake our kingdoms, our names and our thrones. This day and every day. If we can't stop this curse obliterating the land, then no one can. These people know that. They've lost hope."

Karlov forlornly nudged his horse forward away from the village along the lakeshore, the others following behind.

"Theia get a water sample from the Lake and let's get back to Stonegard. Maybe Malum can figure out what's going on."

Within half an hour, the Knot had turned their horses northward to begin the long journey back to the capital. They looked dejected, slumped in their saddles, all conversation died out. As they travelled north, the countryside grew steadily worse. It had only been a few days since they had passed this way, but the decline had been rapid. The plants were decaying in the field, and the smell of blood was carried on the wind. The people looked beaten, and the young sojourners met thinly veiled hostility wherever they went.

16

Khan Scum

Over the next few days they watched the countryside grow steadily worse. There were more confrontations with the people of Trevena, but their hostility was evident. People would spit as the young Guardians passed by, hurling the occasional insults at their backs. The morale of the Knot slipped lower and lower with every mile.

Eventually, late one morning, the castle of Stonegard broke the horizon and the mood of the Knot lifted.

"At last," said Indio, "I need some proper food and a warm bed tonight."

Jaron was too tired to say anything so he just nodded his agreement. Karlov led them through the main gates of Stonegard and slowed his horse to a walk. Mingled in with the normal busy crowds were small pockets of burly, hard-looking men. Pinned on their chests was a small badge, a burning crown pierced with a bloody sword.

"I don't like this," said Ariella. "Something's happened."

"It's Baron Rexsalve," whispered Felix.

"Rexsalve?" asked Ariella, "as in Eugenie Rexsalve? Is he her father?"

Felix nodded, "Baron Rexsalve is no friend of the Guardians."

"What do you mean?" Ariella urged.

"He makes no secret of the fact that he thinks the splitting of Dawnhaven was a cataclysmic mistake," said Felix. "He believes that the island is weakened by the five kingdoms and what we need is a single strong ruler in Stonegard. To him, the Guardians are a symbol of everything he despises. He's always been a bit of a lone voice, powerful in his county but not across Trevena. I guess things might be changing."

Ariella flinched at that comment. "The people of Trevena are turning against the Guardians and Khan. That sounds like something that Baron Rexsalve would like. It seems the Blood Curse is helping his cause, don't you think?"

Felix went white, a state he returned to regularly. "Surely not," he said. "The baron may hate many things, but he loves Trevena. Surely he wouldn't do this much damage just to see the Guardians discredited?"

"I don't know," she said. "I don't know this Baron Rexsalve, but I know Eugenie. I know what an obnoxious, poisonous vixen she is."

"But she's a Guardian. Why would she support this?"

"I don't know. But you said that her father hates the Guardians. What's she even doing here? Something stinks, Felix, and I'm going to find out what it is."

As they rode down the main street of Stonegard, they realised the atmosphere had changed. The people were tense. The street sellers were not as loud; there were no jokes. The food stalls were almost empty and those that did have food had long queues.

"Look!" said Jaron.

He pointed at a large building amongst the finest shops in the city. These were the luxury shops that surrounded the Royal Keep. It was here that the wealthy nobility of Trevena did their shopping. The building Jaron was pointing at was Valdacor's Amazing Bazaar. Valdacor was a popular merchant from Khan. He sold beautiful jewellery, clockwork wonders and all manner of intricate pieces of metalwork from the finest artificers in Khan. They rode past the shop frequently, and Indio would boast of the skill of the Khan craftsmen.

It was approaching midday. The rest of the city was bustling with people about their business. But Valdacor's Amazing Bazaar was closed, the shutters covering the windows. Across the front of the shop, in hastily scrawled letters in red paint was written, 'GET OUT KHAN SCUM'. Karlov's jaw tightened.

Jaron flicked his head around, "She's smiling," he whispered. "Eugenie's smiling. Whatever her father's plan is, she thinks it's working."

"Come on," said Ariella, "Let's get back to the compound. Maybe Malum has figured something out."

Indio had stopped in front of the shop, his mouth tightly closed, a fierce look in his eye. Jaron rested his hand on his shoulder. "Come on, Indio, there's nothing we can do here. Let's go." He led his distraught friend back with the rest of the Knot.

The Guardian compound was even more sombre than the streets of the city. There was no laughter or singing from anywhere. Serious looking people dashed around with concerned looks on their faces.

"Esther, go and find Malum. Tell him we're back with the samples," commanded Karlov. "The rest of you, hand in your weapons, stable your horses and go have a bath. We all smell bad." They didn't laugh. No one could tell if he was joking. Only Eugenie seemed to be in good spirits. She positively bounced out of her saddle.

Ariella bathed and changed, then went down to the mess hall. She bumped into Indio and Jaron on their way back up the stairs, faces like thunder.

"What's happened?" she asked.

Jaron was seething, "Eugenie happened. She's down there with Joachim. They're discussing all that is messed up with the Guardians and how barbaric the people of Khan are."

"Joachim's with her?" she asked.

"Yep, it seems he has as much dislike for the Guardians as Eugenie does," replied Jaron. "They're hacking me off."

"Yeah, for once I had to pull him away. I thought he was going to smash his goblet into Joachim's face," said Indio, smiling for once.

Jaron tried to suppress a laugh. "Come on, let's find somewhere to go. Karlov has given us the afternoon off."

They wandered through the city for a while, their mood darkening with every step. It wasn't just Valdacor's shop that was closed; it seemed every merchant from Khan had left the city. They saw more graffiti in the same red paint.

"It's got to be Baron Rexsalve's men. It's sick," muttered Ariella.

"I've had enough of this," said Indio. "Let's get out of here."

"Come on," said Ariella, "I know just the place."

They followed her around a few more corners, down a wide street, and there it was - the Friendly Phoenix.

"This is where I stayed the last night before I started the Journey," said Ariella. "It doesn't feel like just a few months ago; it feels like years."

Jaron looked up at the opulent exterior of the Inn and whistled. "I've never stayed anywhere like this."

"Really?" asked Indio. "It reminds me of a place we have in Everfrost, just along from the palace."

Jaron laughed, "I've not got a lot of experience with palaces. When I say not a lot, I mean none. The closest I've been to royalty was King Tristan on the day we started the Journey. You two are the noble ones; I'm a commoner."

"Not anymore," smiled Ariella. "You're a sojourner. There are no royals or nobles or commoners now. And don't be too impressed with this inn. The last time I stayed here, I got attacked by a thief in the middle of the night."

The boys' eyes went wide in shock.

"Drinks first," she said, "then stories."

An hour later, the three of them were hidden away in a snug in the back of the Friendly Phoenix. Ariella had regaled them with the story of the thief, the butterfly dart and her first meeting with Karlov.

"Whose room was the thief trying to get into?" asked Indio.

"I don't know," she replied, "but I have an idea."

"Eleazar's," said Jaron.

She nodded, "I think so. I think the thief was the 'old friend' that he spoke about. I think it's something from his past, from Lightharbour."

"But what do butterflies, and midnight assassins have to do with the Blood Curse and Baron Rexsalve?" asked Jaron, leaning back in his chair.

"Beats me," muttered Indio, downing his drink.

"I don't know if they are connected," said Ariella. "If they are, I can't see the link."

"So, which one do we deal with?" Indio asked.

"I can't see us having any impact on Baron Rexsalve," said Jaron. "I say we look out for Eleazar and find out who this butterfly man is."

"Woman," interrupted Ariella.

"Excuse me?"

"It's a woman," she replied. "The person who threw that dart at me was female."

"Okay then," said Indio, "that settles it. We find the butterfly girl, stop her before she kills Ele, all the while avoiding stabbing Eugenie with a fork every time she breathes annoyingly."

"Not to mention surviving the Journey, random Thunderhead attacks and Karlov's mood swings," smiled Jaron. "Simple."

Ariella laughed, "All right then. Let's go find Eleazar and see if we can discover what's going on."

The streets of Stonegard had quietened down as they emerged from the Friendly Phoenix. The sun was setting over the high city walls, casting long shadows.

They had only walked a few streets when Jaron kept glancing high over his shoulder.

"What's wrong?" Ariella asked.

"We're being followed. Don't look round. Up on the rooftops. I keep seeing a flash of movement out of the corner of my eye, but when I turn there's nothing there."

He scanned the streets ahead. "Follow me," and he darted into a side entry. He moved quickly, down one street, then turned sharply into an alley, then another. He came to a halt, finger on his lips. They stopped and waited, eyes on the rooftops.

A minute went past and nothing. Then, a quick flash of movement directly over their heads.

Ariella couldn't stop herself. "Hakeem!" she cried.

A gargoyle the size of a dog leapt down from the rooftops and landed amongst them. Indio leapt back, scrabbling for some sort of weapon to use. Jaron pushed Ariella out of the way, a ball of green Light bursting from his palm.

The gargoyle's face was shaped like a dragon, with long horns and short stubby stone wings. Its blank, stony eyes stared at the boys for a moment and then turned to Ariella. She threw her arms around its neck and kissed its bald head.

"Urgh!" coughed Indio.

"What are you doing?" asked Jaron.

She looked at the stunned expressions on the boys' faces and burst into laughter.

"This is one of the gargoyles of Lightharbour," she said proudly. "and, most importantly, it's a gift from an old friend."

The gargoyle opened up its clawed hand and revealed two pouches of deep blue velvet. Ariella opened the first pouch. The familiar smell of rich chocolate filled the alleyway.

"Here," she said, tossing the pouch to Jaron. He helped himself to a chunk.

"Wow, I like this friend of yours."

She smiled and opened the second pouch. It contained a small scroll written in Hakeem's flowing handwriting she knew so well.

She read the note. Her eyes went wide.

"What is it?" asked Indio.

She ignored him and read it again. She looked up at the gargoyle and then at Indio and Jaron.

"Oh, no!" she whispered.

17

Rexsalve

My dearest Ariella,

I hope my messenger finds you in time. The gargoyles don't often travel far from Lightharbour and are uncomfortable away from the city. I'm afraid that I write to you with dire news. Dawnhaven faces its greatest threat since the emergence of the five kingdoms and the creation of the Guardians.

The Blood Curse that has swept Trevena is being felt across the island. The other four kingdoms rely on the farms of Trevena for the majority of their food. Now that the harvest has been devastated it's not only the people of Trevena that face hardship, but all of Dawnhaven.

Your mother and the council have been working tirelessly to bring in food supplies from outside our land, but the price is high, and delivery is slow.

Our scholars have been searching the archives of the palace library, and our suspicions have been upheld. Dawnhaven, or any other land, has never seen a plague like this. Our research confirms our worst fears. This curse is not natural. Some darkness has created it and unleashed it on us.

As of yet, we do not know who or why. What we can do is discover who is profiting from the disaster. So far, the obvious, in fact, the only candidate, is Baron Rexsalve.

He has never been vocal with his opinions regarding the Guardians and the five kingdoms. Until now. He seems to have seized on this moment to gather popular support. He is playing on the fears of the populace, noble and common alike. He has chosen to direct people's anger towards Khan . There is no evidence to support his claim, but people are scared, so they do not need evidence.

He has managed to gather a number of the influential barons to his side, and they are making life difficult for King Tristan. He is calling a gathering of the monarchs to Stonegard. The tide in Trevena is turning against Queen Abalyne and the people of Khan. Tristan and Abalyne, like many siblings, have never got on, their relationship is strained. Your mother is currently working to find common ground between the two of them, but it is not easy.

To complicate matters further, I am led to believe that Baron Rexsalve's daughter Eugenie is currently on the Journey and in your Knot. I do not know what she plans, but I cannot imagine she has the Guardians' best interests at heart.

I need you to watch her closely, Ariella. Events are colliding that I cannot foresee, but the fate of the Guardians is in the balance. Your presence there is not a coincidence. I sense that you and your Knot will have a significant part to play in the days ahead.

You possess a strength you are not aware of yet. It will serve you well. Use it for the good of Dawnhaven, the Guardians and those you love.

I will see you soon, my dear Ariella. Until then, stay strong, stay brave and enjoy the chocolate.

Hakeem.

"Oh, no!" she said again, passing the note to Jaron.

He scanned it, with Indio reading over his shoulder.

Jaron looked up at Ariella then read the note again. "No!"

"Exactly," replied Ariella.

Indio smiled, "Um, before we all get a bit carried away, there's something important to ask." The others paused, "Can I have some chocolate? It's been ages since I've had chocolate."

Ariella and Jaron both stared at him.

"What?" he protested, "You were both thinking it."

She shook her head as Jaron tossed him the pouch of chocolate. He helped himself to a piece, savouring and making happy noises.

"Oh, Ari, this is good stuff!" murmured Indio. "Tell Hakeem he has a new best friend."

Jaron ignored him, "Ari, who's Hakeem and what," he pointed at the gargoyle, "is that?"

Ariella patted the gargoyle's cold, stone head. "This is a gargoyle."

Jaron shook his head and pointed up at a group of gargoyles on a high part of the city wall. "No, Ari, those are gargoyles. Gargoyles don't move, they don't stare at me and they don't deliver chocolate."

"You've never heard of the Gargoyles of Lightharbour?" she asked.

Jaron rubbed his eyes, "Yes, I've heard of them, I just thought they were stories people made up to scare kids. You know, 'Be good, or the gargoyles will get you,' that kind of thing."

The gargoyle tilted his head and took a few steps towards Jaron, nuzzling its chin against his knee. Jaron's jaw dropped open.

"I think he likes you," smiled Ariella.

"This is too weird," he mumbled.

"Apart from someone who sends you amazing gifts," said Indio through a mouthful of chocolate, "Who is Hakeem?"

"An old friend. He was my father's best friend. He's been around our family for as long as I can remember."

"And he has gargoyles as pets?" asked Jaron, the shock evident in his voice.

At that comment the gargoyle stuck out his forked tongue at Jaron.

"Not pets," said Ariella. "The gargoyles aren't pets, they are wild. I've never seen them respond to anyone else, apart from Hakeem. They seem to be happy to work for him when he asks. How he asks is a mystery. They don't talk, and I'm not sure how much they understand."

She bent to the gargoyle and smiled. "Will you go tell Hakeem that I got his message? Tell him I'm on it, if you can talk or whatever it is you do." She kissed the gargoyle on his head, and Indio made a gagging sound. "And thank him for the chocolate!" The gargoyle leapt from the street, landed on the rooftop above them and was gone.

"Wow," laughed Indio. "I can't wait until we go to Lightharbour."

The sound of heavy hooves passing on the street broke up their conversation. The three exchanged glances, then crept out of the alleyway to see what was going on.

In the main street was a tremendous black carriage. It was fully enclosed with a driver at the front and two footmen standing at the back. With the carriage were huge horses ridden by heavily armoured knights, two in front and two behind. Emblazoned on the carriage door and the shields of the knights was a distinctive sigil: a burning crown pierced by a blood sword.

"Rexsalve," snarled Indio.

"Let's follow him," said Ariella.

They kept to the growing shadows on either side of the road, mingling with the thinning crowd. They followed the carriage with ease as it made its way down the wide Stonegard streets.

Jaron grabbed the arms of the other two and pulled them into a side alley. "He's heading to the compound. Let's get in front of him."

Before they could object, Jaron began crisscrossing the streets, working his way back to the compound and staying out of sight of Rexsalve's knights. Ariella and Indio had trouble keeping up with him as he led them back and forth until they emerged in a tight alleyway by the compound entrance. They could hear the heavy hooves echoing off the cobblestones.

Jaron was breathing heavily when they stopped. "We made it," he glanced out of the alley, "and just in time."

Indio leaned his back against the wall and took deep breaths. "How did you do that? You've never been on those streets unless you're sneaking out of the compound without me."

Jaron had a sparkle in his eye. "My father is a hedge warden, and my mother is a ranger. I've been tracking since I could walk. These streets aren't so different from the forest, once you get your bearings."

"Your father's a what?" asked Indio.

"A hedge warden," replied Jaron with great pride.

"What in the world is a hedge warden?"

Jaron smiled, "In Darcian, we don't use stone walls to protect us. Our capital, Oakenfold, is surrounded by a high, living hedge. The hedge wardens are responsible for looking after it."

"You're saying your father's a gardener?"

Jaron looked shocked and his voice started to rise, "He is not a gardener! He is a hedge warden. It's one of the greatest honours in Darcian. He was personally chosen by…"

"Sshhh," hissed Ariella, "they're here."

The three ducked down into the deep shadows of the alleyway, watching the approaching procession. The Guardians on sentry duty at the compound entrance snapped to attention as they approached. Their hands were on their swords.

"You don't think he's going to start a fight, do you?" whispered Indio.

No one answered him. The two lead knights came to a halt no more than a few yards from the Guardian sentries. The knights wore their visors down and, mounted on their warhorses, they were an imposing sight. The Guardians did not flinch.

For a few moments, there was silence. Nobody moved. Ariella held her breath. Then, on perfectly oiled hinges, the carriage door swung open without a sound. Out stepped a tall man with slightly receding, slicked brown hair. His clothes were exquisite, adorned with jewels. He had narrow, piercing eyes that scanned the Guardian sentries without blinking.

So that's Baron Rexsalve.

He turned back to the carriage and extended a hand. It was taken by an attractive young woman with flowing blonde hair. Standing next to each other, it was impossible to miss the family resemblance.

"Eugenie," muttered Indio. "We should've known. Hag, witch, harpy."

Ariella gave him a withering look and slapped a hand over his mouth, silencing him. The baron leaned towards his daughter and whispered something in her ear. She lifted her head and laughed, loud and clear. She kissed him once on each cheek and walked towards the Guardian compound, calling over her shoulder.

"Farewell father, I'll see you very soon."

What does she mean by that?

The baron climbed back into his carriage and banged the side with his palm, signalling to the driver to move off. The two lead knights turned away from the Guardian sentries and led the carriage back into the streets of Stonegard.

"Hey," whispered Indio, once Ariella had taken her hand from his mouth, "I've been practising."

Before anyone could stop him, he opened his hand and sent a red flash of Light bursting into the faces of the two horses bringing up the rear of the procession. The startled horses reared in fright, toppling one knight from his saddle. He crashed to the ground, his metal armour smashing off the stones. The two horses, one now riderless, bolted past the carriage, spooking the horses pulling it. They took off at a gallop causing the carriage to bump and bounce down the streets. One footman lost his grip and fell; the other was cursing the driver while trying to hang on. There was bedlam as the carriage tore down the streets with a knight and a footman running along behind.

The three young sojourners burst into laughter, falling about the dark alleyway. Their joy was short-lived when a tall figure blocked the alleyway entrance.

"Having fun, are we?"

The three shut up, staring up at the visitor. It was the Guardian leading the sentry duty, and he didn't look happy.

"First years?"

The three nodded in unison, suddenly feeling nervous.

"Knot leader?"

"Karlov, Sir," answered Ariella.

The man nodded. "Get back in the compound and go to your tower."

They did not argue - they sped past the man and into the compound heading for their tower. At first, they didn't see Eugenie, standing in the courtyard, arms folded with a vicious look in her eye.

"I suppose you think that was funny?"

Indio laughed, "It was hilarious! Did you see the way the carriage bounced down the street? I bet whoever was in there got thrown around good and proper. Any idea whose carriage it was?"

Her lip curled in a sneer, "I know it was your Light that scared the horses. Don't play games with me, you Khan scum."

Jaron stepped up to Eugenie, their noses almost touching. His voice was low, calm and steady. "No, Eugenie. It's you who shouldn't play games. I've waited my whole life to become a Guardian. It's what I would give the rest of my life for. I will not allow you, your father, or anyone else to jeopardise that. Do not play games with me. It will end badly for you."

Jaron let the words hang for a moment before turning on his heel and walking to the tower. Indio whistled and ran after him, slapping him on the back. Ariella hesitated as she watched Eugenie. For just a moment, her face changed.

What is that? She looks upset, genuinely upset. What's going on with her?

Eugenie saw Ariella watching her, and her face changed again, the barriers were back up, and it was the cold, hard Eugenie from before.

"What are you looking at?" she demanded.

"I don't know." Ariella answered, honestly. "I do not know." She sighed and followed Jaron and Indio to the tower.

Karlov found them after dinner. They had grabbed three of the soft armchairs and pulled them to the far side of the mess hall and were in deep conversation when he interrupted them.

"Had an interesting afternoon?"

No one spoke. Suddenly the three sojourners found the floor hugely interesting.

Karlov coughed. "When I ask you a question, it's not rhetorical. Interesting afternoon?"

"Yes, Sir," answered Ariella weakly.

"How was the Friendly Phoenix?"

How does he know we went there? Is he having us followed?

Jaron tried to smile, "It was very good, thank you for asking."

"Lovely," said Karlov, grinning. "I don't suppose any of you happened to see Baron Rexsalve this afternoon?"

"Baron who?" asked Indio, "Wait a minute, I know that name. Rexsalve, yes that's Eugenie's family name. Is he her father?"

Karlov's tone went flat and dangerous. "Indio, if you ever assume that I am stupid again, I will bump you off the Journey so fast you'll be back in Khan before you can blink. Do you understand me?"

Indio swallowed hard. "Yes, Sir. Sorry, Sir. Won't happen again, Sir."

"Very good. Now, who would like to explain to me why we had some very scared horses galloping through Stonegard with an even angrier baron bouncing along behind?"

Ariella could have sworn she saw a hint of a smile when he said the word 'bouncing.' The three answered as one. "It was me!"

Karlov rolled his eyes. "Really? It was all of you, together, at the same time?"

"Yes, Sir," they answered simultaneously.

"And you all have red Light, do you?" asked Karlov.

There was silence.

"What did I just say about answering my questions?"

"It was me, Sir," said Indio. "They didn't have anything to do with it."

"That's not true," objected Jaron. "We were all there, we were all involved."

"That's right," said Ariella. "You'll have to punish all of us, not just Indio."

Karlov paused for a moment.

Get it over with, will you? I can't stand the suspense, put us out of our misery.

"We are Guardians. As tempted as we may be, we never use the Light for playing games with people we don't like. Is that understood?"

They nodded.

"Excellent. Lesson learned. Do not do it again." Karlov looked around the mess hall. Several of the Knot had left after dinner. "Now, go and gather everyone. We have a meeting here in ten minutes."

The three looked at each other, slightly startled.

That's it? No punishment? I guess Karlov doesn't like Baron Rexsalve either.

Ten minutes later, the Knot was gathered in the dining hall.

"Listen up, everyone," called Karlov as the conversations died away. "The samples we collected from the Willowbank and Evermere have been passed on to Malum. He is working on a cure for the 'Blood Curse' as, so far, his Light has proved ineffective. As I'm sure you are aware, this is having a devastating effect not only on Trevena but on the whole of Dawnhaven as food supplies run low."

A few of the Knot exchanged nervous glances. Ariella watched Eugenie. Her face was fixed, rigid like she was wearing a mask.

Karlov continued, "King Tristan has called a meeting of the monarchs here in Stonegard for the day after tomorrow to try to resolve the situation."

Theia raised her hand.

"Yes, Theia?"

"Is Abalyne invited as well?" she asked.

"Queen."

"What?"

"Queen and Sir," answered Karlov, coldly. "She is Queen Abalyne, and I am Sir." He stared hard at Theia who shrank back under his gaze. "Yes, she is invited. As yet there is no evidence to back up the claims that Khan are responsible for the 'Blood Curse.'"

Eugenie coughed.

"Something you want to say, Eugenie?" called Indio, rising to his feet.

"Indio sit down. Eugenie, shut up," demanded Karlov. "As I was saying, the monarchs are coming here. Security is tight, as I imagine there will be the tensions in the city. As first years we will have no direct responsibilities during the visit, so tomorrow our training resumes."

There was a groan throughout the room.

Karlov smiled, "So glad you're looking forward to it and as you're so happy, I'll see you on the training ground at seven tomorrow morning. That is all."

"Oh joy," said Indio. "I need my bed."

Lalea Onderskat, Assistant Master of Arms, must have received word from Karlov that the Knot was not enthusiastic about that morning's training. She hammered the sojourners. Drill after drill. Swords, axes, bows, spears and unarmed combat, over and over again.

"I'm going to throw up," moaned Indio.

"Harder! Faster!" Lalea demanded.

Karlov was outside the training ground, arms folded with a wide grin on his face. "Stop slacking!"

"They're twisted," said Jaron, "I think they're enjoying our pain."

By midday, the whole Knot was ready to collapse. Only Joachim and Phoebe seemed to be keen for more. They were duelling with wooden staffs, flying into each other at dizzying speed. Neither could gain the upper hand as their breathing became laboured, but still, they fought on.

Ariella was lying on her back, trying to catch her breath.

Pointing at Phoebe, Esther called, "Ari, look at her."

She stood equal in height to Joachim and was matching him in strength. Blow after blow Joachim rained on her, but she repelled him and came back with attacks of her own.

"She's amazing," gasped Esther.

"She's a freak," muttered Eugenie.

Eleazar laughed, "Do you want to fight her?" Eugenie snapped her mouth shut and walked away. "Didn't think so."

Phoebe and Joachim were almost out of strength. They could hardly lift their staffs to launch another attack.

"That's enough," Lalea called. "Amazing job, you two. Excellent work."

Joachim let the staff drop from his hands, rattling on the stones. He stood up tall and stepped towards Phoebe, a hard look on his face.

"Uh oh," whispered Ariella, and moved to intervene.

"Wait," said Jaron, holding out his hand.

Phoebe rose to her full height as Joachim stepped towards her. They stood facing each other, one pace apart, breathing deeply. Joachim raised his arm and placed his hand firmly on Phoebe's shoulder. He closed his other hand across his chest and thumped his heart twice. Esther gasped. Phoebe didn't flinch. Joachim lowered his arms and smiled a broad smile, then turned and walked back to the tower.

"I don't believe it," said Eleazar. "He smiled, did you see that? Joachim smiled!"

"Esther," asked Ariella, "what just happened?"

"It's an Erestian custom," she said. "It means respect between warriors. It means Joachim believes Phoebe is his equal."

Ariella smiled. "Amazing."

"What about me?" Indio asked Esther, "Does he think I'm his equal?"

Esther opened her mouth to say something, then changed her mind.

"What?" said Indio. "What?"

"Oh, Indio," smiled Jaron, putting his arm around his friend's shoulders. "To Joachim, you are still a worm."

"Or a bug, I don't think he's made up his mind," smiled Eleazar.

"That's not funny," said Indio, "not even nearly funny!"

As they made their way back to the tower, a loud screech reverberated off the stone walls.

Jaron winced at the sound, "What was that?"

Indio's face lit up. "That is the most beautiful sound you will ever hear. That is the sound of a gryphon. Queen Abalyne is here."

18

The Monarchs of Dawnhaven

A flight of nine gryphons flew low over the Guardian compound. Ariella was stunned by the majesty of the great beasts. They had the head and front legs of a powerful eagle and the body and hind legs of a mighty lion. They were even more spectacular than she had imagined.

You're not in the library of Lightharbour anymore Ari, those are real gryphons!

"Oh Indi, they're beautiful," she gasped.

"Told you," he smiled. "You see the one on the far left, black and gold feathers?"

Ariella nodded.

"That's Thrace, my uncle's gryphon. Thrace is the fastest gryphon in all Khan," said Indio, glowing with pride. "My uncle is General Ketil Gryphonfriend. He leads Khan's armies. He's not got much of a sense of humour, but he can fight."

"Savages," said Theia, loudly. "They shouldn't allow that filth into the city."

"I'd be careful what you say, Theia," said Indio. "Gryphons are intelligent and have exceptional hearing. They may take offence at your insults." As if to support Indio's claim, one of the gryphons let out a terrifying cry and the blood drained from Theia's face as she ran to the tower, Indio's laughter ringing around her.

"Hey Ari, I guess this means your mother's going to be arriving in town soon," said Jaron.

"That's right," she smiled, "and I have an idea." She kept her voice low. "Grab Indio and meet me out here after lunch."

The three finished lunch, found a quiet spot in the compound and sat with their backs against the tall inner wall.

"If what Hakeem wrote is true," she began, "then this meeting of the monarchs is going to be vital in halting the curse, protecting Dawnhaven and possibly even saving the Guardians."

Jaron nodded, "Absolutely. What I would give to be at that meeting."

"Funny you should mention that," Ariella smiled. "There may be a way."

Indio tilted his head.

"Go on," said Jaron.

"You remember how I said I overheard Eugenie sounding off to Theia about how Khan had caused the Blood Curse?"

The boys nodded.

"What I didn't tell you is how I overheard them." Out of her pocket, she pulled two marble shaped glass stones. "These are the echo orbs."

"Okay," said Indio, "and what, exactly, are 'echo orbs'"?

"They pick up an echo," she said, matter of factly.

"What kind of echo?" pressed Jaron.

"Well, let's say, hypothetically, one of these happened to fall into my mother's pocket. Then she just happens to go to an extremely important meeting of the Dawnhaven Monarchs. If we had the other orb, then we could hear everything that's being said."

"Are you kidding me?" said Jaron, mouth agape.

Ariella shook her head, "For real. I used to use them to spy on my younger, twin brothers when they were trying to prank me. They never figured out how I was always one step ahead of them. It used to drive them mad."

"Twin brothers, that must've been fun?"

"Yeah, there have been twins in our family for generations, although Osias and Calixto are more like the living embodiment of thunder and lightning."

Jaron suddenly went serious. "How do you feel about listening in on your mother's private conversations?"

Ariella shrugged, "Hakeem made me promise not to eavesdrop on her, but then he also said that we needed to get involved 'for the good of Dawnhaven'. This is one of those 'for the good of Dawnhaven' moments, wouldn't you say?"

"Absolutely," said Indio, nodding enthusiastically.

"Okay," said Jaron, "but how do we get it into your mother's pocket? We don't know when she's arriving, and we've got Light training all afternoon. They're not going to let you out of the compound."

"Pull a sickie," said Indio.

"A what?" asked Ariella.

"You know, a sickie. Pretend you're sick, stomach cramps, headache, whatever you fancy. Then you can go lie down for the afternoon and slip out when no one's looking."

Jaron shook his head. "That used to work for you?"

"All the time. My parents tried to teach me to dance when I was younger. I had lessons twice a week with a fanatical dance teacher. The guy was a lunatic. It's amazing how sick I got just before dance lessons."

"I don't think that'll fly here," said Jaron. "If she feigns a sickie, she's going straight to Karlov. He'll just go all healing Light on her. Reckon you can con Karlov, Ari?"

"Not a chance," she replied. "We need another plan."

Just then Felix came into the courtyard and spotted them. "I've been looking for you all over. Malum has cancelled Light training this afternoon, he needs to concentrate on finding a cure for the curse. Karlov says we can rest up."

The three looked at each and burst out laughing.

"What's so funny?" asked Felix. "I was looking forward to it."

"It's okay, Felix, you can go and train on your own without anyone bothering you," Ariella laughed.

Felix's face lit up, "You're right, see you later!" and he dashed off to the training ground.

"Right," said Jaron, "That was easy. Now, anyone for a drink in the Friendly Phoenix? Who knows who we may bump into on the way? I've always wanted to meet a queen."

The Friendly Phoenix was the perfect location to wait for Ariella's mother. It was on the main route between the Stonegard gates and the Royal Keep. The friends found a table in the window and settled in for the afternoon, watching and waiting.

They did not have long to wait. A sudden burst of trumpets rang out from the watchtowers on the main gate.

"Here we go," said Jaron.

They stood outside the inn as a small crowd gathered and lined the streets, hoping for any kind of spectacle. They heard the sound of many hooves on the stone as a column of Lightharbour guards rode towards them at a steady walk. The guards were three abreast and about ten deep. Behind them, they could just make out a white carriage, and behind that, still more guards.

"That's a lot of guards," said Jaron. "Someone's paranoid."

Ariella sighed, "The Captain of the Guard is, err, safety-conscious."

"No kidding," laughed Indio, as he pointed at one of the guards in the second row. "Isn't that your handsome friend that you arrived here with? What was his name?"

Ariella blushed, "Micah, his name is Micah."

"Micah, that's right, I wondered if you remembered him, but judging by the colour of your cheeks I'd say that's a yes."

Jaron slapped him on the back of the head, "Leave her alone."

"What did I say?" he protested, rubbing his sore head.

Jaron ignored him. "What's the plan, Ari?" he asked, "You just going to leap in front of the horses and shout 'Hello mummy'?"

"I think I'll just improvise," she replied. "I'll see you back here when I'm done."

With that, she started moving through the crowd towards the approaching column.

Improvise? What kind of answer is that? You haven't seen her for a few months. Is she angry? Does she miss me? Guess I'm about to find out.

Riding on the final row of guards, just in front of the queen's carriage, was the captain. He had a stern look on his face, and his hand was on the hilt of his sword.

"Good afternoon, Captain. Welcome to Stonegard!" she called, stepping out from the crowd.

The captain nearly fell off his horse in shock. "Your Highness, what are you doing here?" He raised his hand and halted the column.

"I wanted to see my mother. Do you mind?"

Before the captain could answer, Queen Susanna had leaned out of the carriage window to see why they had stopped.

"Ariella!" she cried, throwing open the carriage door and stepping into the street.

Five of the guards immediately dropped from their horses and formed a ring around their queen, eyes vigilantly scanning the crowd.

Several of the bystanders started to bow when they saw the queen, many others just stared open-mouthed in shock. They were not used to visiting monarchs leaping out of carriages.

Queen Susanna ignored them all, throwing her arms around her daughter and covering her with kisses. "My darling Ariella! I've missed you so much. What are you doing here? What's going on? How are you? You look taller."

"Mother, could we talk inside?" she smiled, nodding at the crowds surrounding them and the nervous-looking guards.

"Of course." The queen led her daughter into the royal carriage and closed the door.

As they wound their way through the busy streets of Stonegard, Queen Susanna regaled Ariella with tales of her brothers and the latest news from Lightharbour. In return, Ariella told her of life so far on the Journey. When she began to tell her of her encounters with the Blood Curse, the queen's face darkened.

"These are perilous times, Ariella. Something is at work in Dawnhaven that has evil at its heart."

The carriage came to a halt as more trumpets sounded. Ariella leaned out of the window.

"We're at the Keep, I had better be off now, I have duties to attend to." Ariella embraced her mother and felt a tinge of guilt as she artfully dropped an echo orb into the deep pockets of her robes.

"I love you," she said, kissing her mother's cheek. "I'll see you soon. The Guardians are with you."

Her mother returned her smile although Ariella saw the strain she carried. "I love you too, Ariella, stay safe."

Ariella opened up the carriage and stepped into the street just as the column set off again, through the gates into the Royal Keep.

Well, Ari, there's no going back now. Let's see what happens.

She made her way back to the Friendly Phoenix and found Indio and Jaron tucked away in a snug at the back of the inn.

"Well?" Indio asked. "How did it go?"

"It's done," she replied. "Now we wait."

For the next hour, the orb was silent. The three friends passed the time telling stories of their homelands. Indio was explaining the rite of passage for the Gryphon Riders when the orb gave a gentle hum.

"This is it," said Ariella. She grabbed a piece of parchment from a pocket and a small stick of charcoal. She wrote on it the names of the five children of King Haldor and Queen Lucia, now the Monarchs of

Dawnhaven. The eldest was King Tristan of Trevena, then Queen Susanna of Lightharbour, her own mother. Queen Tatianna of Erestia and King Ellisedd of Darcian were twins. Ariella always used to laugh at how different they were. Tatianna was as wild and fierce as the Erestian plains, while Ellisedd was calm, almost still. The youngest of the siblings was Queen Abalyne of Khan. She was always Ariella's favourite.

The first voice they heard was male. Ariella pointed to the word 'Tristan'.

"Welcome everyone," began Tristan. "I wish we were meeting under happier circumstances. I want to begin by explaining to you the current situation here in Trevena. I don't know what you have heard, but I cannot underestimate the severity of the problem. This year's harvest is decimated. Nothing has survived: wheat, barley, corn, vegetables, the orchards and the vineyards. They're all ruined. What we don't know is how long-term the damage is. The current thinking is that it is permanent, in which case the food shortage in Trevena is the greatest threat our island has faced since the Rebellion."

"What about the Guardians?" said a female voice, "has their Light not been effective?"

Ariella pointed at the name 'Tatianna,' the Queen of Erestia.

"No," replied Tristan. "Nothing has been effective. Currently, Lord Vantor and Malum Asinum are working around the clock to discover the source of the curse and a way to stop it. On top of the problems with the plants, the curse has polluted our waterways. The fish in the Willowbank and Lake Evermere are dead."

"All of them?" someone gasped.

Ellisedd, King of Darcian, Ariella indicated with her finger.

"Yes, so it appears." Tristan hesitated. "We also need to address the accusations."

"Baseless accusations," interjected a female voice, angrily.

Indio pointed to a name on the paper: Abalyne, Queen of Khan.

Tristan continued. "The findings so far point to the Willowbank being the source of the poison. It would seem that the river is emerging, already polluted, from the Khan mountains."

Abalyne interrupted, "That proves nothing."

"Baron Rexsalve says he has other proof," said Tristan, his voice rising.

"Then let him bring it!" shouted Abalyne.

"Enough!" a clear voice called out.

Ariella pointed to her mother's name on the parchment.

"She's right, Tristan. If Rexsalve has evidence, then he needs to present it," said Susanna. "He cannot continue on his campaign to attack Khan, undermine the Guardians and destabilise Dawnhaven."

"And what would you have me do?" answered Tristan, his frustration bubbling over. "The crops are gone, the people are looking at their livelihoods being wiped away. We're facing starvation, Susanna, and not just Trevena but the whole of Dawnhaven. The people are angry, and the barons are scared. It's easy for people to believe Rexsalve without any evidence. Khan and the Guardians give them a focus for their anger."

"It's convenient that the focus is on my kingdom and not yours," shot Abalyne. "It's not your people who have been threatened and driven from the city."

"It's my people who are starving!" yelled Tristan.

Through the echo orbs, they heard the sound of a heavy wooden chair topple and crash to the ground. There was a long silence before Ellisedd spoke.

"Is there any chance at all Abalyne, any possibility?"

"Of what?" she snapped.

"That it has come from Khan? The furnaces you have up in the mountains, the workshops and mines. Isn't there a chance that some contaminant has come down to the river?"

"You've heard the stories Ellisedd, you've read the reports," Abalyne replied. "Does it sound like pollution from one of our mines? There is evil at work here. Are any of you accusing me of deliberately polluting the river? Of wanting to destroy Trevena? That's madness."

"You've always resented me, Abalyne," Tristan said, without trace of emotion.

"You're an idiot!" she exploded, "A self-righteous, stuck up, moron! You're patronising, smug, superior and you think I'm too young, too immature, too incapable of running a kingdom. That's what you told Father, isn't it?"

Tristan did not reply.

"I thought so," continued Abalyne. "Indeed, I can't stand to be in the same room as you, but do I want to destroy you? I'd be mad to even try. Our father's plan for Dawnhaven was brilliant. If one of the kingdoms falls, we all fall. If Erestia implodes we have no cattle, no horses. Without Darcian our wood is gone, no bows, ships or houses. With Lightharbour gone so is our navy, our defence, and also our trade with the rest of the world. Without Khan, you have no metal for tools or weapons, no jewels or artefacts for trade. And without Trevena, we slowly starve to death. Yes, dear brother, I despise you, but I do not wish you or your people dead. I am not a monster!"

The young sojourners heard the sound of footsteps on a wooden floor and a door slamming closed.

"Do you believe her?" asked Tatianna.

For a moment, no one answered.

"Yes," said Susanna. "I do. I believe what she said, most of it. She doesn't despise you, Tristan, she's angry and lashing out."

Tristan snorted, "I was right, she is too young, too impulsive to be queen."

"You're also, on occasion, a fool, Tristan," she replied. "She is far more capable than you can see. To you, she will always be the little sister, the one who was clumsy and broke things. Who said inappropriate things to important people, who took reckless chances just for fun. She is not that little girl anymore. She has grown to wear the crown."

"As we all have," interrupted Tatianna. "I agree with you, Susanna. I can't believe she wants to destroy Trevena. I can't see any gain in it for her."

"That then leaves us one question," said Ellisedd. "If Khan isn't responsible, who is?"

"Rexsalve?" ventured Tatianna.

"I can't see it," responded Tristan. "Yes, he hates the idea of Dawnhaven and the Guardians. He wants Trevena to rule the whole island again from Stonegard, but to unleash this curse? I think that's a step too far."

"I'm inclined to agree," said Susanna. "I don't know a lot about Baron Rexsalve but what I do know leads me to believe he does not have the power to wield a curse like the one that's raging here. I believe he is an opportunist, a vile one, but nothing more than that."

"Who does have the power to do this?" asked Tristan. "Does anyone in Dawnhaven?"

"Lord Vantor is certainly capable. I'm not even sure we realise how strong he is," replied Susanna, "but he would never harm Dawnhaven?"

"What about Malum Asinum?" asked Ellisedd, "Does he have the power to wield a curse like this?"

"No," answered Tatianna. "Nor has anyone I know or have heard of. What about Ghost Raiders?"

"They have blood magic, that's for certain," replied Ellisedd. "But I've not seen or heard of anything on this scale."

"Besides," said Susanna, "it doesn't make sense for the raiders to wipe out all the crops. They rely on raiding the coasts of Dawnhaven and the other lands for their survival. They don't farm as far as we can tell. Wiping a major food source with no gain seems counterproductive."

"Then who?" said Tristan, his frustration returning.

"There's only one that I can think of that is this powerful," said Susanna. Her voice had changed. The heaviness was evident to those listening in the Friendly Phoenix.

"Yes?" demanded Tristan.

Susanna sighed heavily. "Diatus. Diatus could have done this."

There were gasps around the room, in the keep and around the table at the Friendly Phoenix. Ariella glared at the boys and held a finger to her lips, whispering, "They can hear us too."

"He's dead, my sister. Very, very dead," said Ellisedd

"I'm well aware of that," replied Susanna. "Yet, he is the only one I know of that could do the damage that has been done."

"Dead people can't curse," said Tatianna. "What about one of the other islands or kingdoms, could they be responsible? What are your spies telling you, Susanna?"

"Nothing," she replied. "No one is preparing for war or invasion. Everyone has internal problems to deal with or is too small to challenge us. There's something else, something we're missing."

"We need some answers and we need them quickly," said Tristan. "The land is continuing to die and support is growing for Rexsalve. I wouldn't be surprised if he started calling for war on Khan."

"We cannot let that happen," said Susanna. "Let's meet back here in one week. In the meantime, I will continue to gather food supplies from as many kingdoms as will trade with us. The rest of you, stockpile food and start to ration. It will be a long hard winter."

"I will send out my rangers to the borders of Khan and see what they can find." said Ellisedd. "If the pollutant is carried by the river, then the Thunderrun is vulnerable. We cannot allow Darcian to suffer the same fate as Trevena."

"Tristan, do you think you can keep a lid on Rexsalve for another week?" Susanna asked.

"Yes, hopefully. Lord Vantor and the Guardians will have some good news for us soon."

"Then a week it is," said Susanna. "We can get through this. It is what our father predicted, that evil would strike at us, but we can overcome it when we stick together. You are my brothers and my sisters. I love you and would die for you. We will beat this."

"That's settled then," said Tristan. "Dinner is being prepared for us, just us, no guests. Stay and eat with me and maybe, for just a few hours, we can forget about being kings and queens and just be brothers and sisters."

Ariella slipped the echo orb back into her pocket and sat back in her chair, her eyes closed.

"What do you think?" asked Indio.

"I think we're in trouble," Jaron replied, "and when I say 'we' I mean the entire five kingdoms."

"All right then, what shall we do about it?" said Indio.

"Us?" Jaron laughed. "We're first year sojourners; we're not going to do anything about it."

"But we're in trouble, all of us. You heard the monarchs. It's a mess, Dawnhaven is in danger of falling apart. Baron 'nut job' Rexsalve is going to be calling for war on Khan, the Guardians will be side-lined. We have to do something."

"Like what?" Jaron replied.

Ariella opened her eyes. "We go to Khan."

"What?" asked Jaron in surprise.

"All the evidence points to the Willowbank being the source of whatever this thing is that's killing Trevena. We go to the source of the river and take a look."

"Excellent idea," said Indio, his eyes sparkling.

"No, not an excellent idea, it's a crazy idea," said Jaron. "Everybody take a deep breath. How exactly are we going to get to the source of the river? It's got to be over one hundred miles away; it'll take us days. In that time Karlov will have realised we're gone and send people after us. We'll be kicked off the Journey, permanently."

Ariella shrugged, "That's a fair point."

"As well as that," Jaron continued, "Lord Vantor has already sent Guardians across Trevena. If there's anything to find, then surely they would have found it."

"That's another good point," she replied, "but I'm not going to sit around, we've got to do something."

"Even if there was something to find, it's so far away. How would we cover that distance?" Jaron demanded.

"I don't know," she replied.

"I do," smiled Indio. "What if I could get us there and back in a day?"

"How?" Ariella asked.

"Leave that to me. Jaron, if I could do that, are you in?"

Jaron hesitated. "It's different for me. If you two get kicked out, you go back to being a princess and a noble. If I get kicked out, nothing is waiting for me in Darcian. Being a Guardian is my way out. It's all I've wanted to be since I was a kid."

Ariella leaned forward and put her hand on Jaron's. "I get you, I do. I want this more than I can say. I gave up the throne of Lightharbour for the Guardians. But if someone doesn't do something, if *we* don't do something, if Rexsalve has his way, there won't be any Guardians."

Jaron looked at her, then at Indio. "You two are crazy."

Indio nodded enthusiastically, "It'll be an adventure!"

"It'll be our deaths," sighed Jaron, "either from the Blood Curse, some wandering beast in the mountains or Karlov when we get back."

"Karlov will not find out," assured Indio.

"Really?" shot back Jaron, "he's not going to find out?"

Indio hesitated, "He's probably not going to find out."

Jaron slumped back in his chair "Oh great, this is going to be great."

"This is a big ask, Jaron," said Ariella. "You don't have to come."

"Of course, I have to come," said Jaron with a scowl. "Someone has to watch your back with a bow, and I've seen you two shoot." He took a deep breath "So, what's the plan?"

Indio grinned, "Thrace."

"Thrace?" coughed Ariella "Thrace? Are you joking?"

"Nope."

Jaron had a confused look on his face. "What is a Thrace?"

"Not a what, my friend," said Indio, "but a who. Thrace is a who."

"Okay, who is Thrace?" Jaron asked.

"Thrace is a gryphon."

"You said Thrace was your uncle's gryphon," said Ariella. "Are you saying we're going to steal your uncle's gryphon?"

"Ariella!" protested Indio, "steal is such an ugly word. We're not thieves, we're not going to steal my uncle's gryphon. We're simply going to borrow it."

Jaron groaned, "What could possibly go wrong?"

19

Indio falls in Love

"Come on," said Indio as they left the Friendly Phoenix. "I'm guessing the gryphons will be stabled somewhere near the keep."

"The Royal Keep?" said Jaron, "The Royal Keep that houses the royal family of Trevena? The most heavily guarded building in the whole of Stonegard? That keep?"

"Yep," laughed Indio, "it'll be fun."

"Ari, please, help me with him," Jaron pleaded.

"It's the only option I can see," shrugged Ariella. "We can't walk or ride to the mountains. Somehow we have to get that gryphon."

Jaron's eyes rose skywards as he shook his head.

They made their way through the busy streets towards the Keep. They were passing a row of woodcarver's shops in one of the streets usually occupied by the Darcian merchants. A flash of white hair caught Ariella's eyes, and she stopped walking.

"What's up?" asked Jaron.

"Over there," she indicated, lifting her chin, "I think that's Eleazar."

Jaron and Indio followed her gaze towards a figure obscured in the crowd. Their hair was bright white.

"Eleazar!" Indio called before anyone could stop him.

The figure froze and turned their head, just a fraction. Then they lifted a hood over their head and slipped into the crowd.

"Hey!" Indio called.

But the white hair was hidden under the hood, and they lost track of it in the bustling streets.

"I guess he didn't want to say hello," said Indio, shrugging his shoulders.

Jaron's eyes scanned the crowd. "That didn't look right," he muttered. "Something about that didn't look right."

"What are you thinking?" Ariella asked.

"I don't know. Just something. I can't put my finger on it..." Jaron hesitated.

"He was probably just in a bad mood," said Indio. "Come on, the gryphons are waiting."

Indio set off for the keep with Ariella and a reluctant Jaron following behind. As they grew closer, the shops and houses were larger and more extravagant. Intricate wooden fascias ordained the buildings, and brightly coloured pennants fluttered in the gentle breeze.

Indio slowed to halt outside one of the grander looking shops. Valdacor's Amazing Bazaar still had the shutters closed, and no lights could be seen flickering inside. The scrawl they had seen had faded slightly, as if someone had been scrubbing it, but it was still visible: 'GET OUT KHAN SCUM'.

Jaron stood by his friend and gripped his shoulder. "Come on, Indio. Let's go get us a gryphon."

The walls of the keep loomed high above them, the bright pennants of Trevena adding splashes of colour to the grey stone. The massive gates were closed and in front of them stood a group of stern-faced royal guards.

"Any ideas?" asked Ariella. "I don't suppose they're going to let us wander in there and help ourselves to a gryphon."

"They don't look the friendly sort, do they?" said Jaron.

"Could you go all 'princess' on them?" asked Indio.

Ariella's eyes narrowed. "Go all 'princess' on them? What exactly do you mean by that?"

"You know, like a princess," smiled Indio. "Massive fuss, diva moments, loud tantrums, hand waving, 'Do you not know who I am?' type of thing. Like a princess. They'll have to let us in."

Ariella's voice was icy, "And that's what you think princesses do?"

"Of course," Indio replied. "You know what I mean, don't you, Jaron?"

Jaron stepped back, watching Ariella's mouth twitch in anger, "Leave me out of this."

"What's up with you?" asked Indio, noticing Ariella's look.

Before she got a chance to answer, a gruff voice interrupted them.

"What are you doing?" It was one of the Royal Guards. "We don't allow loitering around the Royal Keep. Be on your way."

"I don't think so mate," said Indio squaring up to the guard.

The man bristled and laid his hand on the hilt of his sword. "Mate? Mate? You think I'm your mate?"

Indio sensed danger and back-pedalled, pointing at Ariella "She's a princess!" he blurted out.

The guard turned his attention to Ariella, who was giving Indio the filthiest of looks and clenching her fists.

Things were about to unravel when Jaron stepped in front of the guard. "I do apologise on behalf of my exuberant friends. I assure you, they mean no harm or offence."

The Guard raised an eyebrow but said nothing.

"They saw the gryphons flying overhead and were desperate to get another look. We assumed they would be stabled here, at the Keep."

The Guard snorted, "Here? In the Royal Keep? Stabled with the finest horses in Trevena? I don't think so. The gryphons are filthy animals. Vile beasts." The guard spat on the ground in disgust, and Indio's face darkened, his jaw clenching.

"If you don't mind me asking Sir," Jaron continued, "Where are they being kept?"

"Outside the city, in one of the fields. We don't want their Khan stench drifting in here."

"Of course not," smiled Jaron. "Thank you for your time."

Before anyone could speak, he grabbed Ariella and Indio by the arm and led them away from the guard.

Indio was furious. "Vile beasts! He called them filthy! Compared to horses, gryphons are the cleanest animals on Dawnhaven. Horses dirty their stables; you wouldn't catch a gryphon doing that. What a jerk. I need to get Malum to teach me how he set my hair on fire. I'd like to use that on him. Idiot."

Ariella ignored him. "Great work, Jaron. Let's go see if we can find Thrace."

They retraced their footsteps back through the city, this time toward the main gates and the farms beyond. The streets were thick with people heading home, their minds on their dinner. The three friends started to push themselves through the crowds, but the going was slow.

"This is taking too long," muttered Ariella, "could you find us a shortcut, Jay?"

Jaron stood on his tiptoes and got his bearings. "Sure, follow me."

He darted off into a side street, the others following quickly behind. The crowds started to thin as Jaron led them down one back alley after another, working their way steadily towards the main gate. He led them down a narrow passage that wove its way behind a network of tall buildings. Other passages and alleyways criss crossed their path so frequently that Ariella was hopelessly lost.

"Do you know where you are?" she called as Jaron quickened his pace.

"He's making it up as he goes along. There's no way anyone can find themselves in these alleys. It's a maze," said Indio.

"Nearly there," he called over his shoulder as he jogged along. "Just a couple more turns and then…"

Crash!

Jaron stumbled headlong into a hooded figure that had emerged from one of the side alleys. The force of the impact knocked them both to the floor. Jaron cracked his head against the stone wall and lay on the ground for a moment, stunned by the impact.

"Are you all right?" asked Indio, bending down to help his friend.

The cloaked figure sprang to its feet, its hood falling as it rose.

Ariella froze, stepping back into the darkness of the passageway.

Indio glanced up at the stranger, "Wow, you're beautiful," he whispered. The unmasked woman was a few years older than the sojourners, her snow-white hair cut short around her chin. But it was her eyes that Indio noticed, her perfect ice blue eyes.

The stranger scowled at Indio and Jaron, before pulling up her hood, casting her face in shadow. Just as quickly as she had entered the passageway, she was gone, moving effortlessly through the gloom.

Jaron rubbed the back of his head and rose unsteadily to his feet. "What just happened?"

"Did you see her?" Indio asked with a faraway look in his eye.

"See who? The crazy spook that just smashed me to the ground? No, I didn't see her. I was busy trying to recover from my head being cracked against the stone."

"I think I'm in love," smiled Indio.

Jaron stared at him, "What? You're what?"

"In love."

"You're crazy."

"That's right, crazy in love with a hooded stranger with the most sensational eyes I have ever seen."

"Oh, do shut up, my head hurts."

"Did you see her eyes Jaron? Did you see them?"

Jaron ignored him.

"Ariella, did you see them? Please tell me you saw her eyes?"

"Yes, I saw her eyes." Ariella stepped out of the shadows, the blood had drained from her face.

"Ari, what's wrong?" asked Jaron.

"I've seen those eyes before."

"You have? That's amazing, tell me where! Who is she?"

"She's the girl that tried to kill me."

Indio hesitated, "You what?"

"It was her, I'm certain it was her."

Indio looked heartbroken, "Are you sure?" he pleaded, "You could be wrong? Right?"

Ariella shook her head. "I'll never forget those eyes."

Indio's shoulders slumped. "Great, I finally fall in love, and she turns out to be an assassin with butterfly darts. That's what excellent taste I have."

"If she's the one who threw the dart at you, then what's she doing here?" asked Jaron.

Ariella's eyes grew wide. "Eleazar. She's still after Eleazar. We have to follow her. Which way did she go?"

Indio pointed down a side alley, "That way. But did you see how she moved? It was effortless, like a ghost on glass. I don't think we'll be able to sneak up on her."

"We'll have to try," answered Ariella, "We can't let her get to Eleazar. How's your head, Jaron?"

"Good enough, let's go."

"What about the gryphons?" asked Indio.

"Later. We need to help Eleazer," said Ariella.

They set off after the girl with the ice-blue eyes, trying their best to follow her path as quickly and quietly as possible. After a few minutes of trying to sneak through the alleyways, they emerged back onto the main street of Stonegard only a few metres from the main gate.

Jaron sighed. "We've lost her."

"Now what?" Indio asked, scanning the crowded streets trying to catch a glimpse of the girl.

"We've got to keep looking," said Ariella.

"In this crowd," said Indio. "It's hopeless, she's gone. We'll never find her."

"Then we find Eleazar," she said. "If she's hunting him then once we find him, we find her."

Ariella looked over at Jaron, "Any ideas?" but Jaron wasn't looking at her. The sound of raised voices had grabbed his attention.

Outside the city gates, two men were haggling over the price of a horse. The one holding the horse's bridle was a short, squat man, with a heavy belly, thick beard and a filthy mouth. Every third word was a curse, and he was getting louder as the haggling continued. The man buying the horse was hooded and spoke so softly they could not make out what he was saying.

"I think that's Eleazar," said Jaron.

"How can you tell?" asked Indio, "It could be anyone."

"Maybe I'm wrong, but I don't think so," he replied. "Wait here."

Before they could object, Jaron had ducked into the mass of people streaming out of the city and disappeared.

"How does he do that?" sighed Indio. "I sound like a deranged cow rampaging through a dinner party when I try to be silent."

"Yes," Ariella nodded, "you do."

Indio gave her a filthy look but stayed silent, keeping his eye on the horse seller and the hooded figure.

The minutes seemed to drag by and Indio was growing restless.

"What is he doing, Ari?" he asked. "Do you think he's lost?"

"We're talking about Jaron," she said, "not you."

Before Indio could answer back, Jaron emerged from the crowd.

"It's him. He's trying to buy a horse, but it doesn't seem like he's got enough money."

"What does he want a horse for?" Indio asked.

"How should I know," replied Jaron. "Maybe he wants some fresh air."

"Or maybe he's running," said Ariella. "He knows she's here."

"Well then, let's find her and fast," said Indio, "then smash her face in so she doesn't hurt Eleazar."

"Smash her face in?" said Ariella, "A few minutes ago you were in love, 'Oh those beautiful eyes'"

Indio shrugged his shoulders, "I'm fickle, I got over her. Now, what's the plan? Watch Eleazar until she tries to kill him? Kind of like baiting a trap."

Jaron winced. "Yes, but let's never tell him we used him as bait."

"It's for his good," smiled Indio. "He'll understand."

Jaron rolled his eyes.

"Look," pointed Ariella, "I don't think he got the price down low enough."

A tirade of swearing erupted from the horse seller, and Eleazar hastily backed away, his shoulders slumped. He turned on his heel and walked back into the city against the flow of the crowd.

"Come on," said Jaron, "and stay quiet." He glared at Indio who held his hands up in protest.

The three friends set off after Eleazar. The sun had begun to sink behind the tall buildings of Stonegard casting long dark shadows across the busy city streets. Jaron kept them in the shade and far enough back so as not to arouse his suspicion.

Eleazar seemed to be heading in the direction of the Guardian compound, but he was walking slowly, dragging his feet and bumping into people. Suddenly Jaron grabbed Ariella's arm and pointed through the crowd. Fifty metres in front of Eleazar, standing in a side street with her hood pulled up, was the girl with the ice-blue eyes. She was watching Eleazar's slow march back through the city. His head was down, and it seemed he was not paying attention to anything around him, least of all the imminent danger up ahead.

"Ari, stay close to him in case we don't make it in time," whispered Jaron as he grabbed Indio and pulled him off into an alleyway.

"Where are you going?" she whispered but they were gone, dashing as quietly as possible out of sight.

Great, now what? I'm supposed to protect Eleazar from a maniac with butterfly pins? She's already hit me once, and that knocked me out. I'm not too thrilled about a rematch.

Eleazar was still walking, nearer and nearer to the girl with the ice blue eyes.

156

Ariella got as close to him as she dared, trying to keep out of sight of the girl, whose focus seemed to be entirely on Eleazar. They were only thirty metres from her now. She stood perfectly still, her hands hidden in the depths of her sleeves, her eyes unblinking as Eleazar drew ever closer.

Where are the boys?

Ariella was starting to get desperate. A few more seconds and Eleazar would be in the range of the mysterious girl's darts.

Then what? Throw yourself in front of him? Start to scream? A lot of good screaming did for you last time.

She rubbed her shoulder where the first butterfly dart had hit her. Another second went by and Eleazar was still coming. Ever so slowly, the girl withdrew her arms from her sleeves and lowered them to her side. Ariella could make out a tiny sliver of metal in each hand. Still, Eleazar kept walking.

Okay, Ari, this is it.

The girl raised her arm and Ariella opened her mouth to scream. But before either of them could move Jaron emerged from the shadows behind the girl. He threw his arm around her neck and yanked her off her feet. She landed on the stone floor with a crash, and before she could react, Indio had slammed his knee into her chest, driving the air from her lungs.

The violent assault had startled the crowd around them, but after the initial shock, they simply shook their heads and walked away, keen to stay out of trouble. All except Eleazar. Jaron and Indio's display of strength had snapped him into action, and he covered the ground towards them in a sprint, Ariella at his heels.

"What are you doing?" Eleazar yelled. "Indio, get off her."

"What?" demanded Indio.

"I said, 'Get off her,'" he repeated, pulling at Indio's shirt.

"Easy, Ele," said Jaron, "this is the girl, the one with the butterfly darts. We caught her."

"I know who it is, you idiots," sighed Eleazar.

"What?" asked Indio again.

"I know who she is."

Jaron and Indio were left speechless, one with his arm around the girl's neck, the other with his knee pressed onto her chest. The girl lay still, her ice-blue eyes taking in every detail.

"You better start talking, Ele," said Ariella. "I was about to leap in front of a dart for you. Again."

"You were?" asked Indio, "I'm not sure I would've done that for you, Ele. Maybe she does like you after all."

Eleazar ignored them both and looked at the girl on the ground, "Indio, get off her, please."

The tone in Eleazar's voice was gentle and kind. It confused Indio and Jaron and just for a moment, they loosened their grip. The girl lashed out a fist and connected with Indio's jaw, toppling him into Jaron. With a twist she was free, and before Ariella could react, she was gone, flying through the busy city streets. Ariella thought about giving chase, but Indio's moan changed her mind.

"Ow, ow, ow!" he shouted. "That witch broke my jaw!"

"Calm down, you big baby," said Ariella, pushing him off Jaron and helping them both to their feet. "You'd hardly be talking if it were broken. It's just bruised."

Indio rubbed his jaw and glared sulkily at Ariella but did not answer back.

Eleazar turned and pulled down his hood. His eyes had dark rings under them and his face was drawn.

"Heck, Ele, you look rough," said Indio.

"Indio!" glared Ariella punching his arm.

"It's okay," said Eleazar, cracking a smile. "I'm sure he's right. I've...I've not been sleeping very well recently."

"No kidding," said Indio, rubbing his arm where Ariella had punched him. "I'd have trouble sleeping if darkness-creating, butterfly dart-throwing nut jobs were creeping into my room trying to turn me into a pincushion."

"It's your room too, genius," shot Ariella. "Maybe they were after you."

Indio shut up as he mulled over that possibility.

"You were leaving," said Jaron. It wasn't a question.

Eleazar nodded. "I thought it was best."

"Who is she?" asked Ariella.

Eleazar shifted uneasily from foot to foot, staring at the cobblestones.

"It's okay, Ele," said Ariella. "You can tell us, we're on your side."

He didn't look up, "It's complicated."

"Doesn't seem that complicated," muttered Indio. "Some crazy girl with spiky darts is trying to kill you, and you seem content to die."

Ariella glared at him.

"There's something you're not telling us," said Jaron.

Eleazar looked up at them, "There's a lot I'm not telling you."

"You wanted us to let her go, didn't you?" Ariella asked. "You didn't want us to hurt her."

He went back to staring at the cobblestones.

"You're not leaving us with many options, Ele," she continued. "We're going to have to go back to Karlov and tell him what's been going on. Is that what you want?"

He did not answer.

"All right then, I guess we go to Karlov." She turned to leave.

"Wait," said Eleazar, his voice dropping. He took a deep breath and held it for a moment. "She's my sister."

20

It's Borrowing

"Your sister?" gasped Jaron.

"Are you joking?" said Indio. "I've had fights with my cousins before, but none of them actually tried to kill me. What did you do to her?"

Ariella rolled her eyes and ignored him. "What's going on? Why is she trying to kill you?"

"Like I said, it's complicated."

The four friends stood for a moment in the silence trying to take in the events of the last few hours.

Finally, Ariella spoke.

"We need to carry on with the plan."

"What about him?" said Jaron, nodding at Eleazar.

Ariella smiled.

"He's coming with us."

Indio coughed, "He is?"

"Of course," she replied. "If we left him here, he'd end up as target practice for his sister."

Indio sighed, "We're going to need another gryphon."

"Really?" Jaron asked.

"Yes. Thrace is impressive, but four of us would be too much for him to fly for any long distance. We'll need another one. That means one of you will have to fly it."

"I will!" said Ariella, trying to keep the broad grin off her face. "I will. Definitely. Me. I'll do it."

"Fine with me," said Jaron.

Eleazar raised his hand in the air. "Excuse me, mildly crazy people. What exactly are you talking about? Where exactly are you off to. Who's got a gryphon and does Karlov know about it?"

"Karlov?" Indio asked innocently "I really like Karlov, a great guy."

"And?" pressed Eleazar.

"And what?"

"Does he know, Indio? Does he know you three are planning a trip on someone's gryphon?"

"Well. How can I put this, err…no. No, he doesn't. Not a clue. Totally oblivious. We kind of think that's the best way to keep it. Ignorance is bliss and all that."

"What about you?" asked Ariella, eyebrows raised. "Does Karlov know about you trying to buy a horse and riding off to who knows where?"

Eleazar was silent.

"I didn't think so."

Eleazar sighed, "So what's the plan?"

"We're going north," said Ariella.

"How far north?"

"To Khan."

"You're going where?"

"Not 'you'," said Jaron. "'We', it's a 'we' now. You're coming with us."

"Khan was not exactly what I had in mind," said Eleazar.

"And where did you have in mind?" Ariella asked, watching him closely. "Back to Lightharbour?"

Eleazar dropped his gaze.

"No, I didn't think so," she continued. "You didn't have anywhere to go, you just wanted to run. Well, now you can run with us."

"Fly," interrupted Indio, "fly with us. Running gets so boring after a while. Flying on gryphons is way more fun."

"You three are crazy," muttered Eleazar. "What are we going to Khan for?"

"To shut up that vicious witch and her psycho father," snarled Indio.

Eleazar's eyes widened.

"He means Eugenie," explained Jaron. "She and Indio have a personality clash."

161

Indio spluttered, "Personality clash! She's a harpy, a rabid troll."

"How is flying off to Khan going to sort that out?"

"It's a long story," Ariella began as she filled Eleazar in on what they had seen and heard.

"You really think we're going to find anything?" he asked once Ariella had finished. "Lord Vantor has had all the Guardians in Trevena out searching for the source of the curse. What makes you think we stand a chance?"

"We have to help. We have to do something. We can't just sit around and allow Trevena to starve, Khan to get blamed and the Guardians discredited. Eugenie's father has to be stopped. I'm not staying in Stonegard when everything I've dreamed of gets turned to garbage." She felt her voice rise with the anger stirring in her.

"Okay, okay," said Eleazar, raising his hands in apology. "I was just asking. How are we going to do this?"

"Simple," said Ariella nonchalantly. "We steal a couple-"

"Borrow." interrupted Indio. "We're not stealing, we're borrowing."

"Without permission?" asked Eleazar.

"Details," answered Indio. "Everyone always seems so fixated on details."

"You finished?" Ariella asked, folding her arms.

Indio nodded.

"Excellent," she continued. "We 'borrow' a couple of gryphons, fly to the border of Khan where the Willowbank flows from the mountains. Malum and the others think the river is the most likely carrier of the Blood Curse. We should be there before daybreak."

"Then we just have to find the cause, cure it, exonerate Khan and shut up Baron Rexsalve. Simple." added Indio. Eleazar and Jaron exchanged glances and shook their heads.

"What?" asked Indio. "What? It'll be simple, trust me."

"Sure, Indio. How could it possibly fail?" sighed Jaron.

"I don't suppose you have thought about weapons, have you?" Eleazar asked. "We seem to have a knack for finding trouble."

"That's a good point," conceded Ariella. "I hadn't thought of that."

"Obviously, you guys have never flown with the Gryphon Cavalry before," smiled Indio. "Weapons won't be a problem. Gryphons are not pets; they're flying balls of fury, trained for combat and ridden by the finest warriors in Khan. Each of the gryphons will have their own weapon holsters bursting with all the best axes, bows and spears that our weapon smiths can make. They are remarkable creatures."

Indio was brimming with pride.

"Okay then," said Eleazar, "I guess that's it then. Let's go pinch a gryphon."

"Borrow," said Indio with a pained expression on his face.

"Of course. My mistake. Borrow a gryphon."

"I'm guessing they'll be guarded?" Ariella asked.

"Certainly. But only nine flew in. Some of the riders will have gone with the queen and my uncle certainly. I reckon there will only be two or three left behind.

Gryphons don't need guarding like horses. If a gryphon decides it doesn't want to go with you, it'll just tear your head off."

"As far as theft deterrents go, I bet that's pretty effective," said Eleazar.

"So, we need to get past a couple of guards and get to Thrace and the other gryphons without anyone noticing?" said Jaron, mulling over their options.

"Is no one else scared that the gryphons will rip our heads off?" asked Eleazer.

"Relax, you're with me," said Indio.

"Oh, excellent," said Eleazer, rolling his eyes. "That makes me feel so much better."

"Let's go check out where they're staying, and we can assess our options then," said Ariella, and she led them on towards the distant farm.

The evening sun was obscured by thick clouds allowing the four companions to pass unseen through the fields. The occasional cry from a gryphon helped them to navigate, and they quickly found the field where they were tethered. Even in the low light, the nine beasts looked majestic. Their orange eagle eyes seemed to glow, taking in all that was going on around them.

There were three tents pitched next to the gryphons, striped blue and white in the colours of Khan. A small fire had been lit, and they could make out two figures roasting something over a spit. When they were about a hundred metres from the field, Ariella called them to a halt, crouching low to the ground.

"Okay Indio, this is your territory, what do you think?' she whispered.

"Two guards, that'll be simple. One of the tents will be for sleeping, one for food and the final one will probably be for the baggage."

Jaron kept his voice low, "What exactly do you mean, two guards, that'll be simple?"

"I mean, in a moment I'm going to stand up and stroll over to the two guards. They'll almost certainly recognise me. I've been around the palace since I was a child. I'm then going to introduce you and tell them that I've bought my dear friends to meet Thrace. We'll stand around for a while admiring the magnificent beast, and they'll get bored and go back to their dinner. Once they do that, we'll hop on and fly off to Khan. Simple."

The other three sat for a moment, stunned by the plan.

"Are you serious?" Eleazar asked, his eyes wide.

"That's the plan?" Jaron chipped in.

"Actually," Ariella said, "I think it's pretty brilliant. The alternative is we have to sneak around the guards. If we try that and the gryphons hear us..."

"Which they will," interjected Indio.

"Then the guards will come running," she continued. "Then we'll have to explain what we're doing. They'll never let us near Thrace, so we'll have to knock them out, and I'd rather not resort to that."

"I suppose not," said Indio.

Eleazar looked at Jaron who shrugged, "If Ariella's up for it, then I'm in."

"Excellent," said Indio, jumping to his feet and making his way through the field, followed by the others.

"I can't believe we're doing this," sighed Eleazar, "I must be out of my mind."

As they got nearer to the gryphons and the guards, Indio started waving.

Really, Ari, this is the best idea you could come up with? If you get caught, Karlov is going to erupt, not to mention dear Aunt Abalyne. I don't think she's going to be thrilled about you 'borrowing' her gryphons.

"Good evening!" called Indio, "welcome to Trevena. Not like the mountains back home, is it?"

Oh heck, no going back now.

The guards jumped to their feet, and each grabbed a tall spear that glinted menacingly in the firelight.

"Halt, who's there?"

"It's Indio Gryphonfriend. I've been telling my, not very smart, friends here, that gryphons are the finest beasts in all Dawnhaven. They've foolishly doubted me, so I've dragged them down to see for themselves."

"Indio?" one of the guards asked, lowering his spear.

"I think we just got lucky," whispered Eleazar.

"Rapha! What are you doing out here? I thought you were out in the far north fighting off Ghost Raiders?"

Rapha laughed, "Nope, I've just got married, so they allowed me back to the capital for a year's posting. I'm part of the Royal Guard, so I got to fly down here."

"You're married! Congratulations, how did you convince her?"

"I begged," said Rapha, "and then I begged some more. She eventually took pity on me. How's the life of a Guardian?"

"Tough Rapha," said Indio, shaking his head. "I miss the mountains and the gryphons. That's why I brought my friends with me to show them what amazing creatures they are. May I introduce three of the finest sojourners the Guardians have ever had the privilege of training: Ariella, Jaron and Eleazar."

The friends nodded and smiled.

"Greetings. Friends of Indio's are friends of mine," said Rapha.

"Do you mind if I take them to see Thrace?" asked Indio, his voice dripping with innocence.

"Be my guest," said Rapha, "as long as you don't mind going on your own. I'm starving."

"Not at all, enjoy your meal," said Indio as he led the others away from the fire, the roasting pheasant and the two guards.

"How lucky can one person be?" said Jaron, shaking his head.

"Told you," said Indio smugly. "Simple."

Ariella ignored them. She was staring beside the nearest gryphon, her mouth wide in wonder.

"She's beautiful," she whispered.

"How did you know it was a she?" asked Indio suspiciously.

"I've no idea, she just looks like a 'she'."

The gryphon's feathers were shining in the far off firelight. They looked like bronze shards of armour covering the beast's upper body. The gryphon stared at Ariella, fixing her with a penetrating gaze. Ariella did not look away, and for a moment, she was lost in awe of the creature in front of her.

"That's the queen's," said Indio. "Her name is Lavina."

Ariella reached out her hand and held it a few inches from the gryphon's beak.

"Ariella," Indio whispered, "be super careful. Remember what I said about gryphons ripping people's heads off?"

But Ariella ignored him, captivated by Lavina's gaze. She kept her hand outstretched, her eyes never leaving Lavina's. After what seemed like an eternity, the gryphon leaned its head forward and placed its beak on Ariella's hand.

Eleazar exhaled sharply, "Oh my!"

"You sure you've never been around gryphons before?" Indio asked.

Ariella shook her head.

"Well, in that case, that was pretty amazing. Now, let's find Thrace and get out of here."

Ariella stayed with Lavina while the others moved quickly through the gryphons and found Thrace. The gryphon recognised Indio and gave a soft cry as Indio threw his arms around Thrace's feathery neck.

Jaron and Eleazar checked down Thrace's side and found the weapon holster as Indio had promised.

"Check it out, Jaron," said Eleazar. "A couple of swords, a bow, a spear and a few knives. These boys from Khan certainly came prepared for a fight."

Ariella joined the boys as they were sorting the weapons.

"I'll take Jaron with me," said Indio. "Ele, you can fly with Ariella."

Eleazar hesitated "Err...."

"What's the problem?" she asked.

"Well, it's just that, well...you've never flown before and...." he stammered.

Ariella smiled, "No problem, you can stay here and explain to Rapha where we've gone."

He pulled a face at her, "Fine, I'll fly with you."

"Excellent idea. We'll take Lavina. Indio, are you ready?" she asked.

"Yep. You sure you're okay taking the queen's gryphon?" he asked.

"She's my aunt. How mad can she be?" asked Ariella.

"Pretty stinking mad," mumbled Eleazar.

Ariella ignored him. "Give us two minutes to get on Lavina and untether her. Then get airborne and we'll follow you."

"Got it," said Indio, climbing onto Thrace and giving Jaron a hand up.

Ariella and Eleazar made their way back to Lavina. Ariella began to untether her.

"Just thought of something," said Eleazar. "Back in a moment."

"What?" she hissed. "Where are you going?"

Eleazar had already slipped into the shadows.

Idiot, what is he doing?

Ariella carefully climbed onto Lavina's back and sat down low, trying not to attract Rapha's attention.

Where are you, Ele?

Just then he slipped out of the shadows and sheathed the knife he'd taken from the weapon holster.

"What have you been doing?"

Eleazar climbed up behind her. "Don't worry, you'll see in a moment."

Ariella looked over her shoulder through the twilight and could make out Jaron and Indio on Thrace's broad back.

Time to go Indio, give the signal.

"Hey! What are you lot doing up there!?" bellowed Rapha. "That's the queen's gryphon. Get off!"

"Now would be a good time, Ari," said Eleazar.

"Go!" she heard Indio yell through the night. Out of the corner of her eye, she saw Thrace spread his massive wings and kick into the air.

"Wow," she whispered.

"Get going!" said Eleazar as Rapha came storming towards them with his spear held high and anger all over his face. At that moment that Ariella realised she had no idea how to fly a gryphon.

What have I done? You're a fool Ariella, and this is the dumbest thing you've ever done.

Rapha was only twenty yards from them now and closing fast.

"Ari!" said Eleazar squeezing her waist tight, "I'm sorry I was mean to you, but please make this thing fly."

Think, Ari, think!

Rapha was five metres away then a loud voice called from up above them.

"Ride it like a horse! It's been trained the same as a horse!"

A horse!

Just as Rapha reached out his hand to grab Ariella, she kicked both her heels into Lavina's flanks, and the gryphon rose into the night sky.

21

A Night Flight

Ariella gasped as Lavina's powerful wings beat, again and again, driving them higher and higher. Below them, she could hear Rapha's shouts of anger grow faint as they climbed. The chill of the evening air blew on her face, but she smiled and began to laugh an exuberant laugh.

"This is amazing!" she cried.

She heard a groan behind her.

"Enjoying the flight, Ele?"

"I think I'm going to be sick."

"Not here, you're not. I don't think Lavina would take it well if you threw up on her feathers. She may be inclined to take you for a spin."

"That's not funny," grumbled Eleazar. "I thought we were finished back there. I can't believe I let you talk me into this. We've just stolen the Queen of Khan's gryphon."

"Borrowed," she corrected, "besides, what was your alternative? Buy a horse and ride off to who knows where, with no friends, no help. You'd be miserable and probably end up dead with a butterfly dart in your neck."

Ariella felt him slump behind her, but he said nothing. She scanned the sky around them trying to get a bearing on Indio and Jaron, but the clouds had blocked out the light of the moon and stars.

Where are you? I can't see anything up here except great black clouds.

Just then she heard the cry of a gryphon ahead of them but higher up. Lavina gave an answering call and beat her wings again, taking them up towards the low hanging clouds. Then, to Ariella's surprise, she heard another gryphon give an answering cry, just off to her left. Then another to her right. And another, and another. Then three more in quick succession.

"They're after us," she called to Eleazar.

"Don't panic," he replied, "Look a little closer at them, I was hoping this would happen."

"What would happen?" but he ignored her.

I guess flying doesn't agree with him. What did he mean by 'I was hoping this would happen'?

She peered through the gloomy night, trying to make out the nearest gryphon. It was only about twenty metres from them and was flying parallel but a little behind.

That's weird - he's not chasing us. Something's not right.

Then it dawned on her, "There are no riders."

"Well spotted, genius."

"I don't think Lavina likes sarcasm, Ele," she replied. "I think if she hears any more sarcasm, then she might be inclined to make a few loops, maybe some rolls. What do you think, Lavina?" Ariella stroked the great gryphon's feathers, and she gave a friendly squawk. "I think she agrees with me."

"Easy, no need to be hasty. What I meant to say was, I figured the guards may give chase, so I cut the tethers of the other gryphons. I guessed there would be a good chance if two of them flew the other seven would follow."

Actually, that was an excellent idea.

Not sure I should let him know that, don't want him getting an even higher opinion of himself, do I?

Ari, you're being unkind. Give credit where credit is due.

"Ele."

"What?"

"That was a really good plan."

There was a moment of silence.

"Thank you."

Before they could say any more, Lavina plunged into the low lying clouds. Immediately their visibility was down to only a few metres either side of them. The moisture of the clouds soaked their hair and clothes. Lavina didn't seem to object. Droplets ran off her feathers and down her back.

"I hope she knows where she's going," said Eleazar. "I couldn't find my feet in this cloud."

On and on Lavina flew. They neither heard nor saw any of the other gryphons and just as Ariella was about to start panicking, they burst through the cloud and out into the clear night sky.

"Oh, my," whispered Ariella in awe.

The bank of cloud was laid out below them like a soft feather bed, stretching for miles in all directions. Around them, the sky was filled with a million stars and the twin moons, Owr and Cashak, shining brightly together. They were so close they seemed to be almost touching, the smaller, Cashak, orbiting its larger sibling.

"I have never seen anything quite as beautiful as this," she murmured.

A cry above them drew their eyes to Thrace. Majestic, soaring on his great wings. Indio was riding high on his back, waving frantically down at them.

"I think he wants us to go see him. Any ideas on how to make a gryphon obey you?" inquired Eleazar.

"Give me a moment," she replied.

Alright Lavina, how do we do this?

Ariella noticed a thin metal collar hanging loosely around the gryphon's neck. Attached to the collar was a leather strap fashioned like a horse's bridle.

Like a horse he said, they're trained like horses. Okay, I can ride a horse, how hard can this be?

She reached down and gripped the bridle.

"Go easy," said Eleazar. "I don't want her to suddenly decide she's not happy with us riding her and ditch us through the clouds. I don't think I'd bounce."

"Thanks for the encouragement, really helpful. Any more gems of wisdom to throw in?"

"I thought Lavina didn't like sarcasm," he said.

"Your sarcasm. She doesn't like your sarcasm. It's a girl thing. You wouldn't understand."

With that, she gave a gentle pull on the bridle and kicked with her heels into Lavina's soft flanks. She immediately rose gracefully up towards Thrace with a few beats of her wings.

"Heck, it worked," said Eleazar, unable to keep the surprise out of his voice.

Ariella ignored him as she guided Lavina to where Indio and Jaron were circling on Thrace.

"How's it going?" called Indio when they were in earshot.

"It's amazing!" she shouted back. "I've never felt anything like it. I've never been this free."

"What about you Ele, enjoying the trip?"

Eleazar waved a hand but didn't answer.

"What's with him?" called Jaron.

"Ignore him," she said. "He's in a bad mood because Lavina doesn't like him. He thinks she's going to tip him off if he says anything mean to me."

"Ari, you're hilarious," said Eleazar.

"Was that sarcasm, Ele?" she asked as she gave Lavina a sharp tug on her reins and dug her foot in on one side. Instantly Lavina tucked in her wing and dived sharply.

Eleazar locked his arms around Ariella's waist and screamed. "Knock it off, Ari! Now! Right now!"

Ariella turned Lavina back towards Thrace and levelled her off. "I did tell you she didn't like sarcasm. It's not my fault if you can't help yourself."

Eleazar sighed, "Okay, you win. No more sarcasm."

"Excellent." She called over to the others. "Which way to Khan? I can't see any landmarks through the clouds."

"Landmarks?" scoffed Indio. "We don't need landmarks. You see that constellation over there?"

Ariella followed his gaze to a cluster of bright stars on the far horizon.

"That's Elbrathon, the chief of the Frost Giants. We follow those stars, and we'll be in Khan in a couple of hours."

"Frost Giants?" said Jaron. "Did you say Frost Giants? They don't sound like the kind of people I want to bump into wandering around the mountains."

"Just legends," laughed Indio. "There are plenty of real dangers without worrying about imaginary ones."

With that, he pointed Thrace toward the constellation of Elbrathon and led them on through the dark. Behind them flew the seven other gryphons, rider less but following Thrace's cries. After a couple of hours, the clouds began to thin beneath them, and the foothills of the Khan mountains came into view.

Ariella knew from the stories in the great library that these foothills were only the beginning of the massive range. There were peaks in the Khans that were so high you would have trouble breathing on the summit.

Indio pulled Thrace in beside Lavina and pointed to a valley that Ariella could just make out in the gloom.

"That's where the Willowbank flows down from the mountains into Trevena," he said.

"Then that's the place to start. Let's get the gryphons down and find a safe place to rest until morning. Then we can begin the search."

Indio guided Thrace down close to the foothills, looking for a place for them to land. Thankfully, the clouds had all but gone and the moons shone bright enough for them to see a small piece of flat grass on the side of one of the hills.

Thrace landed without a sound, Lavina following behind.

"I'm not sure I want to get down," sighed Ariella.

Eleazar didn't hesitate, sliding down to the ground and collapsing in a heap. "That was not the most fun experience of my short life," he muttered.

"I can't believe you didn't enjoy it," scolded Indio. "The way the wind blows in your hair, the way the land drops away from you as you soar up through the clouds, the way..."

"Enough," pleaded Eleazar. "I think I'm going to throw up."

"Hey," called Jaron. "Our new friends are sticking around."

The others turned to look as the seven remaining gryphons landed next to them and gathered around Thrace.

"I guess he's the boss," said Jaron. "Is that how gryphons live?"

"Pretty much," replied Indio. "Good news is we won't need a sentry tonight. Nine gryphons make us as safe as we could ever be."

"Then let's get some rest and be up at first light," said Ariella. "Who knows how long we've got before an irate Karlov comes rampaging through the hills looking for us."

"Wow, that's a cheery thought. Sweet dreams, Ari," said Eleazar and he pulled his hood over his head and settled down for the night.

Jaron and Indio found a soft patch of grass and made themselves comfortable, quickly dropping off to sleep. Ariella went to say goodnight to Lavina. The queen's gryphon was lying with the others, preening her bronze feathers and swishing her long tail. She watched as Ariella approached, her orange eyes bright in the dark night, following every step she took.

"Hello, beautiful," whispered Ariella, holding out her hand. This time Lavina didn't hesitate. She nuzzled Ariella's palm and gave a squawk.

Ariella threw her arms around Lavina's neck and buried her head in the soft feathers. "Good night, you amazing thing."

With that, Ariella curled up next to her warm pelt and fell fast asleep. A hard beak knocking against Ariella's cheek woke her from her deep sleep. She batted away the beak as Lavina gave a low cry. "I'm awake, I'm awake," she mumbled, wiping her eyes.

The sun had not yet risen above the hills, but Ariella could see the warm glow in the sky and the promise of a bright day to come. The others had started to stir as Ariella took a quick look around. The place they had landed was a natural bowl in the side of a hill covered in rich green grass. The sides sloped gently upwards, blocking their view of the surrounding hills. Off to the north, Ariella got a glimpse of the scale of the Khan mountains. Before her, peak after peak towered into the sky.

Indio saw her taking in the view.

"Those are just the small ones," he said. They get bigger the further you go north. Some in the far north have never been climbed. The air is too thin to breathe. Many have died trying, but only the gryphons go up that high."

Eleazar strolled over to where they were talking and reached into his backpack. "Here," he said, tossing them each an apple. "I had a few supplies for the road. Had to pay through the nose for these, there's not much that's been spared from the curse."

"Thanks, Ele," said Indio, crunching down on the apple. "What do you reckon, Ari, have a look around?"

She nodded, "Yep, we need to find the Willowbank and track its source. Any idea in which direction to look?"

"No," said Indio, "I think it's over that way," pointing to the west of the bowl, "but I could be totally wrong."

"Gather your weapons," she replied, "just in case. Then we'll take a look."

The friends spent a few minutes getting their gear together and then set off towards the edge of the bowl where Indio thought the Willowbank would be.

"What about the gryphons?" asked Jaron. "Are we just going to leave them here?"

"They'll be good for a few minutes until we get our bearings," said Indio. "If we need to, we can use them to scout around."

The edges of the grassy bowl sloped upward at a steep angle. The morning dew made the ground slippery underfoot, but they made it to the top.

The green foothills of the Khans spread out before them. Pockets of woodland dotted the hills here and there. A few hundred yards below them was a winding river, narrow and fast.

"That's it," said Indio proudly.

"It's pretty small," said Eleazar. "Are you sure that's it?"

"Definitely," he replied. "This is just the beginning. It grows the further south you go. This is the Willowbank."

"It looks easy enough to get down to. Let's check it out," said Ariella.

She had just stepped over the edge of the bowl when Jaron grabbed her shoulder and pulled her down. She hit the ground hard, banging her hip.

"What was...?"

Before she could finish, Jaron's hand was over her mouth, and he was pointing at the gryphons. Eleazar and Indio followed his lead and were lying down flat in the grass.

"Look at the gryphons," Jaron whispered.

Each of the nine gryphons had pressed their bodies hard against the grassy bowl. Their eagle heads were erect, eyes narrowed. Their tails were twitching and their claws were extended.

"They've heard something," said Indio. "Something they don't like."

The gryphons' eyes were locked on the far side of the bowl.

"I can't hear anything," said Ariella.

"Me neither," said Eleazar.

"That's because you two aren't gryphons," said Jaron. "We better go see, slowly, and stay low." Jaron rose to a low crouch and inched his way across the bowl without making a sound, the others following, although only Eleazar could match Jaron's stealth.

How do they do that? I'm going to have to get them to teach me that when we get home. If we get home.

Just to confirm her thoughts, Indio stepped on a stick hidden in the grass. The sound of the snap seemed to be amplified across the bowl. The gryphons swung their heads round and glared at him. Jaron winced, and he put his finger to his lips. Indio held his hands up in apology.

Nice one, Indio. So glad that wasn't me.

They followed Jaron and Eleazar as they approached the steep sides where the gryphons were staring. Jaron flattened himself on his stomach and crawled forward. The others copied him, inching their way slowly after him.

They reached the top of the bowl and lay still. The rising sun was breaking the horizon, the glow of dawn gliding across the hills.

"I don't see anything," Indio whispered but fell silent after Jaron gave him a withering look. They lay there in silence for a long while before Jaron slowly reached out his hand and pointed.

"What?" Ariella asked, "I can't see..." Then she saw them. A long way in the distance moving down the side of a steep hill was a small group of people, maybe six, it was hard to tell from this range. They moved quickly, with purpose, down towards the young, free-flowing, Willowbank River.

"Who are they?" asked Eleazar.

Jaron did not say anything. He kept watching.

The group disappeared out of view as they dropped behind an outcrop. They emerged again, closer, heading towards the river. Ariella could make out more details now. There were definitely six of them, all men she thought, except one - a hooded figure in the middle of the group. They were talking, but she could not make out any words.

"Blast!" muttered Jaron, turning to look at the gryphons. They seemed agitated, tense. One of them was clawing the ground.

"What?" asked Ariella. "Who are they?"

"These gryphons," Jaron asked, "they're trained to fight?"

Too right," answered Indio.

"And who, specifically, are they trained to fight?

"Well, anyone really," said Indio, "but I suppose the people they love to fight is....oh no!" Indio looked at the gryphons and then at the group.

"Will someone please tell me what is going on?" pleaded Eleazar. "Who are those people?"

Then Ariella saw it. A shaft of light broke out from behind a hill, and the group was fully illuminated. Their weapons glinting in the sunlight, bleached white skin and red tattoos in full view.

Ariella gripped the grass in front of her, her voice almost a snarl. "Ghost Raiders."

22

Ghosts in the Sunshine

"This is mad," said Indio. "Ghost Raiders are never this far from the sea. It must be a couple of days walk from the nearest coast to here, across half of Trevena."

"They must be up to something important to risk the journey," said Jaron. "If any of the knights of Trevena caught them crossing their land they would have been killed on sight."

Ghost Raiders were a tribe from a distant chain of volcanic islands, far to the north of Dawnhaven. They came to raid the coastline, stealing whatever they could, enslaving people and killing any who opposed them. Their skin was painted white and they covered their bodies in blood red tattoos.

The four watched in silence as the Ghost Raiders moved across the hills in front of them. They left no marks on the soft grass of the foothills and made little sound save for the odd, brief conversation.

"They're heading for the Willowbank," said Jaron. "I wonder..."

"Could it be them?" asked Eleazar.

"I don't think so," he replied. "I've never heard of Ghost Raiders having the kind of magic that would do as much damage as the Blood Curse."

"Besides," said Ariella, "they spend their lives raiding the coast of Trevena for food and supplies. I'm not sure it'd be in their interest to poison the whole country."

"Unless," said Jaron, "someone is making it worth their while."

"You mean paying them to do it?" said Indio.

"Maybe."

"Who?"

"No idea," said Jaron, shrugging his shoulders.

"What do you reckon?" asked Indio, looking over at Ariella.

"They're Ghost Raiders. We kill them." Her voice was soft but angry. Jaron and Eleazar exchanged nervous glances.

Jaron spoke up. "There are six of them, Ari, and only four of us. We wouldn't stand a chance."

"They're Ghost Raiders," she stated again as if that was answer enough.

Ariella felt the blood rise in her with every step the Ghost Raiders took. It was the first time she had seen one in the flesh. She had heard stories and seen pictures in books. But here, on a lonely hillside, miles from anywhere, she saw them. And she hated them.

She hated them for everything they had taken from her. The precious moments she should have spent with her father. The days hunting in the woods around Lightharbour. Long summer walks through the palace gardens. They had taken his smile, his laugh, his arm around her shoulder. And she hated them.

"We kill them, we kill them all." She glanced over her shoulder. "Not four, thirteen. I think these gryphons hate Ghost Raiders almost as much as I do."

Lavina flicked her tail and stretched out her talons in agreement.

"Good girl," Ariella smiled. "Le's stalk them and see where we can set an ambush. Then we'll come back for the gryphons."

"Are you sure you want to do this, Ari?" Jaron asked. He had a worried look in his eye. "We're talking about killing people."

"No Jaron, not people. Ghost Raiders. They're monsters. We show them the same courtesy they showed my father."

"And mine," said Indio.

The young redhead had tears running down his cheeks and a determined look in his eye. "They killed both my parents. It's time to repay some debts."

"That settles it," said Ariella. "Are you with us?" She stared long and hard at Jaron and Eleazar.

They looked at each other and nodded. "We're with you," said Jaron.

"We're a Knot, right?" added Eleazar. "The harder you pull us, the tighter we get. Let's go stalk some Ghost Raiders."

The Ghost Raiders had dropped out of sight, down into a valley. The four slipped over the crest of the slope, keeping low to the ground.

Jaron led the way, parallel to the path the Ghost Raiders had taken. He kept them behind the ridges of the hills, stopping regularly to listen to the murmurs of their enemies and keep them on track.

After half an hour, they came to the top of a steep slope. Below them was the fast-flowing stream that would eventually become the massive river that watered all of Trevena. Jaron led them along the ridge, keeping them from becoming silhouetted against the bright blue sky. They stopped to listen.

Silence.

Jaron led them on slower than before. He was bent low to the ground, almost crawling. The Willowbank was on their left as they crept up towards a ridge where they heard low voices. Jaron flattened himself on the ground and held his hand up, stopping the others. He slid forward the last ten yards to the ridge top, pulled his dark green hood over his head and peered over.

After a minute he beckoned the others up to him. The four looked down at the scene unfolding below them. The Ghost Raiders had stopped at a bend in the river where a small pool had formed before the water rushed off again down through the hills.

They were only a hundred or so yards away, and Ariella could see them clearly. Their hard faces seemed to be fixed in permanent scowls. Blood red tattoos covered their bodies, in sharp contrast to their snow-white skin.

As she watched them move about the banks of the stream, Ariella's mind was suddenly filled with flashes of her father's smiling face. Tears filled her eyes, and she shut them tight. She still imagined his face, so full of joy, but lost to her forever. She shoved her fist into her mouth to stifle the sob.

She lay there for a moment then opened her eyes, blinking away the tears. The Ghost Raiders had stopped moving. Five of them remained on the bank while the hooded figure waded into the water, thigh deep.

What is going on?

The figure stooped down, stretching out both hands and stroking the water, making small ripples that flowed outwards. They stood again and held out their left hand. One of the Ghost Raiders stepped forward, drawing a vicious looking dagger with a curved blade. He took the hooded figure's wrist and slipped his blade across their open palm. Drops of scarlet blood fell into the stream. Ariella could see tiny spots of pink, expanding outwards where the blood had hit the water.

179

Then, ever so slowly, the figure began to speak. It was low and rhythmic, the syllables drifting in the still air.

They're chanting. Some kind of spell? Blood magic? This is wrong, this is very wrong.

Ariella glanced at the others, but they were transfixed by the proceedings below them. The chanting changed pace, growing faster and louder. She could hear every syllable clearly, but none of it made any sense to her. She had never heard the language before, not from any of the sailors she had listened to back in Lightharbour.

As the chanting rose, Ariella noticed the blood that had dropped into the river. The small patches of pink had grown dark, almost black.

It's exactly like the colour we found on the plant roots. This has to be it, they're cursing the river.

Louder and swifter, the chanting grew. The hooded figure seemed to be shaking under the intensity of the words. The dark patches of blood were growing at the speed of the chanting.

Soon, all around the hooded figure, the water had turned darkest red and seemed to be pulsating. The figure was screaming now, and their shoulders were moving violently, almost convulsing.

Suddenly, at the height of the figure's crescendo, the pool of blood seemed to explode down the river in a violent surge. The water kicked up, spilling over the banks and withering the grass it touched. The whole stream, for just an instant, turned blood red, as the figure collapsed backwards into the arms of the waiting Ghost Raider.

As the figure fell, their hood slipped down, revealing a thick braid of blonde hair and beautifully pink skin.

"That's no Ghost Raider," said Indio.

"Hush!" Ariella snapped.

Too late.

The raiders spun as one, with cold, cruel eyes spotting the four watching faces. In an instant, weapons were drawn from their sheaths, and they began sprinting up the steep hill towards them.

Jaron reacted first, leaping to his feet and fitting an arrow to his bow in a blur of motion.

"Run!" he screamed, firing an arrow at the leading raider. The raider swung his curved sword in a sweeping arc, cutting the shaft from the sky.

"Run!" Jaron screamed again, fitting another arrow.

The others had recovered from their shock and tore off in the direction of the gryphons.

Ariella hesitated as Jaron took aim again. "You too, run!"

Jaron had learned his lesson as the Ghost Raider drew closer. He aimed low, catching the raider off guard and sending the arrow deep into his thigh.

The raider toppled like an oak, cursing and screaming in pain.

"Now, Jaron!" Ariella cried, pulling his arm before he had time to notch another arrow. Three of the Ghost Raiders were now only fifty yards from them.

They ran together down the slope following Indio and Eleazar. Ariella kept her head low and ran with all her strength. They were gaining on the others as they struggled up the next steep slope, taking the quickest route back to the gryphons.

She felt her lungs begin to burn as she gasped for breath. They were about a minute away from the grass bowl where they had spent the night. Indio and Eleazar were just in front of them, running full speed. She glanced over her shoulder and saw the three Raiders barrelling down the hill towards them.

They're gaining on us. We can't outrun them. How long until we reach the gryphons?

She looked again at the pursuing Raiders. Their swords reflected the sunlight as they ran, their heavy boots thudding across the turf. Closer and closer they came. Forty metres, thirty metres. The ground started to rise again, and Ariella looked up.

We're nearly there. We're going to make it, we're going to be okay, we're going to...

"Aarrgghh!"

Eleazar let out a cry of pain as Ariella saw his foot stick in a hole and his knee twist horribly. He stumbled to the ground in front of her, a look of anguish in his face.

Indio glanced over his shoulder at his fallen friend and then at the oncoming Raiders. He tucked his head down and accelerated forward, leaving Eleazar sprawled on the grass clutching his wrecked knee.

Ariella pulled up next to Eleazar and drew her sword.

"What are you doing?" he screamed. "Run, you idiot, run!"

Jaron notched an arrow and spun, releasing the arrow in one movement. The point of the arrow struck the angled armour plate on one of the Raider's shoulders and flew harmlessly into the air.

Eleazar struggled to his knees and drew his dagger, flipping it over and catching it by its point.

The Raiders were almost upon them, swords raised. The one in the centre, a massive thuggish looking man with a blood-red moon etched across his cheek, snarled as he approached.

"You're children," he spat.

"We're Guardians," replied Jaron aiming an arrow at the Raider's throat. The Raider anticipated the move and, spinning sideways, he dodged the arrow, leapt forward and drove his sword towards Jaron's head. In a moment of desperation, Jaron raised his bow to deflect the oncoming blade. The bow splintered in two, and he was knocked to the earth, dazed by the impact.

The Raider laughed as he advanced for the killing blow, Jaron lying helpless at his feet. Before the strike could land, Eleazar flung his dagger. End over end it flashed in front of Ariella and sliced the Raider's arm. He howled in pain, dropping the sword and lashing out with his boot, catching Jaron on the side of his head. There was a sickening crunch, and Ariella saw Jaron's eyes roll back as he lay deathly still.

The Raider laughed at Jaron's broken body. Rage filled her mind as she leapt towards the unarmed Raider, her sword point driving towards his heart. But the other Raiders were quicker. One of them intercepted her blade, knocking it downwards, the second pummelled her jaw with his fist and she spun to the ground.

The pain was intense. It felt like her head was going to explode. She saw bright flashes in front of her eyes as she tried to recover. She heard the laughter of the Ghost Raiders as they drew closer. She kept blinking, trying to clear her vision, but all she could focus on was Jaron's ashen face.

She felt a firm hand grip her hair and snap her head back.

Come on, Ari, you can do this.

She opened her palm, and a flash of Light exploded out, blasting back the Raider holding her. Then she felt a fist hit her stomach, and the air was driven from her lungs.

"This one's learned to use the Light."

"We don't like the Light," one of them snarled and kicked her hard in the side causing her to cry out in pain.

Eleazar ran to her defence and slammed his remaining dagger into the side of one of the Ghost Raiders. He screamed in pain and smashed the hilt of his sword against Eleazar's, knocking him to the ground.

182

He grasped his side, where the dagger had pierced his armour. Blood had begun to ooze from the wound. "How much time do we have? Kill them quickly or slowly?"

"Quickly," came the harsh answer. "There's still one left. We can't have any witnesses."

Indio, at least Indio got away.

"Quickly it is then." She felt her head pulled up, the fullness of her neck exposed for the killing blow.

But it never came.

She felt a rush of powerful wind fly past her head, and the grip was gone. She heard a thud as the Ghost Raider fell to the ground beside her.

There was another rush, another thud.

What's happening?

She managed to focus her eyes as she heard Thrace's cry. The last Raider screamed in terror as he was impaled on the gryphon's razor sharp claws.

23

Polly

As she lay on the grass, Ariella felt the gryphons landing softly around her. She heard one of them approach and then the hardness of Lavina's beak nudging her, trying to get some response. The gryphon let out a cry as Ariella stirred.

"Hello, you wonderful creature," she mumbled through her pain.

She pushed herself to her feet and looked around. Next to her were the broken bodies of two of the Ghost Raiders. The third Raider had been flung back and was lying a way off, his chest torn open by Thrace.

Eleazar was leaning against one of the gryphons, standing on one leg.

"You okay?" he asked.

She nodded.

"I thought we were dead. Indio sure has a knack for timing. That Raider was half a second away from slitting your throat."

Ariella felt her neck and shivered. "Where is Indio?"

"I think he's with Jaron, on the other side of Thrace."

Ariella turned and saw Thrace lying on the ground, facing away from her. She walked over to him, wincing with each step. The pain in her side was intense. As she moved past Thrace, she stopped. Indio was on his knees beside his friend. Jaron's face was still white, and he wasn't moving.

Indio was sobbing as flashes of Light erupted from his hand. He looked up at Ariella.

"It's not working, Ari, it's not working," he said as another flash of red Light sparked. The Light rippled across Jaron's chest then faded away.

"I was too late. They've killed him. I was too late."

Ariella knelt beside Jaron and felt his wrist. Nothing. She moved her fingers and pressed harder. Nothing.

No, no, no.

She reached up to his neck, her fingers searching for a pulse. Nothing.

Come on, please.

She closed her eyes.

Beat, will you, beat, just beat.

Then, ever so faintly, she felt the tiniest movement under her fingers.

Come on, come on.

The pulse grew stronger, and she felt Jaron stir. She opened her eyes and turned to Indio. His eyes were wide, and his mouth was hanging open.

"Ari, look at your hand."

For the first time, Ariella was aware of warmth around her hand as it felt Jaron's pulse grow strong. She looked down and gasped. Her hand was covered in shimmering red Light.

"How are you doing that?"

"Urgh," groaned Jaron, opening his eyes. "My head hurts."

Ariella closed her hand, lifting it away as the Light faded.

"Hurts? Hurts? You should be dead, you idiot," said Indio. "I thought that Raider had caved your head in. I guess it's tougher than it looks. Must be all those rocks you have for brains."

"You're hilarious." He propped himself up on his elbow and took in the scene around him. "Where are the Ghost Raiders? What happened?"

"Indio rescued us," said Ariella. "I thought it was all over and then the gryphons tore into the Raiders. They didn't know what hit them."

"Gryphons," smiled Eleazar, limping over. "I've always liked gryphons."

"Yeah right," she laughed. "You and Lavina are the best of friends."

"Thanks, Indio," said Jaron, "I owe you one."

185

"Yep, you do" he replied, wiping away his tears. "You all do. And you can repay me in chocolate. Chocolate and a daily appreciation of my awesomeness."

"Yeah right," said Eleazar. "Your awesomeness. That's exactly what's going to happen." He winced in pain as he tried to rest on his damaged knee.

"Reckon you can use that Light on his knee Ari?" Indio asked, "I don't want to be stuck carrying him around."

Ariella shrugged. "I don't know how I used it on Jaron, it sort of just happened."

"That was you?" Jaron asked. "I saw the red Light, and I thought it was Indio."

Indio shook his head. "No way. I was trying but couldn't get it working."

"Come on then, princess," said Eleazar, "give it a shot. I don't want Indio dragging me around the rest of the day either."

Ariella knelt by Eleazar. She stretched out her fingers and lightly touched his knee. He flinched and clenched his jaw, stifling a scream. She closed her eyes and let her fingers move across the joint, feeling the swelling.

All right, Ari, let's get this sorted. Come on, Light, do something. Err, you're talking to the Light, Ari. Not sure that's how it works. What did you do with Jaron? Nothing. I did nothing except... sort of... wanting him to be well. Suppose I could try that.

She took a deep breath, clearing her head. She could feel where the knee had swollen. The ligaments were wrenched and the muscles torn. She felt the sharpness of the pain that Eleazar was feeling.

This knee must be agony. That's not right. That needs to change.

Just then she felt the knee straighten and the swelling reduce. She opened her eyes and saw her hand covered by a beautiful green Light.

"Wow," whispered Indio.

"How's your knee?" Jaron asked.

Eleazar had a shocked look on his face. "It's... it's perfect," he said, putting his full weight on his damaged leg. "It's as good as new."

"Good skills, Ari," said Indio. "Red and green. Two colours of Light. Never heard of that."

"I'm sure it's common," she replied, suddenly nervous. "Maybe the Light is just figuring itself out."

"Yeah," said Jaron, trying to reassure her, "that's probably it."

Ariella watched Jaron's face. He was trying to be kind, but there were questions and confusion in his look, and she felt decidedly uncomfortable.

"We need to get going," she said. "There are still two Ghost Raiders out there and the blonde witch. We need to find them and get the Blood Curse stopped or reversed or whatever we can do."

"You good to fly?" Eleazar asked Jaron.

"Yeah, I can hang on to Indio."

"Great. You want to ride with me, or you think you can handle one of these now?"

"I got this. No problems, always loved gryphons, remember?"

He walked to a sleek, silver feathered gryphon who gave him a friendly peck with its beak.

"I think he likes me," he said, jumping up on to its back.

Ariella shook her head and climbed on Lavina, stroking her bronze feathers. "Ready for another hunt?"

Lavina gave a loud cry, echoed by Thrace and then by the other seven.

"I almost pity those Ghost Raiders," said Indio. "Almost." He gave Thrace a nudge and the gryphon leapt into the sky.

The nine gryphons fanned out in a wide 'V' formation, Thrace in the lead. They raced across the hillside, searching for their enemies. After less than a minute, they spotted a figure sprawled on the grass. Indio looked over at the others and made a circular motion with his hand. Eleazar gave Ariella a confused look, and she called over to him. "I think he wants us to circle and keep watch."

Eleazar nodded and turned his gryphon into a high arc. Ariella banked Lavina underneath him into a tighter circle, eyes scanning the hills looking for any signs of the other Ghost Raiders.

Indio and Jaron swooped low on Thrace, the gryphon's hind legs parting the tips of the grass. The figure didn't flinch. Indio banked hard and settled Thrace next to him. It was the Raider Jaron had felled; the arrow he had fired was sticking upright from his thigh.

"He's had his throat cut," said Jaron.

"By whom?" asked Indio looking around in case the attacker was still nearby.

"By the other Raiders. They don't allow themselves to be taken prisoner and that arrow would've slowed them down. They're running."

"Then let's get after them." Indio launched Thrace back into the sky and rejoined the others.

When they were in earshot, Indio called across to Ariella and Eleazer, "There are only two left, and our guess is they're running."

"Any ideas which way?" called Eleazar.

Indio shook his head.

"Then we split up," said Ariella. "Three gryphons each. We fly high and in wide arcs. These gryphons have incredible eyesight, they'll pick them up. Once you've spotted them, send one of your gryphons back to the others. And Indio -"

"Yeah?"

"Do not attack them until we are all together. I've had enough healing for one day."

"Okay," he muttered.

"I mean it, Indio."

"Don't worry, Ari," said Jaron "If he tries it, I'll chuck him off when he's not concentrating. Then we'll get to see if Thrace can catch." Jaron smirked.

"Not funny, Jay. Not funny,"

"All right, you two fly down the Willowbank and see if they've kept to the stream. Ele, you go west and check in case they've gone inland to throw us off. I'll go east. See you soon." Ariella pulled up on Lavina's reins drawing the two nearest gryphons with her. She looked over her shoulder as the others parted.

Let's get going Ari, these two are not going to escape.

Lavina opened her wings wide and caught the thermals rising off the hills. High up in the sky, they swung back and forth, looking for any signs of the escaping Raiders. The wind whipped through Ariella's hair as she studied the ground, looking for a trail. After half an hour of searching, she was ready to call it quits and head back to the others.

There's no way they could've travelled this far, this fast.

She looked back west and south, searching for any signal that the boys had found them.

Not a thing. Where have they gone?

She turned Lavina and began following a deep valley carved out of the hills by some ancient river. The valley wound its way back towards the Willowbank but then turned sharply north as if something had blocked the flow, years ago.

Instinctively, Ariella pushed Lavina down into a dive. They flew down the valley, its steep sides casting long shadows across Ariella's face. As the river turned sharply, Lavina dipped her wingtips and banked hard, causing Ariella to cling tightly to her feathers. They flew around the corner, and Lavina let out a sharp screech and tucked in her wings. The hiding Ghost Raider leapt from a crack in the valley wall and swung his curved sword. The blade caught Lavina on her wing joint sending her tumbling from the sky in an explosion of blood.

The great gryphon crashed into the rocky valley floor throwing dust, rocks and Ariella up into the air. She spun twice and thudded to the ground. Her head swam, and she saw stars for the second time that day.

Not again.

Get up, he's coming. Get up!

She heard the Ghost Raider moving across the rocks and she struggled to her knees, reaching for her sword. Lavina was whimpering from the pain in her wing then she let out a terrifying shriek that caused Ariella to wince. She jumped up and tried to focus. The Ghost Raider had stamped down on Lavina's wing, pinning her to the ground. He grinned viciously and raised his sword above the gryphon's head.

As the blade fell, Ariella screamed, stretching out her hand.

"No!"

A burst of blue Light flew from her and smashed into the rushing blade, shattering it in a shower of sparks. The Ghost Raider fell backwards with the force of the impact and looked at Ariella in horror.

She drew her sword and advanced on her fallen enemy, a look of determination etched on her face.

He killed your father. He took him from you.

She started to move quicker, fury rising with every step, her blade poised to attack.

The Ghost Raider was still holding the shattered hilt of his sword, and he flung it at Ariella as she rushed towards him. It caught her on the side of her head, causing her to stumble. She put out her hand to steady herself, then instinctively reached up to her head. She felt her warm blood ooze down from the cut above her ear.

The Ghost Raider grabbed his opportunity as she faltered. Jumping to his feet, he sprinted down the valley, sending dust up behind him. Ariella set off after him, but he was quicker, easily outdistancing her.

She screamed in frustration at his escape. As if in response a gryphon screeched just above her head. She ducked as the two mighty beasts that had followed her and Lavina streaked past, down the valley.

189

The Ghost Raider glanced over his shoulder, a look of terror on his face. He caught his foot on a rock and began to tumble to the ground. Before he could recover, the gryphon was on him with a shriek, and the valley fell silent.

Ariella sunk to her knees and tried to steady her breathing. The adrenaline was coursing through her and she felt her hands shaking. Lavina's whimpering roused her. She ran to her fallen friend.

"Easy girl," soothed Ariella, "easy. Let's take a look."

The Ghost Raider's blade had cut deep into Lavina's wing, and it looked like her bone was broken. The gorgeous bronze feathers were matted with blood. Ariella felt the sting of tears as she studied the wound. Without thinking, she placed her hands over the gash, and a deep green Light flooded out, covering Lavina's wing. Ariella felt the warmth of the Light as it moved back and forth. Lavina's moaning stopped, and she emitted a heartfelt cry, stretching out her wing. She beat it lightly. Once, twice, three times, each time increasing the speed, then with a leap, she rose into the sky.

She spun over and dived back down to earth, landing on Ariella and knocking her to the ground. Lavina cried loudly and nuzzled Ariella's face.

"Get off, you lump!" she laughed. "You weigh a ton, get off me!"

She managed to push off the gryphon's feet and stand up, throwing her arms around Lavina's neck. The other two gryphons landed next to them, gathering around Lavina, touching beaks. Ariella rested her hand on one of the gryphons and spoke softly.

"Can you go and get the others?" she asked. "Bring them back here. Can you do that?"

The gryphon let out a cry and was gone in a cloud of dust, heading off in the direction of the boys.

"I guess he understands," she said out loud.

"Gryphons are intelligent creatures," said a weak voice.

Ariella spun round, her sword flashing in her hand. "Who's there?"

She was facing the cleft in the rock where the Ghost Raider had ambushed them. The area was covered in shadow by the steep sides of the valley.

"Show yourself, slowly," Ariella commanded.

Out of the cleft, hesitantly, came the hooded figure they had seen by the stream. She was older than Ariella but just as tall and slim.

Her hood was down, allowing her braided blonde hair to fall across her shoulders. Her face was a mess. Her left eye was swollen and almost closed over. Her bottom lip was bleeding, and she had a gash somewhere on her head, the blood mixing with the blonde tresses. She walked out of the cleft wincing with each step.

"What happened to you?" Ariella asked.

The lady gave a half-smile. "I wasn't moving quickly enough. I thought that if I slowed down there was a chance that you would find us. He didn't like my plan."

"You wanted to be found?" Ariella asked, suspicious.

She nodded. "I thought being your prisoner would be better than being their prisoner." She shuddered and looked away. "Anything is better than being their prisoner."

Ariella was shocked. "You're a prisoner?"

The lady looked confused. "Of course. Do I look like a Ghost Raider?"

"Well, err, no. I guess not. But we saw you cursing the Willowbank. That was you?"

The lady slumped and nodded.

"Do you know what you've done?" said Ariella, feeling her anger rise. "You've poisoned the whole country! People are starving because of you. They're blaming Khan and the Guardians when all the time it was you and the Ghost Raiders."

"I'm sorry," she mumbled.

"Sorry. You're sorry?" Ariella's voice was getting louder, and she stepped towards the lady, lifting her sword. "You think I could care less about your sorry?"

The lady lifted her hands, backing away from her. "I, I, I didn't want to do it."

"What's that got to do with it? You're in league with Ghost Raiders and you cursed the river. That's what matters, and you're going to pay for it."

"They killed my parents!" The lady screamed, her eyes filling with tears. She sunk to her knees in front of Ariella and began to sob.

Ariella stopped, her anger disappearing in an instant. "What did you say?"

The lady had to take a couple of deep breaths to compose herself. "They killed my parents. They said they'd come back for my brother if I didn't do what they said."

"Your brother?"

The lady nodded. "I have a brother. They said they'd...." she hesitated and began sobbing again

Nice one Ari, real sensitive. Look at her, she's a mess. Of course, she's not a Ghost Raider. Get a grip.

Ariella knelt beside her. "It's okay, you're safe. You're not my prisoner; I'm not going to hurt you. Ghost Raiders killed my father too. I understand."

The lady stopped sobbing and looked up at Ariella. "My name is Polly," she said.

"I'm Ariella."

Polly tried to force a smile through her tears.

"What I need to know, Polly, is can the curse be stopped?"

Polly stopped crying. "Yes, at least, I think so."

"What do we need to do?"

"We need to go back to the stream," Polly replied, "where you first saw me."

"Then let's go. Have you ever ridden a gryphon?"

Polly shook her head, looking nervously at Lavina and the other gryphon.

"It'll be all right," Ariella reassured her. "They'll do all the work, you just have to hang on."

Ariella swung up on Lavina's back and pointed to the gryphon. "Let's hurry, we've got to get this curse broken."

Polly edged up to the gryphon and gently patted its feathers. The gryphon stared at her for a moment, then lowered its back, making it easy for her to climb up.

"You settled?" Ariella asked as Polly fidgeted on the gryphon's back.

"Yes," she said, "I think so."

"Good, come on Lavina, fly," she nudged the gryphon's side with her heel, and the great creature rose with a single leap. Ariella heard Polly's shocked scream behind her and turned to see her hanging on tightly to the gryphon's feathers, her eyes firmly shut.

24

Broken

Ariella and Polly soared up into the blue sky and headed towards the pool where the Blood Curse had started. After a few moments, they saw three gryphons heading towards them from the south, flying fast in their direction.

"My friends," Ariella called over to Polly who still hadn't opened her eyes. "Never mind. Just hang on."

She waved as Indio and Jaron approached. When they spotted Polly clinging on to the other gryphon Indio's face darkened.

"What's going on?" he yelled.

"I'll explain when we land," Ariella called back. "Trust me."

Jaron nodded, but Indio remained motionless, his eyes fixed on Polly.

As they got closer to the pool, they saw Eleazar flying in from the west with the other gryphons. They landed together on the hillside. Indio jumped down from Thrace and advanced on Polly, his sword drawn. She gave Ariella a terrified look and dropped to the ground putting the gryphon between her and Indio.

"Back up, Indio," said Ariella.

"She's a witch, Ari, a Ghost Raider witch. Why is she still alive?" he growled.

"Because she can break the curse," said Ariella.

That stopped Indio in his tracks. He stared hard at Ariella as Polly started to sob.

"Is this true?"

She nodded.

"You better fill us in, Ari," said Eleazar stepping up beside Indio.

Ariella nodded and told them about the incident in the valley and how she met Polly.

"You healed Lavina?" Jaron asked.

"Yeah," she replied.

"What colour was the Light?"

Ariella shifted uneasily. "It was green."

"Green?" said Indio.

"And when you shattered the sword, what colour was that?" Jaron asked.

Lie, just lie! Why can't you just lie? Because we're a Knot, that's why.
She sighed, "It was blue."

Indio snorted, "That's weird. You're an odd one, Ari."

"Not helpful, mate," said Eleazar.

"What did I say?"

"It's okay," said Ariella, "I know something's not right."

"Forget about it for now," said Jaron. "Let's get this curse broken. You reckon you can do that, Polly?"

Polly was still staring at Indio and the bright blade he was holding.

"Indio," said Jaron, "put that sword away."

"Oh, yes, sorry." Indio sheathed his sword and tried to give Polly a reassuring smile.

"What do we need to do, Polly?" Ariella asked.

"I need to go back to the stream," she said nervously.

"Lead on then."

The four of them followed Polly down the hillside to the stream. Polly waded out in the water up to her thighs.

"I need some blood," she said, quietly, looking at the four sojourners.

"What about yours?" asked Indio. "Your blood cursed the river."

"Exactly," answered Polly.

"Huh?" said Indio.

"My blood cursed the river," she said, her voice tinged with sadness. "Now I need someone else's blood to remove the curse."

"Take mine," said Ariella, stepping into the pool.

194

"Wait," said Indio, placing his hand on his sword. He took a step towards Polly. "If anything happens to her, you die. No questions, no hesitations, no remorse. Do you understand?"

The blood drained from Polly's face and she nodded.

"Easy, Indio," said Ariella. "It'll be okay."

Ariella waded next to Polly and drew her sword. She pressed her palm against the blade, just enough to cut a thin line. She squeezed her hand into a fist, and the blood began to drip into the pool. Polly stroked the water as she had before, then the chanting began. It was the same rhythm, but the words were different this time. Ariella still couldn't understand what Polly was saying, but she sensed the shift.

She looked down at the pool and gasped. Her blood had started to turn a vibrant forest green. It began to shimmer and pulse as Polly's chanting grew louder and faster. Her shoulders began to shake and convulse, as the chanting reached its crescendo. The green blood spread and pulsed quicker and quicker. Then suddenly, the pool seemed to explode and a wave of green flew down the stream and out of sight.

Polly's knees buckled and Ariella had to scoop her up to stop her head going under the water. Jaron strode into the pool and helped pull her to the bank and lay her down. She was breathing heavily, but her eyes were closed.

"Is she all right?" Jaron asked, kneeling beside her.

"I think so," replied Ariella. "She's breathing but I guess the whole chanting thing takes it out of her."

"What do you think?" asked Indio. "Did it work?"

"Look," said Eleazar pointing downstream, his eyes wide.

"What?" said Indio. "I don't see anything."

"Look at the riverbank."

"Oh, wow," said Jaron.

"What?" said Indio "What are you guys looking at?"

"The grass," said Ariella, grinning. "The Blood Curse killed the grass on the banks of the stream. Now, look at it."

The withered grass that had been there a few moments ago now looked fresh and vibrant, swaying in the breeze.

"It worked," said Indio. "I can't believe it worked."

Polly began to stir and open her eyes, blinking in the sunlight.

"You did it, Polly," said Ariella. "You broke the Blood Curse. It's over."

"What about the rest of Trevena?" asked Eleazar. "The whole land was covered in the curse. How long ago did you start all this?"

"A few months ago, I think," said Polly. "They would bring me up here every week or so to reinforce the curse."

"Do we need to do that then," asked Eleazar, "come back here each week?"

"I don't think so," she answered. "I think it's broken. The land should be able to recover now."

Jaron stood. "Time to face the music," he said.

"You don't think Karlov will be mad, do you?" asked Indio.

"Mad?" laughed Jaron, "he'll be nuts, crazy, wild. He'll probably try to have us strung up by our thumbs and have people throw rotten food at us."

"But we broke the curse," said Indio. "We saved Trevena and Khan and the Guardians."

"And disobeyed orders, deserted our posts and abandoned our Knot," Jaron answered.

"Don't forget stealing the Queen of Khan's gryphons," Eleazar added.

Indio winced, "Borrowed. We borrowed the Queen of Khan's gryphons."

"I'm sure that's how she will see it, Indio." said Eleazar, "I'm sure she's understanding of people who wander off with her gryphons, without permission."

Indio's head dropped. "O dear," he muttered.

"What about her?" asked Eleazar. "We can't leave her here. She's defenceless."

"She's coming back with us," said Ariella. "She needs to explain what's been going on."

Polly looked scared. "Explain? To whom?"

"To the king," said Ariella, matter of factly.

"The king? The actual king?" Stammered Polly, "I can't talk to the king."

"You can, and you will. You need to clear Khan of all wrongdoing in this." She turned to the boys. "Ready to fly?"

"No," said Indio.

Eleazar and Jaron nodded.

"Let's fly," said Ariella, ignoring Indio and climbing onto Lavina. "Polly, it's time to go."

"Err, excuse me," said Indio. "Did no one hear me? I said 'No', I thought I was pretty clear."

Polly and the others climbed onto the waiting gryphons, ignoring Indio.

"I think this is a nice spot," Indio called. "No need to rush back to Karlov or the queen. We could stay for a while."

Ariella smiled at him and called over to Indio's gryphon. "Could you help me out with him, Thrace?"

Thrace gave a cry, grabbed Indio's shirt in its sharp beak and dumped the young redhead on its broad lion back. Before Indio could protest, Thrace leapt into the sky, the other gryphons following in quick succession.

They climbed rapidly, the young Willowbank flowing along underneath them stretching as far south as they could see. They followed the ribbon of the river as it passed through the foothills into the vast farms of Trevena. An extensive orchard nestling along the bank came into view.

Ariella called out to the others. "I want to check something out, give me a minute."

She banked Lavina and pointed her towards the edge of the orchard, landing on the banks of the river. The orchard was deserted.

I guess no one is interested in fruit when it's saturated with blood.

She walked to the first tree and plucked the nearest apple. The fruit was so soft that her fingers broke the skin. The familiar dark red blood seeped through the marks Ariella had made. She took the apple down to the river and crouched, holding the fruit under the flow.

The others landed next to Lavina, waiting for Ariella to finish. She lifted the apple out of the water. The blood had been washed away and it felt firmer to the touch. She walked back to the others.

"Ele, can I borrow your knife?" she asked.

He handed it down to her and, taking it, she slit open the apple. The flesh was a pale green and the aroma made her smile. She took a bite, savouring every crunch.

"It's broken," she said, a broad smile spread across her face.

The boys dropped from their gryphons and raced to the apple trees. They each grabbed an apple, Indio grabbed three and ran to the river to soak their fruit. It was the same result. The apples were as perfect as they should have been.

"This is great," laughed Indio. "We know it worked. The question is, how do we get the whole of Trevena into the Willowbank? That's going to be a tough ask."

"We won't need to," answered Jaron. "The Willowbank feeds every stream from here to Lake Evermere. Every farm gets its irrigation from this river. The curse will be broken across the whole country. We just have to wait for it to take effect."

"You did it, Polly," said Ariella, smiling up at the blonde lady on the gryphon.

She smiled weakly, "Do I still need to talk to the king?"

"Sorry, Polly, there's no other way. It'll be okay, he's a good king."

"He's Ariella's uncle," said Eleazar. She'll put in a good word for you won't you, Princess?"

Ariella rolled her eyes and jumped onto Lavina. "I wish I was still a princess," she said, giving him a withering look. "Then I could have you thrown in the dungeon."

"Oh, Princess, don't be like that. You'd miss me."

"Like a hammer to the head," she laughed as Lavina lifted her back into the sky.

There were no clouds as they made their way back to Stonegard. The setting sun turned the sky a lush shade of pink and orange. The Royal Keep came into view.

"I think we should avoid Rapha," called Indio. "Let's get in trouble with him another day."

Ariella nodded. "Let's see if we can land in the Guardian compound without too much attention."

"And then the fun begins," said Eleazar, his face worried.

The group fanned out and came in low over the city, heading as fast as possible to their compound. Their timing, however, was bad. Masses of people were heading home from the day's work. They stopped and gawped at the incoming gryphons. Some shook their fists and shouted; others made obscene gestures and swore at what they thought were more Khan Cavalry.

"Welcome home," muttered Indio. To make matters worse, a small detachment of royal guards was making their way back to the Keep and spotted them. Orders were barked, and men ran off in various directions, no doubt carrying messages.

"They know we're back," called Jaron.

So much for a quiet entrance. Let the fireworks begin.

They landed the gryphons in the training area, much to the shock of the Guardians on duty. There was more shouting and people running to and fro.

Ariella dropped to the floor, the boys following her. They waited in silence for the coming storm. They did not have to wait long. Karlov came bursting out of the weapons room with Lalea close behind.

"He looks pretty ticked off," whispered Indio.

"Why do you think that is? Maybe someone burnt his dinner?" answered Eleazar.

Ariella gave them both a cold stare.

Karlov came storming towards them, shouting the whole time.

"You stupid, impudent, idiotic, foolish morons! I ought to string you up by your thumbs..."

"Told you," whispered Jaron.

"Shut up," hissed Ariella.

"...but that would be too good for sojourners as spectacularly dumb and reckless as you four. We've got two kingdoms at each other's throats, and you think it's a great idea to steal the Queen of Khan's gryphons."

"Err..." started Indio.

"Don't," hissed Jaron.

"Err, pardon me for interrupting, Sir, but," began Indio.

"What? You have something to say, do you? You have something to contribute that could justify your cataclysmic stupidity?"

"Just wanted to clarify."

"Clarify what?"

"They were borrowed, you see, not stolen. We brought them back." Even Indio managed a smile.

Karlov's face turned bright red, and green sparks flashed across his fingertips. He opened his mouth to answer, but Lalea leaned a gentle hand on his shoulder.

"You four, step away from the gryphons." She then noticed Polly, still perched nervously on her mount. "And who are you?"

Polly gulped, and tears welled in her eyes.

"It's her," said Ariella.

"What kind of answer is that?" Karlov demanded.

"It's all been her," said Ariella, trying to remain calm. "She's the one that started the Blood Curse."

Karlov was stunned. "Her? Are you serious?"

The four of them nodded.

"She was being forced by Ghost Raiders to put a curse on the Willowbank," explained Ariella. "We saw her do it. Then we rescued her, and she broke the curse. It's over."

"Are you kidding me?" demanded Karlov, eyeing Polly with disdain.

"It's true," said Jaron. "I swear it."

Karlov clenched his jaw and looked at Lalea. She nodded.

"Wait here," she commanded. Turning on her heel, she strode to the central building.

Karlov called over to the guards on the gate, "Watch them, closely. Do not let them leave." He turned and followed Lalea.

"Uh oh," said Jaron.

"You don't think they're going to get..." Eleazar's voice trailed off.

"Who?" asked Indio looking at the others, but they were avoiding eye contact. "What are they talking about, Ari?"

"Vantor," she replied. "They've gone to get Lord Vantor."

Indio sighed. "Someone stab me now."

25

Homecoming

"So, you've come crawling back then?" Eugenie's voice echoed across the courtyard.

The rest of the Knot emerged from the tower, Eugenie and Theia taking the lead.

"Great!" sighed Eleazar, "this is exactly what we need."

"Get lost, Eugenie," called Ariella.

"You've got some nerve coming back here," Eugenie continued. "You take off to who knows where abandoning your Knot and…"

"Oh, do shut up!" snapped Jaron. "You don't give a rip about the Knot, the Guardians or anyone but yourself. You're a spoiled little rich girl, happy to play a part in daddy's schemes, even if that means betraying the Guardians and spreading lies about Khan. You make me sick."

It was the first time Ariella had seen Eugenie lost for words. She stood there for a moment, eyes fixed on Jaron. Then she turned, flicking her hair behind her, marched through the rest of the Knot and back into the tower. Theia followed behind. Before she turned, Ariella had seen a look on Eugenie's face that didn't quite fit.

She was hurt, genuinely hurt. Not defensive or angry but hurt. Jaron hurt her.

"You're not dead then?" said Joachim. Ariella was not sure if it was a question or statement. Either way, he did not seem to want an answer; he was more interested in the gryphons.

"We missed you too," said Eleazar, but the tall warrior did not even acknowledge him.

"It's so good to see you all," said Esther, a bright smile on her face.

"We were pretty worried when we heard you'd taken the gryphons," added Felix. "Karlov was erupting. I thought he was going to burst something."

"There's still time for that," said Indio, trying to be funny. No one laughed.

Phoebe came and stood in front of Ariella. The tall girl stooped sheepishly, looking at her.

"It's good to see you, Phoebe," she said. Phoebe nodded and gave Ariella a nervous half smile.

The reunion was brought to a sudden halt by a disturbance at the entrance to the compound. A detachment of the Trevena Royal Guard had arrived and was arguing with the Guardians at the gate. Their voices carried across the courtyard. The commander was toe to toe with one of the Guardians, neither backing down.

"They stole her gryphons! Queen Abalyne of Khan's gryphons!" their commander was shouting. "I have orders from King Tristan to arrest them!"

"I work for Lord Vantor," the Guardian shot back, "not the king."

"Then Lord Vantor can come and see the king and ask for his sojourners back. I am arresting them now. If you wish to stop me, you'll have to draw your sword."

"This could get ugly," muttered Indio.

Ariella was already off and running, the others following quickly behind. "Stop!" she called. "Stop! We'll go with you."

"We will?" asked Eleazar, "Err…are you sure about that?"

Polly went pale.

Ariella nodded. "It'll be all right; the king is a good man."

"He may be," said Jaron, "but we did steal his sister's gryphons."

"Borrowed," said Indio. "We borrowed them."

"Without permission? In Trevena we call that stealing," said the commander. He nodded to his men, "Put them in irons."

At that moment, the doors of the main Guardian building were swung open by Karlov, emerging into the sunlight. Lalea was still with him followed by Malum, Elsa and lastly Lord Vantor.

A hush descended on the courtyard as the Lord Guardian strode towards the young sojourners and the Royal Guard.

"This is not going to be pretty," muttered Eleazar.

"I think being strung up by my thumbs looks like a more attractive option than facing this lot," said Indio, shifting from one foot to another.

Lord Vantor addressed the commander of the guard, "What is the meaning of this, commander?"

The commander stood to his full height but appeared like a boy when faced with the Lord Guardian.

"The king's orders, my Lord. They stole the Queen of Khan's gryphons." To emphasise his point, the commander waved his hand towards where the gryphons stood in the courtyard.

Vantor said nothing. He stood and stared at them, taking in every detail. Malum stood on one side of him, his usual bored expression on his face. He was causing small flickers of Light to fly between one index finger and the other.

Ariella glanced at Elsa, her childhood hero, standing on the other side of Vantor. She had always dreamed of meeting her, of being this close to her.

Excellent. You finally get to meet the Lioness of the Guardians on the day you get arrested by your uncle and expelled from the Journey. That'll be a fun day to tell your grandchildren about.

Lord Vantor stood in front of them like a statue. Only his eyes moved, from the sojourners to the royal guard. Soaking in everything.

Enough already! Speak, will you! Say something!

He turned toward Polly, "I think the king should meet you," he said

"Splendid idea," said Malum with a broad grin.

"Really?" asked Elsa

"Really," replied Vantor.

"Err..." began Indio.

Vantor spoke slowly, his eyes fixed on Indio. "This would not be a good time to speak."

Indio shrank back and clamped his mouth shut.

Lord Vantor turned to the royal guards, "Commander, I do not believe the chains are necessary. You have my word that they will accompany you without hesitation."

"But my Lord, they may try to escape," said the commander.

"I have given my word. Do you doubt my word?" Vantor spoke slowly, emphasizing each syllable.

The commander shrank back, "No, my Lord. Of course not, my Lord," He motioned to his men who quickly released the prisoners.

"Excellent decision, Commander."

Ariella tried to give the others a reassuring smile.

Within a few moments, the four sojourners and Polly were following Lord Vantor and the commander through the streets of Stonegard heading to the Royal Keep.

"And I thought this day couldn't get any worse," said Eleazar. "Now we're off to see the king."

The Royal Guards were expecting them and parted as they approached the Keep. The iron doors swung inward, revealing a spectacular entrance hall, as high as it was wide. Crystal chandeliers hung from the ceiling and a luxurious red carpet covered the floor.

Polly began shaking, her eyes darting around. Ariella moved closer to her and touched her arm.

"It'll be okay," she whispered, "The king is a good man. Nothing will happen to you."

Polly tried to smile, but her lip quivered.

As they stepped into the entrance hall, they were greeted by a tall, thin courtier with an aloof expression. He was dressed in elegant orange and red robes, a golden phoenix brooch pinned to his chest. He nodded at the commander and Lord Vantor.

"His Royal Majesty, King Tristan of Trevena will see you now."

The courtier's robes swished grandly as he spun on his heel and led the group onward. They arrived at a pair of stunning gold doors with a Royal Guard at each handle. As they approached, the guards swung open the doors, and they stepped into the throne room.

At the far end was a great golden throne, a phoenix rising from the flames emblazoned on its back. In front of the throne was King Tristan and the other four Monarchs of Dawnhaven.

"Oh no, they're all here," said Ariella under her breath when she saw her mother.

Standing just behind Queen Abalyne was Indio's uncle, Ketil Gryphonfriend, General of the armies of Khan. "I am in so much trouble," muttered Indio.

The rest of the throne room was filled with people, all dressed in their finest clothes. Lords, ladies and courtiers from across Trevena.

"The king spoke: "Lord Vantor, I was not expecting you, but you are always welcome in this court."

"Your Majesty," answered the Lord Guardian, bowing to the king.

Tristan looked past Vantor to the sojourners and Polly. "Are these the ones that stole my sister's gryphons?"

"They are, Your Majesty. We found them in the Guardian compound."

Vantor said nothing. Even in the presence of the five Monarchs of Dawnhaven, Vantor was still imperious. His presence seemed to fill the whole throne room.

"Tell me," asked Tristan, "whose idea was it to steal the Queen of Khan's gryphon?"

"It was mine, my Lord," said Ariella trying desperately to sound strong.

Indio coughed and stepped forward. "Your Majesty, it was my idea to borrow the gryphons."

"Hold on, I think going to Khan was my idea," said Jaron, moving to Ariella's side.

"I thought they were all foolish, Your Majesty," said Eleazar, "but I thought they needed someone to keep them out of trouble."

Elsa frowned, Malum smirked, Vantor did not move.

"Do you think this is funny?" asked the king, rising to his feet. "Theft against the royal household is a grievous crime."

"No, Your Majesty," answered Ariella. "It's just…"

"Just what, child?"

"We thought that…"

"You thought? You thought that because you are royalty you are above the law?"

"No," replied Ariella, her voice starting to waiver.

"Or perhaps you believed the Guardians would protect you?"

"No."

"Or your mother?"

"No."

"Then what? What possible justification could you have for such an act of stupidity?"

"We broke the curse!" she yelled, her voice filling the throne room. All around her were gasps of astonishment. "We broke it, it's over. The Blood Curse is broken."

Tristan's voice became dangerously soft, "Do not play games, child."

"She's not," said Jaron. "It's true, the Blood Curse is over."

Lord Vantor stepped forward. "Your majesty, I believe it would be best if we allowed the sojourners to tell their story."

Vantor turned and looked at Ariella. She suddenly felt every eye in the throne room fixed on her, studying her.

Ground, please swallow me now.

Ariella looked at Vantor, her eyes begging for his help. His face was impervious, unreadable. He simply stood and waited.

"I can tell our story, Your Majesty," she whispered.

"Speak up, child," demanded Queen Abalyne, her voice frosty. "Then perhaps you could explain why you stole my gryphons."

Ariella made eye contact with each of the Monarchs: her uncles, aunts and her mother. Their faces were still.

Seriously? They're not going to help at all? Some family they are!

For the second time, that day, Jaron squeezed her hand while Indio and Eleazar gave her a nod and smiled.

At least they're with me. My Knot.

She took a deep breath and retold the tale, skipping past the echo orbs but including everything else. She watched their faces while she talked. Not a twitch, not a movement. They listened like statues, betraying no emotion.

What are you thinking? You make me want to scream!

When she had finished, she stepped backwards. The king turned his attention to Polly.

"And you, my dear," he asked gently, "where are you from?"

"From across the eastern sea, Your Majesty," she said, her voice weak. "A small chain of islands where my family have lived for generations. The Ghost Raiders came to our village one night and killed my parents. They threatened my brother with the same if I did not help them."

"It was not the Light that wrought the Blood Curse, and no Light was able to break it," said Tristan, his eyes narrowing as he studied Polly.

"Magic," said Malum, his face darkening. "Blood magic."

Nervous whispers broke out across the throne room.

"Our people use it for good," said Polly, taking a step away from Malum and the king.

Tristan studied Polly for a moment then turned to the Lord Guardian. "Have you confirmed any of this Lord Vantor?" Tristan asked.

"No, Your Majesty."

"Actually," interrupted Indio, "would this help?" He held out two apples.

"Would you play games with us, child?" asked Tristan.

"No, Your Majesty," Indio protested. "I took these from an orchard we passed on the way back from Khan. We wanted to test if the curse had been broken."

"How does that prove anything?"

"Well," began Indio, "they're from the same tree; they look the same."

"And?"

Indio dropped one of the apples onto the thick carpet that covered the throne room and stamped down hard. The fruit exploded in a shower of dark red blood, splattering across the floor and Karlov's boots.

"Oops, sorry about that. Didn't think that one through," said Indio.

"Keep going," Karlov growled.

"Err, yes, well, as you can see, that apple was affected by the Blood Curse. But today I soaked this other one in the Willowbank."

Indio bit down on the second apple, taking a huge bite. Tristan winced, expecting a shower of blood but all they got was the sound of Indio crunching."

"See?" said Indio.

"Nice job," whispered Jaron, giving Indio a wink.

Tristan snapped his fingers together, and a guard with a gold chain around his neck and a helmet with a large red plume stepped forward. "Commander, send your men and check the wells in the city, they are fed by the Willowbank through underground streams. If the child's story is true, then the wells will be clean, if not…" Tristan let the words hang in the air.

He keeps calling me a child. Is he trying to annoy me? Well, dear uncle, go check your wells, and we'll see what this child has done.

The commander snapped to attention and swiftly left the throne room, a detachment of Royal Guards falling in behind him. The room descended into excited whispers, the courtiers staring at the sojourners, trying to determine how trustworthy they are.

The Monarchs turned to each other and talked in hushed tones. Ariella tried to catch her mother's eye, to get some token of reassurance, but nothing. Vantor, Malum and Elsa stood still. Malum had even stopped sparking Light across his hands. They waited patiently for the minutes to tick by and the guards to return.

The sojourners exchanged uneasy glances, but none of them spoke. Ariella started to doubt.

What if the river hasn't flowed down this far? What if the power has run out and it only cleansed the northern section of the river? What if it's going to take days for the river to be whole again? What if, what if...?

Get a grip, Ari, there's nothing you can do now but wait.

Just as she thought she couldn't take the suspense any longer, there was movement at the throne room door. The commander had returned, his helmet under his arm. A hush descended as King Tristan beckoned him forward.

"What is it?" demanded Queen Tatianna.

The commander leaned forward and whispered in his king's ear. No one spoke; it seemed everyone in the throne room was holding their breath. The king nodded and stood tall. The commander retreated to his sentry position. Tristan's eyes swept the throne room, resting on Ariella.

"Their story appears to be correct. The curse is broken."

All around the throne room, excited conversations broke out, a few people left at a run. The Monarchs gathered and whispered together, then King Tristan raised his hands and silence fell.

"It appears we owe you our thanks," said Tristan, eyeing the four friends. "Trevena is in your debt."

To Ariella's surprise, spontaneous applause echoed around the room, someone even cheered.

"Oh my!" said Indio.

Jaron grinned and Eleazar whistled.

The king raised his hands again and silence descended. Before he could speak, a man stepped from the crowd into the middle of the throne room, bowing to the king.

Baron Rexsalve. Ariella felt her jaw tighten.

"Your Majesty, if I may be so bold, there are a couple of questions that remain unanswered."

"And what would they be, baron?" asked the king.

"First, there is the issue of the Guardians and their utter incompetence in this matter."

Elsa flinched at his words. Malum rolled his eyes but said nothing.

"They proved completely unable to fulfil their roles as defenders of Dawnhaven. Their Light was powerless against the Blood Curse. It makes me wonder what good they are doing and if we need them here in Trevena."

Rexsalve smiled at Vantor, then continued. "Then, there is the question of judgement on the witch that unleashed this horror on our land. Such a crime cannot, must not, go unpunished."

Malum's fingertips flashed with tiny blue flames, but he remained silent. Vantor did not move.

The throne room was still for a moment before Queen Susanna spoke up in the same tone that Ariella had heard her use so many times before.

"My dear, Baron. I wonder, were you actually listening to the child's story, or perhaps your mind was elsewhere?"

"Your Majesty? I am not sure what you mean."

"No, it appears you do not. Let me explain it to you, in simple terms. The Blood Curse was a dire threat to Trevena and the whole of Dawnhaven. That threat has been averted, not by your knights, Baron, but by the actions of four brave sojourners. They put the safety of the nation above their own. For that, the Guardians should be applauded, not accused. Do you understand, Baron?"

Baron Rexsalve merely gaped for a moment and then closed his mouth.

"As for the matter of punishment for the 'witch' as you so delicately put it, I do not believe you were listening to the story, or perhaps its contents were too complicated for you to understand. The young lady was forced, against her will, with threats of violence by Ghost Raiders. You do realise what that means, don't you, Baron? Ghost Raiders do not make idle threats. This woman needs refuge, safety and security, not some twisted threat of revenge."

Rexsalve bristled with rage at her words. "With all due respect, Your Majesty. You are not Queen of Trevena, and I believe…"

"You are right, Baron," interrupted Tristan, "But I am the king, and I have decided that my sister's words are wise and true."

Rexsalve and Tristan locked eyes, neither willing to give ground. "Step back, Baron," commanded Tristan, his voice menacing.

Rexsalve hesitated, then gave a short, half bow and stepped backwards.

Tristan signalled to one of his courtiers. "See that Polly is treated for any wounds she has. Get her a change of clothes and somewhere to rest. She is now our guest."

Polly's eyes went wide, staring at Ariella.

She smiled and nodded at her. "It's going to be okay," Ariella whispered. "I told you it would."

The courtier escorted Polly from the throne room as Tristan addressed the gathering.

"Lord Vantor, we are in your debt," said Tristan. "You have the thanks of Trevena and all the Kingdoms of Dawnhaven."

"Thank you, Your Majesty," said Vantor, turning and striding from the throne room, the other Guardians following in his wake.

Ariella tried to catch her mother's eye, but she was deep in conversation with Tatianna. She tried to slow down, to get some sign from her, but Karlov put his hand on her back and ushered her out of the room.

They made their way back to the Guardian compound. When they arrived, Lord Vantor turned to speak to the four young sojourners.

"What you did was exceptionally foolish. It was also courageous." His eyes lit up as he spoke, and his face broke into a smile. "Well done."

Then he was gone, leaving them with Malum and Elsa.

"How many different types of Light?" Malum asked Ariella. It sounded like an innocent question, but something in his look made Ariella uneasy.

"Three," she answered.

"All three? Interesting," said Malum.

What's interesting? What are you getting at?

But Malum fell silent.

"Now the question remains," began Elsa. "What shall we do with you four? Expulsion seems the obvious course."

"On what charge?" asked Malum. "They did not disobey any direct commands as far as I can see. They missed one day of their Journey through their actions. That should be punished, of course. And I believe they didn't steal the gryphons, they merely borrowed them, isn't that right Indio?"

"Err, yes, exactly," said Indio. "That's what I've been saying all along. Borrowed, definitely borrowed."

"So, you see, expulsion seems to be too severe a penalty. Especially as it appears, they have broken the Blood Curse," added Malum.

Elsa shook her head. "Fine, have it your way. Karlov, these four are to be confined to the compound until the High Winter Festival.

During that time, they are to take personal responsibility for the cleaning of all the stables as well as their normal duties."

"Yes, ma'am," nodded Karlov.

They didn't expel us!

"And Karlov,"

"Yes, ma'am?"

"If there are any more indiscretions, string them up by their thumbs."

"Yes, ma'am." Karlov was scowling.

The four friends gave a collective sigh of relief, smiles breaking out.

"We're alive!" shouted Indio.

Eleazar grinned, "Barely. Next time you have a hare-brained scheme to pinch someone's gryphon, you're on your own."

"Borrow," corrected Jaron with a wink. "We borrowed the gryphons. Besides, Ele, we're a Knot. You're obliged to go with him on all of his hare-brained schemes."

Eleazar groaned and Indio laughed.

"I don't know what you lot are laughing at," barked Karlov. "The stables need mucking out before you get anything to eat. Get to it!"

The four friends tramped across the courtyard towards the stables, dreaming of the High Winter Festival.

25

Next Stop

Ariella mounted her horse and took one last look around the Guardian compound. Twelve months had always seemed like such a long time to her. But this year had passed in a blur.

The Blood Curse had been purged from the land and the fields around Stonegard were green and lush. The High Summer Festival was only two weeks away. The whole city was preparing for the festivities. Soon fifty nervous, young sojourners would be beginning their own Journeys.

She looked around at the other nine. Her Knot. Tighter this summer than last. Joachim was still aloof. Phoebe was still silent. Esther and Felix were spending a lot of time together. Theia was still cold, and Eugenie was still, well, she was still Eugenie, although it did seem that she was less edgy since the Blood Curse had been broken.

Eleazar had experienced no more butterfly incidents and seemed lighter, more comfortable around the others. Jaron was still the wisest and Indio was still the most reckless, but she realised she loved them like her brothers.

Since High Winter, the training had gone up a notch. Karlov, Lalea and Malum had driven them hard. At first, she resented it. The constant pushing, criticism and correction. But over the months the Knot started to click. They could fight together now, watch each other's backs, respect each other. Their ability to harness their Light had been challenging but they were getting there. Ariella's Light still had not settled on a colour yet, but Malum seemed more relaxed about it. All in all, it had been a good year.

"You ready?" called Indio.

"For what?" she replied.

"To see the most glorious sights in the whole of Dawnhaven," he laughed: the majestic peaks, shining glaciers and the jewel of the north, Everfrost!"

"Everfrost? It's hardly a hospitable name for a capital city is it?" said Eleazar. "Why couldn't you name it, 'Always hot' or 'Warm and cosy'?"

Indio looked hurt.

"Leave him alone, Ele," said Jaron, "or he's going to spend the whole trip telling us how wonderful Khan is."

"That's a great idea," said Indio. "Have I told you about the...?"

"Sorry," Eleazar interrupted. "Karlov's leaving."

Eleazar nudged his horse into a trot, following Karlov and the rest of the Knot out of the compound.

Ariella laughed as Indio tried to catch up with him to continue his story.

And that was that. They were leaving Stonegard and the first stage of the Journey. In a week or so they would arrive in Everfrost. Phase two would begin.

They took it easy as they left the city, knowing the horses would appreciate a gentle start to the long ride. As they passed out of the main gate, no one noticed a hooded figure standing in the shadow of the wall, watching them leave.

"They're going," the figure said in a hushed tone.

A dark shadow moved next to the hooded figure. "Excellent. The first stage is complete."

"Yes," the figure answered. "The unforeseen circumstances worked out in our favour. The second stage is already in motion."

The shadow laughed a hollow laugh.

"It's nearly time. The dark moon is rising."

Printed in Great Britain
by Amazon

37754839R00128